IMPRINTS OF THE PAST

GARETH IAN DAVIES

CONTENTS

Dedication		V
1.	I Don't Wanna Go Back	2
2.	My Name is Rosalind Hill	10
3.	Ghosts Don't Exist	18
4.	Can I Go Home Now?	27
5.	Listen	33
6.	Tell Me What You Remember	42
7.	We Don't Do Moderation	49
8.	Take The Lead On This One	58
9.	There's Something You Should Know	66
10.	Stop	78
11.	Always Room For Improvement	86
12.	You Want To Do This?	96
13.	Get Out!	103
14.	So Much Sorrow	113
15.	I Don't Do Exorcisms	121

16. Care For A Little Wager?   132

17. There's Always Hope   143

18. When Can You Get Here?   156

19. Leave Well Enough Alone   164

20. But The Notes   174

21. Let's Do This   180

22. A Token Of Our Admiration   193

Acknowledgments   200

About the Author   202

Stay Connected   203

To my mother, Carol Price, who isn't here to see this book published and who would have been proud of me.
I love you, Mum.

Excerpt of email recovered from closed account, owner untraceable. Destination account also closed and untraceable.

From: (address withheld)
To: (address withheld)
Subject: US Midwest 2022/2
Sent: 2022-05-10 22:43:07 UTC

… so with the addition of these resources, I believe the Chicago situation is well in hand.

Moving further south, there are some concerning developments in St. Louis. Ground observations report a surge of intrusion activity in and around the downtown area since the beginning of the year, well outside the three sigma of the 2020 model. I forwarded the data to Astbury myself; she'll be thrilled at another opportunity to refine her algorithms. From a practical standpoint, I am told there is at least one freelancer operating in the area, and this has the potential to go south in a hurry. Given our current active deployments, I am making the call to take myself there for at least the next three months to assess the situation. I hope we can keep a lid on this without further stretching resources.

On the other hand, Memphis appears to have quietened considerably…

CHAPTER ONE

I DON'T WANNA GO BACK

"Um, I ordered a *large* coffee, like I do every morning."

I stared at the kid and tried to keep my voice calm. He might have just been old enough to be out of high school, tall and gangly in his ill-fitting uniform. He stared back at me from beneath the beginnings of an afro with the vacant disinterest of someone who didn't really want to be working the register at McDonalds at ten-thirty on a Wednesday morning. I got it, I did. Been there, done that, but I also wanted my coffee the way I'd ordered it.

Without comment, he reclaimed the medium-size paper cup he had just offered me, and set in on a rear counter, its fate uncertain. I glanced at the heavyset black guy with the tattered Kobe Bryant jersey behind me, and shrugged in semi-apology without getting a reaction. Behind him, a young blonde woman with horn-rimmed glasses and a nose ring shook her head, before rattling off a torrent of what was probably Bosnian into her cellphone. It was a pretty eclectic crowd at this restaurant, but then you could say that about any establishment on South Grand Avenue. It's why I loved the area so much.

"Here, sir," the kid mumbled as he thrust a larger paper cup at me, an edge of defiance in his eyes. I stifled a sigh and picked it up, but was interrupted before I could head for the exit.

"D! D, how the hell are ya, man?"

Turning back toward the line of waiting customers, I saw him. Colton Lynn. And I couldn't pretend I hadn't seen him.

"Can't complain, Colton. How are you?"

"Ah, you know," he said, gaze flittering around the room. I didn't, and I wasn't sure I wanted to, but I'd known Colton since high school, the better part of two decades now, and our lives had both taken unfortunate turns. I couldn't just blow him off. "Say, are you drinking that here or taking out?"

"Taking out. On my way to work, actually."

"Oh." He looked so crestfallen that I dug my phone out of my jacket pocket and checked the time.

"I got a few minutes to spare," I said, trying not to sound reluctant. "I can wait outside if you want to catch up for a bit."

"Sure," he nodded, grinning. "Lemme grab a coffee first." He shook his fist and coins clinked reassuringly.

I nodded back and walked out into the uncertain sunshine of an early Midwestern spring day. It was late enough that the pedestrian traffic had fallen below commuter levels, so I hovered beside the lamppost on the street corner without fear of being bumped into oncoming traffic. A cool, fragrant breeze hinted of rain later. I didn't mind. I enjoyed walking to work, putting my mind in idle, and simply allowing my senses free rein. I'd spent too much of my life inside to waste the opportunity.

However, I didn't have all morning to wait. I sipped my still-too-hot coffee, checked the news feed on my phone - Cardinals won last night, fears of another new COVID strain were subsiding - and was considering just leaving and feeling guilty about it later, when Colton emerged from the restaurant, blinking as he searched for me. I realized I hadn't seen him since last summer, when we were both still at the New Hope re-entry facility. He looked in slightly better shape, a neat buzz cut disguising his premature baldness, clean shaven, albeit with what looked like a slight paunch to his short, wiry frame. His shirt, sports jacket and pants were less tatty than I remembered, although I swore he still wore the same damn scarlet tie he'd owned since high school. I waved, and he hurried over.

"D! What's it been, six months, seven? Can't believe we haven't run into each other, man. It's been too long."

He grinned, hands cradling the life-giving warmth of his to-go cup. His face was pale and his eyes were a little bloodshot, but he really didn't look that bad. The programs must be helping.

"It's St. Louis, you'd have thought our paths would've crossed," I agreed.

"Yeah, though it's been a while since I've been down this way."

Well, that's reassuring, I thought, and instantly disliked myself for it.

"Oh, what brings you this way now?"

"A client," he beamed, and looked around to see if any of our fellow pedestrians were as impressed as he was.

"A client? You're not... Are you practicing again?"

He grimaced and his eyes clouded before he smiled again, but more soberly. "No, D. You know I can't practice law anymore. They don't let you do that after you're convicted of a felony. I'm a courier now."

He looked away, embarrassed, and an awkward silence descended. I'm not good at this stuff. Too many years keeping my own counsel, nursing my own problems, had left me ill-equipped to ease others' anxieties. I groped for something to say that wasn't glib, and resisted the urge to make my excuses and resume my walk to work.

"Well, we all have to start somewhere," I tried at last. "At least you're working, and back in the real world."

"That's true!" he said, standing up straight and beaming. "Most of my clients are downtown or in Clayton, so I'm outside most of the day. I don't mind, even when it's cold or wet."

"I hear that," I said, nodding. "Good for you."

"Thanks. Hey, where are you working now anyway? I remember you got a job, but my memory... well."

"Cooking, same place." I hoped he'd let such vagueness slide, but he just looked at me, expectant. "At Hickory, down on Cherokee Street."

"The barbecue place? I've heard of it, but I've never eaten there. All staffed by ex-cons, right?"

"That's right."

"Good, good. Bit far for me. I'm living on Locust these days, a couple blocks from the City Museum."

"Really?" I had looked in the neighborhood myself last year and didn't remember any apartments on Locust Street.

"Yep!" he said and puffed up with pride. "There are a couple new buildings opened up. They take people like us, who're ready to move on from places like New Hope, who've got a steady job and need more stability. Mostly studio apartments, but I got a one-bedroom! I moved in last month."

I smiled, glad to have something I could feel good about in this conversation. "That's great, Colton. I'm happy for ya."

"Thanks, man," he beamed, toasting me with his cup and taking a cautious sip, and grimaced. "Ugh. There's gotta be better places for coffee around here."

"Sure," I said. "There's supposed to be a great place two blocks south if you want to pay seven bucks a cup. I don't go there." And not just because of the price of the coffee, but he didn't need to know that. I shivered in the warming sun and glanced at my phone again. He took the hint.

"You gotta go, huh? I won't keep you. Hey, speaking of coffee, there's a great little diner next door to my building. You know, the fifties era, twenty-four hour, fuel-oil coffee kind. Although they're only open four through eight. You should come over and have dinner one night."

"Sure," I heard myself saying, far from sure I would take him up on it. "Although I work most evenings."

"Well, when are you next free?" He leaned forward, earnest, insistent.

And that's how I happened to be at 1500 Locust the following Tuesday.

The City of St. Louis has been trying to reclaim and gentrify the neighborhoods just north and west of downtown since the late 1990s. Washington Street gets most of the buzz, both good and bad: the City Museum justifies its place as one of the highlights of the Midwest, but even I get nervous wandering past the bars and other nightspots in the early hours of a weekend. Locust Street, two blocks south and on the edge of its more famous namesake's Historic District, gets less attention, but began showing signs of life after the COVID-19 pandemic, especially in its rather organic mix of repurposed living spaces. The five floor brick and stone building in which Colton now lived, with the uninspiring if accurate moniker of 1500 Locust, was built in the late 19th century as one of the area's many garment warehouses. Following the decline of that industry after World War 2, it had fallen into disuse and increasing decrepitude, but its bones were still good. Renovations had begun in the early 2000s, but a series of property developers had run afoul of financing, or inspections, or both. It wasn't until late last year that the "clean and affordable studio and one-bedroom apartments" were available to those taking the next step towards re-entering mainstream society, a few months after I had been fortunate to find my own place on the south side, far enough away from the people and things I needed to avoid.

I looked all this up online after work that Tuesday afternoon, while concocting and discarding one guilty excuse after another to cancel on Colton. I regretted agreeing to dinner with him and felt bad because of it. While not that close, we'd shared enough classes at high school that I considered him one of the good guys. However, our paths had diverged since then, both mostly downhill, and he reminded me of parts of my life I was trying to move on from. I told myself I owed him nothing, and if we didn't eat dinner together, I doubted either of us would worry much. But I didn't cancel.

And I hated it. Locust Street was too far to walk from Tower Grove South, even if I had been willing to endure cold, whipping wind and persistent drizzle. I didn't feel like dealing with the parking nightmare courtesy of the happy hour crowd, so I took a chance on the Metro bus. Big mistake: it was crowded and slow, and I could feel the coil winding inside me with every jolt, every lurch, every uncovered cough from the kid across the aisle. I gave it up several blocks shy of Locust and escaped onto the busy, rain-slicked sidewalk of Market Street, hurrying through too many people swarming around me, too many I couldn't see, perhaps other ghosts from my past that would force me to have coffee or dinner with them. My left hand snaked underneath the opposite sleeve of my jacket, gripping my right arm and twisting the strands of leather that encircled my wrist. It was a relief to finally duck through the doorway of Joe's Eat Rite, for all that I didn't want to go there.

Colton sat huddled in a low-backed booth at one end of the shallow room, dominated by the aluminum-accented formica counter that ran most of its length. Iconic fifties music played at a not quite conversation-stifling volume from a period jukebox against the far wall. The twin scents of fried potatoes and delicious bacon competed for my attention as I made my way toward Colton's booth. He was facing the entrance, likely to make it easier for me to find him, but that wasn't going to work.

"Hey, Colton," I said, waving as I approached. "Sorry to be a pest, but do you mind if I take that seat? I prefer to face the door."

He stared up at me, but otherwise didn't react. Uh oh. I hoped I was misreading the signs. I stood there for another few seconds before his bloodshot eyes focused and he stirred.

"Uh, hey D. Sit down?"

"Yeah, like I said, can I get that seat? I just can't sit with my back to the door."

"Huh? Oh. Yeah, sure."

He moved with exaggerated care, like someone plagued by chronic back pain or who had been bedridden for days. As he shuffled onto the opposite bench, I glanced at the other patrons in the mostly full diner, but they all seemed wrapped up in their own conversations. Not so the bland-faced redheaded waitress in the sky-blue dress, who watched from behind the counter as she wiped a glass tumbler with a dish towel. As I slid into the seat Colton had just vacated, she exchanged glass and towel for a pad and pen and approached our table.

"You alright, hon?" she asked him, with the tone of someone wondering if he might upset her other clientele. Her voice was deeper than I'd expected, and after a swift and, I hoped, stealthy appraisal that located a red plastic name tag, I realized this was Joe.

"Yeah, uh, guess I got sleepy waiting for this slacker," Colton said with a smile, and almost without slurring.

Joe looked at me and arched an eyebrow.

"First time here," I offered with what I hoped was a reassuring smile. "Do you have coffee?"

Joe snorted. "This is a diner, hon."

"Two coffees, then. And a minute to look at the menu."

Joe scribbled rapidly, stared at Colton with faint disapproval, and returned back behind the counter.

"Glad you could make it, D. Good to see you. Real good."

I leaned forward and kept my voice down. "Are you clean?"

He looked away, covered his mouth, and started trembling. Was he laughing? I gripped the edge of the table and tried to resist turning it over.

"Jesus, dude," I snarled, glancing around the diner to make sure none of the other patrons were police. "If you're high, I'm fucking out of here. I'm not gonna be a party to that shit. I can't be."

His eyes widened, and suddenly he was reaching over the table, gripping my forearms. "Don't leave!" he gasped, eyes wide with what I could have sworn was terror. "I'm not high, I promise! Not really. I can't go back. I promise!"

"Can't go back where?" I disengaged his hands and set them flat on the table.

"It doesn't feel right," he mumbled, shaking his head and slumping back in his seat. I waited, but he didn't say any more. Our coffees arrived, and to keep Joe's attention elsewhere, I ordered two slingers. Colton didn't object, but I don't think he really noticed.

"What doesn't feel right?"

"The apartment. New Hope didn't feel that way. It's so hot, I can't breathe."

"You got a bad thermostat, or is the AC on the fritz?"

"No, it's not that. I don't wanna go back."

There was genuine despair in his voice. I didn't need this. Why had I ordered food? I could've finished my coffee, made an excuse, and got the hell out of there.

But I hadn't made an excuse earlier that day, and I couldn't bring myself to make one now.

"Look," I told him in what I liked to imagine was my best bedside manner. "I don't understand, but I can see you're upset. How about we just sit here for a while, drink coffee, and eat what I hope is really greasy food. I ordered slingers: you like slingers, I hope?"

"Love slingers." He ran his hand over his scalp, and lapsed back into a semi-trance, staring over my shoulder at something I doubt even he could see.

The food came and, along with the coffee, was everything I expected. My chances of a good night's sleep diminished with every bite of chili and runny egg yolk. Colton ate listlessly, and in a silence I had no desire to break. I wasn't sure what was going on. Despite his protests, I was sure he was on something, something I was pretty sure he shouldn't be touching; he had to still be in some kind of substance abuse program. He was also terrified. I wanted to put it down to paranoia, but I couldn't shake the impression that there was something more at work.

"I don't feel well," Colton announced and dropped his fork on top of his half-eaten slinger. He didn't look good either, his face pale and sweat beading on his brow. Cursing under my breath, I swallowed my mouthful and stood up, tugging at his sleeve.

"C'mon buddy, let's find the restroom," I said, keeping my voice as quiet as possible. Joe was busy taking an order from a table of college students, and could only spare us a narrow-eyed glance as I half-dragged Colton towards the far corner, where I hoped the restroom was. There was one door, a unisex deal, and I mumbled a prayer to some unspecified deity that it was unoccupied. It was, and we just made it inside before Colton threw up. At least most of it went into the bowl, but as he curled up dry heaving on the floor, I had to clean up the rest with paper towels. Somehow I managed to keep my own dinner down, but I wouldn't be ordering another slinger anytime soon. I cleaned him up too and mopped his brow with a damp towel.

"Sorry, man," he croaked, when he had recovered enough to lift himself up on his knees.

"Don't worry about it," I told him. "But I think we should pay up and leave."

He nodded, then shook his head, but followed me out of the restroom. Some of the other patrons stared at us in curiosity, and I briefly considered offering some kind of explanation, but I couldn't think of anything that would make the situation seem any better. I opted for hustling back to our table, grabbing our jackets and throwing a twenty and a ten down.

"Am I gonna have to clean up in there?" hissed Joe as we passed, and I shook my head as reassuringly as I could. Then I grabbed Colton's arm, and we escaped onto the street.

Chapter Two

MY NAME IS ROSALIND HILL

The rain had returned with something approaching enthusiasm, and I zipped up my jacket before asking Colton which way to go. He gestured resignedly to the left, and I guided him to the entrance of 1500 Locust, double-glass doors in a classical white stone portico surmounted by terracotta ocean waves and what looked like a pair of mermaids. A strong scent of pine wafted over us as we passed through the doors into a small, brightly lit lobby. Steel-fronted mailboxes lined the wall to our right, while an unoccupied security desk supported a monitor, keyboard and mouse ahead of us. Colton stopped and frowned at the desk.

"Where's Rashard?" he asked.

"Who's Rashard?"

"Building security. Does the night shift."

"Maybe he stepped out for a piss. You don't need him to get into your apartment, do you?"

"Don't want to go to my apartment," Colton whined and took a step backward.

I sighed. "Dude, you just lost your dinner, and I don't think you need to be going anywhere else tonight. C'mon, I'll go up with you and check it out if you want."

"Would you? Thanks, D."

"Sure." *And I'll punch myself in the nuts later too.*

Colton waved a key card over a reader next to a big white button, which lit up and allowed him to summon the elevator. According to the red LED display over the doors, it had been hanging out on the third floor, and the mechanical groaning emanating from the other side of the doors as it descended didn't thrill me. The elevator cabin itself was small, but bright and reassuringly clean. Colton flashed his keycard at the panel and punched "3".

"I'm not in the penthouse, I'm afraid," he said with a weak smile. I returned it, but as soon as the elevator rose, what little good humor I still had evaporated. The skin on my arms prickled as the temperature dropped, and my breath caught as the air thinned. I grew aware of a... well, I've always had trouble describing this, not that I've often tried with anyone other than myself. If I said "presence", you'd think I was talking about ghosts, and I'm not sure I believe in ghosts, not real ones, not really. But something was there, something I couldn't explain, something I had felt before. I hadn't liked it then, and I didn't like it now.

"You okay, D?"

"Yeah," I muttered, fighting the rising panic and for breath.

"Maybe there was something in those slingers. Don't puke in my elevator, okay?"

I was out of witty replies anyway, but at that moment, the door opened. Neither of us moved at first, and if it had closed and Colton had pressed "L", I wouldn't have objected. We'd have returned to the lobby, I'd have finally made an excuse and left, and my life would have stayed much simpler than it has since become. But then we heard voices.

"*That's* Rashard," Colton said and stepped out of the elevator, leaving me little choice but to follow. Any brief hope the disturbing sensations would ease was immediately dashed. If anything, I felt colder still and my nose twitched at the unmistakable tang of blood. I took a deep breath before shuffling behind Colton down a short, well-lit corridor toward his apartment door, the last one on our left. Three people stood outside.

"Whassup, Rashard!" Colton greeted a dark-skinned man in a slate-gray uniform and peaked cap, who was by far the tallest of the three. His companions were a pretty bleach-blonde who looked my age, and an older, severe-looking woman with shoulder-length brown hair, both dressed in navy-blue skirt suits. They all turned to look at us, but while the first two focused on Colton, the older woman looked straight at me, and her hazel eyes narrowed. I returned her scrutiny with an edge of defiance: I get that reaction sometimes from those who recognize my Hispanic ancestry and disapprove.

"'Sup, Mr. Lynn," said Rashard. "Sorry 'bout this. I know it's irregular, but these ladies wanted access to your apartment."

"Why? Are they police? Do they have a warrant?"

"I represent building management," said the blonde, holding out a business card. "Nicole Kelly. This isn't a legal matter, Mr. Lynn. It's a..."

She stopped and looked at the other woman, who gave a brisk nod before turning toward Colton. "Have you experienced any discomfort in your apartment recently? Changes in temperature, drafts, things of that nature?"

Her accent was British, not in a Downton Abbey way, but she would have sounded right at home in one of those gritty police dramas set in bleak post-industrial towns where it rained all the time. Colton stood up straighter, obviously impressed. I like a British accent as much as the next guy, but what I was sensing left me unsettled, and her staring at me hadn't helped.

"It's too hot, ma'am," he said. Ridiculous. All he needed was a cap to doff.

"Consistently? Can you not control the temperature?"

"Thermostat doesn't work, even if I turn it all the way down."

"I see. And have you tried to fix it?" She turned toward the security guard, who shrugged.

"Maintenance came last week. Said it was all working normal."

"They're wrong," sulked Colton.

"Who are you, exactly?" I asked her. "Are you with building management too?"

She turned her gaze back on me, and I resisted the urge to flinch, as if caught misbehaving in class. She was a striking woman. Her skin was too pale and lips too thin for my taste, and was clearly much older, but she drew the eye and commanded the attention of those around her.

"My name is Rosalind Hill," she said brusquely. "I'm a consultant. You can think of me as a building inspector." She didn't offer me a business card, but I got the impression she wasn't looking for maintenance issues or building code violations. She turned back to Colton. "Mr. Lynn, I may be able to help, but I need your permission to enter your apartment. Do you give it?"

"Uh, sure," Colton said slowly, licking his lips. "But I need to use my bathroom."

"Of course. After you."

Colton opened the door with his key card, and the ensuing frigid blast of air almost knocked me over. I took an involuntary step back toward the elevator, and Rosalind cocked her head as she glanced at me. No-one else reacted, simply following Colton inside.

"You didn't introduce yourself," she said without moving.

"D. Colton and I go back a ways."

"D? Well, D, are you up to this?" She sounded concerned and considerate. "You don't need to come inside if you don't want to."

No, I don't want to. I want to be back in my own place, or anywhere other than here. But I don't want to be out in the corridor by myself either.

"I'll come in. It's just an apartment."

She nodded. "Very well. You should feel better soon."

I forced myself to relax and followed her inside, wondering what she meant by that. Did she think I looked high, like Colton? Or did she see something else?

The space was small despite the high ceilings, and tidier than I had expected. A charcoal-colored fabric couch dominated the main living space, facing the wall to our left upon which hung a flat screen TV. A tall window pierced the back wall, rising above a kitchen sink and flanked by a stainless-steel fridge and an electric cooktop. A plain wooden table and two chairs squatted in front of the sink. To the right was a door, presumably leading to the bedroom and bathroom, but it was closed. I wondered if Colton was being sick again, or perhaps hiding evidence of substances he should no longer possess. The neutral white walls held no decorations of any kind, certainly no photographs. Colton's past was as much his own business as my past was mine.

"It feels fine to me," Nicole whispered to Rashard, who shrugged and turned toward Rosalind.

"What now, ma'am?"

Her lips twitched as she studied the room, head tilted to one side and nostrils flaring. The door to our right opened, and Colton emerged with a guilty glance in my direction.

"I need time, and some peace and quiet," she said. "You may wait outside or in here, but please do nothing to distract me."

"I need to go back to my desk," said Rashard, and Nicole said she'd wait for Rosalind downstairs.

"You'll stay with me, won't you D?" Colton pleaded, and I bit my lip and nodded. This room was the heart of it, of everything I could feel. I could barely breathe, much less speak, and the sharp iron taste of blood was making me nauseous.

"Sit on the couch and be quiet," Rosalind commanded, and we did. She stood behind us and closed her eyes. We sat in uncomfortable silence, me shivering and sweat beading on Colton's brow. He was clearly experiencing something strange, but in an entirely different way. We watched Rosalind, both awed by this diminutive British woman who had taken charge of the situation, whatever the situation actually was. Colton opened his mouth to speak, but I shook my head and he subsided. Her lips moved silently, but otherwise there was no sign of what she was doing, or if she was doing anything at all.

Suddenly, the room shifted somehow, and the pressure changed, like when your ears pop during an airplane descent. My eyes lost focus, and I closed them, which was when I saw the two men: one older and one younger, both dressed in stiff white-collared shirts, dark waistcoats and suit pants. They faced each other across a huge, wooden desk with papers strewn across its surface, in a room of a size with Colton's apartment. I couldn't hear anything, and the scene flickered erratically, like an improperly tuned station on the old analog TV back in my childhood bedroom. But they were arguing, that was clear, eyes wide as they yelled at each other. The older man's white-bearded face was bright red as he waved papers in his right hand while stabbing at them with fingers from his left. The other man, sporting the most improbable mustache I had ever seen, kept shaking his head, then suddenly stopped and took on a look that I knew all too well, the human equivalent of a cornered beast. As soon as the older man turned his back, as if heading for the door, I knew what was going to happen. The younger man picked up a large brass paperweight from his desk, raised it as he strode forward and...

The scene dissolved. Before the inevitable blow fell, the image faded as if the tuner had finally given up on a weakening signal. At the same time, all the pressure, the freezing cold, and the other sensations that had threatened to overwhelm me ever since I stepped off the elevator ebbed and disappeared, like a retreating storm surge after the front has passed. I opened my eyes, and I was back in Colton's apartment, sprawled on the floor, clutching the short pile carpet, my breathing ragged. Colton stared at me in concern and confusion, standing next to his overturned couch. Rosalind was nowhere to be seen.

"What the *fuck* was that?" I croaked and broke into a fit of coughing that doubled me over. My throat felt parched, as if I had drunk nothing all day. As the fit passed, a large red plastic tumbler appeared in front of me, and I looked up to find Rosalind holding it. Sweat beaded her brow and she was panting as if she'd just run a 5K in the Midwestern July heat.

"That," she said, as I took grateful gulps of water, "should be the end of your discomfort, Mr. Lynn."

I spent perhaps three more awkward and mostly silent minutes in Colton's apartment, drinking water and recovering from something I still could not wrap my head around. I mumbled an apology and helped set his couch back on its feet. Apparently, I had screamed something incoherent and swung my arms around, and between that and him defending himself, we had toppled the furniture over, almost knocking Rosalind off her feet.

"That's a new couch, dude," was the only thing he had said to me. He couldn't meet my eyes and flinched if I moved toward him, his head sinking into his shoulders like a startled turtle. He assured Rosalind that he now felt fine, thank you, and obviously didn't want us there any longer. I doubted I would be receiving any more dinner invitations anytime soon, which suited me down to the ground, which was exactly where I wanted to be.

Rosalind, on the other hand, watched me with what I can only describe as a gleam in her eye. I didn't know what I had just seen, or what she had done to cause it, but I knew she was responsible. And I didn't like it. Back in college, I'd flirted with hallucinogenic drugs, Ecstasy mostly, a little acid, and some of those trips had been wild and not all of them pleasant. Seeing weird shit was part of the package, arguably the entire point. But at some point, the weird shit started following me into the sober parts of my life, making me jumpy and undoubtedly less pleasant to be around, and likely less reliable for my former employer. I got to associate it - the temperature swings, the scents no-one else could smell, the certainty of being watched - with specific places, and I laid off the drugs altogether. Although, if I'm being honest, and I'm more honest with myself than I used to be, I'm not so sure it all started with the drugs.

The point being that seeing a vision of some old-time murder wasn't unfamiliar, but something I associated with choices I no longer made or wanted to make. I felt dirty and needed to be home, to shower, to call Jess and ask her to come over after her shift. I'd worked hard to get where I was today, and heaven help anyone who messed that up for me.

After a mumbled farewell, I left Colton's apartment and tried to ignore the fact that Rosalind followed me out the door. Out of the corner of my eye, I briefly saw a face poking into the hallway from the adjacent apartment, but it vanished immediately, followed by the thump of a closing door and the rattle of a deadbolt. Great, so I'd entertained the neighbors too. I didn't think anyone who lived in this building would be quick to call the police, but I needed to get out of there just in case.

Rosalind said nothing as we shared the elevator ride down, merely watched my blurred reflection in the doors as we descended. Maybe I could've left the building unchallenged, while she reassured Nicole and Rashard that the "issue" had been taken care of. But I didn't, and I still can't explain why.

"So, the usual arrangement then?" Rosalind asked Nicole at the conclusion of her brief and devoid of detail report.

Nicole nodded, then paused. "My friend tells me they're having more trouble at Chouteau Village," she said quietly. "I'd really appreciate it if you would call her."

I could have sworn Rosalind gave me the most fleeting of glances before answering. "I promise I will, but only when I'm ready. And I'm not, yet."

Nicole sighed. "I said I'd try. Well, I'll let you know if I hear of anything else that might interest you."

She thanked Rashard, seeming unsure what to do with me, before offering a tight smile, and set out into the rainy night.

"Now then, D," Rosalind said, collecting a long black raincoat from a rack next to the security desk and guiding me with one hand to the far corner of the lobby. "Perhaps I can have a word before we go our separate ways."

It didn't seem to be a request, or at least there seemed little chance I would refuse if it was. I shrugged in acquiescence. I could spare a minute or two.

"First, the most important question. Are you alright?"

I couldn't answer at first. She peered up at me with what appeared to be genuine concern, so a dismissive "Fine" didn't work. But I struggled to articulate what I was feeling, because I really wasn't sure myself.

"I don't understand what just happened up there," I said finally, honestly. "It... reminded me of things I'd rather not be reminded of."

Her lower lip twitched, and then she gave me a sad smile. "We all have things of which we'd rather not be reminded. And they're private, and quite right too. Yet, forgive me, but I guess this is not the first such experience you have had."

Lie. A simple lie, and you are out of here and can forget about the whole thing.

"Maybe," I heard myself say. "But maybe it was as simple as next-door's slinger getting the best of me, as it got the best of Colton."

"Maybe, although I suspect there was more to your friend's illness than a poor dinner choice."

"Colton's had a rough night, as have I, and right now, I don't want to relive it. Even to find out what you think you were doing up there. I want to go home."

Her expression hardened, then she sighed. "I see. Well, D, I can hardly blame you for that, not if you experienced even a tenth of what I have just endured. Not all of us welcome our responsibilities."

"What responsibilities?" I asked in spite of myself, but she shook her head.

"Not now. Go home and do whatever you need to do to relax and put this out of your mind." She withdrew a pen and moleskin notebook from her raincoat's inside pocket, scribbled something on a page, then ripped it out and offered it to me. "If you want to discuss this more, please call me at that number. But not after 9pm, or I fear my husband will be quite cross with you."

CHAPTER THREE

GHOSTS DON'T EXIST

I kept Rosalind's phone number - even though she was married and at least fifteen years my senior, you don't throw away a phone number a woman offers you - but I didn't do anything with it for a while either. Well, that is after stashing the note in the drawer of my bedside table, because it wasn't worth trying to explain such an item to Jess.

She texted me as I left 1500 Locust, asking if I wanted her to pick up anything for dinner on her way over. We'd been dating for six months, and she knew I didn't enjoy cooking in the evenings after my lunch shifts. She arrived not long after I got home, carrying a brown paper bag of Thai food. I held my apartment door open and waited after buzzing her into the building.

"What the hell happened to you?" she demanded. Her mesmerizing emerald eyes narrowed as they looked me up and down.

"Do I look that bad?" I said, closing the door behind her.

"You look like you're on something. You're not, are you?"

"No!"

"Okay, just asking. It's either that or you've seen a ghost."

At that point, I dissolved into a giggling fit, strong enough to drive me to my knees and send sane men scampering from the room. Jess just watched me with a curious smile, twirling strands of her long, dark hair between her fingers. Eventually, she left me to it and poured us each a glass of water, draining hers and offering mine at arm's length.

"Want to tell me about it?" she said once I'd recovered enough to take the glass and drink without spitting everywhere.

I did. Most of it anyway, and while devouring my pad thai, I told her about Colton, about him getting sick at the diner, me cleaning up and helping him home, and told her of his complaints about how hot his apartment was, but I stopped there. I said nothing about Rosalind and Nicole, and offered no hint of any ghostly visions. I would tell her, but I just wasn't ready, not yet.

"You think he was on something?" We had moved to the couch, where she nestled inside the crook of my arm. I loved the way her brow furrowed when she thought, her eyes bright as they gazed into an unguessable distance.

"I'm not sure. He got addicted to some serious painkillers, was still trying to kick them when I met him at New Hope. This wasn't like that. It was like he was afraid of something."

"Paranoia, maybe? Nina's ex was all but an alcoholic, and he thought anything out of the ordinary was a plot against him. I felt sorry for him. How'd he get addicted?"

"Nina's ex?"

She thumped my chest. "No, Colton, you dumbass."

I hesitated. You don't just spill someone's secrets without their consent, especially when those secrets land you in jail. But this was Jess, not just anyone. And I had withheld enough from her already for one evening.

"I never got the full story. His fiancé, Kyle, had an accident during a routine dentist appointment, ended up with suicide disease, that thing where you get constant excruciating pain in your jaw. Can't sleep, can't think straight, it's so bad. Colton used to pick up his painkillers from the pharmacy. At some point, he started taking them too. He never said why. Kyle left him, broke off the engagement, and Colton had to get the drugs, or something like them, via less legal means. Started faking the prescriptions and eventually got caught. Ended up spending a year inside. He came out through New Hope like I did, and with just as much family support."

Jess reached up and cradled my cheek with one gentle hand, then kissed me, slow and soft. "He's lucky to have a friend like you," she murmured, pressing herself against me.

"Don't know about that," I said, my body responding to hers. "But I know I'm lucky to have you."

She kissed me again, this time with urgency. "You're about to get lucky," she purred. After that, I forgot about Colton, ghosts, and Rosalind for the rest of the night.

I was too busy the rest of that week to think about the events at Colton's, much less calling Rosalind. Hickory's other cook got clipped by a drunk-driver on 40 going home that night, and ended up with a broken arm and nose, so someone had a worse night than I did. But that meant I had to pull doubles the rest of the week until a restaurant owned by a friend of my boss loaned us a short-term replacement. And then I had to train that replacement on our menu. It was a testament to how much I needed the job, that the worse expression of my temper that week was a few very choice words for one of my line cooks when his ten minute break became more than fifteen. I was exhausted, irritable, and had no interest in ghosts, visions, or other weirdness from that far off time when I worked less than seventeen hours a day.

The following Wednesday, I at least got the lunch service off, and I seized the opportunity to sleep until 2pm. Then, after closing on Thursday night, Mike, my boss, clapped me on the back and thanked me for all my hard work. "I do appreciate it, D. You've stepped up and I won't forget it. But you need to take a day off before the rest of the kitchen becomes permanently terrified of you!" He gave me all of Friday, and I was grateful, even with his little joke. At least I hoped it was a joke.

Jess was working a big convention that weekend, so I wasn't able to turn my free day to quite the advantage I had hoped. After pretending to do chores around my apartment for a while - how clean do hardwood floors need to be? - my thoughts returned to 1500 Locust and the note sequestered in my bedside table. With the week and a half I had endured, the events and my reaction to them seemed dim and less convincing. But there was an itch that needed scratching, a desire to understand more, and Rosalind claimed to have answers. When I found myself rummaging for beer in my fridge just after noon, I decided I needed a distraction.

"Hello, you've reached the voice mail of Rosalind Hill. Yes, I loathe these things too, but unfortunately I can't answer my phone at the moment. Leave a message and I promise I'll call you when I can."

"Uh, hi. This is D. From that thing at 1500 Locust the other week. I guess I'm ready to find out more. Please call me." I hung up. And then realized I was a moron and called back to leave another message with my damn phone number.

I hate waiting for people to call back. When I'm ready for a conversation, I want to have it right then. I bounced from one room to another for almost an hour before my phone finally rang.

"Hello, D," she said, accent undiluted by the cell carrier. "I'm afraid you called me at work, and this is the first chance I've had to reply."

"No problem," I said, wondering where she worked, but not enough to ask. "Work's been crazy for me too since, well, since we met."

"And you're ready to talk about it?"

"As ready as I'll ever be, I guess."

"I see. Are you free later this afternoon? I can meet you somewhere. This sort of thing is best done in person."

"Uh, sure."

"Don't worry," she laughed. "I promise this will be strictly professional. We can meet somewhere public if you like. Do you enjoy the zoo?"

The St. Louis Zoo is one of the best in the country. Not least because it is free to get in; fees for some of their premium exhibits supplement public donations. It's a fantastic place to go for families, and even for those like me who desire an open space to wander alone with their thoughts. On a fair-weather day, I would walk the four miles from my apartment to Forest Park, at least in one direction. That afternoon was still overcast and damp, but I had nervous energy to burn off before I met Rosalind, so I threw on a Cardinals hat - visor facing forwards, thank you very much - and set out. I skirted the southern edge of Tower Grove Park and threaded my way through the narrow streets of The Hill, fragrant with Italian cooking, as its many restaurants took a collective deep breath before the weekend bustle, then headed north on Hampton. One of the nice things about being a pedestrian on that route is that few other people do it.

Rosalind was waiting for me on a bench near the sea lion enclosure. She wore a dress-suit, as she had done before, although this was a rather unflattering chocolate brown, accompanied by a large black shoulder bag that gaped open beside her. On her lap sat a stack of paper, which she studied with a frown, and made an occasional mark with a red pen. I hesitated as I approached, but she glanced up and sighed before stuffing the papers back into her bag, and I resisted the urge to zip it up for her.

"I weep for the future, D," she said, shaking her head. "There's only so much I can do."

I made the connection. "You're a teacher?"

She nodded. "Gold Cross." An all-girls Catholic high school, just west of Forest Park. I briefly dated a girl from there in my high school days. It hadn't taken long for that novelty to wear off, for her at least.

"How is your friend, Mr. Lynn?"

"Colton? Fine, I guess. I mean, I don't know for sure. I haven't talked to him since that night."

She frowned, and I felt my defenses engage. I wasn't quite sure what I expected from this conversation, but I wasn't interested in it being judgment.

"Just wondered if it was only you. I think it depends on one's nature as well as one's experiences, you see."

"No, I don't. What are you talking about?"

She raised an eyebrow. "Why don't you have a seat, and I'll tell you."

I sat, keeping a comfortable distance between me and her bag. I'm tall and well-built, and I know I can look intimidating, especially when my temper is fraying, and I was here for answers not to scare anyone.

"Good. Now, would you like to tell me what you saw that night? What you heard, smelled or otherwise experienced in your friend's apartment?"

So I did, keeping my voice low to avoid attracting the ear of the growing number of passers-by. Ten days had not dulled my memory of that evening, and that was a good thing. She listened to my account and then probed me with relentless questions. She was interested in everything, from when I first sensed something odd during the elevator ride, until the moment I reclaimed my grasp of reality while gasping on Colton's floor.

"Who are they?" I asked at last when her examination was complete. She hadn't flinched at anything I had said, just frowned at one or two details.

"I can't tell you their names," she said, perching on the edge of the bench, observing me. "But from what I saw of their dress and the furnishings of the room, I guess it was an office when the building was still a garment warehouse. Early twentieth century, perhaps."

"They've been trapped there for a hundred years? Why can't they move on?"

She cocked her head. "Are you a religious man, D?"

"Not practicing," I answered, a little wary. You never know where someone is coming from with a question like that. "My mom raised me Catholic, but I sort of lost my faith in high school. In a lot of things."

"But you believe in life after death?"

"Maybe. I mean, but we don't know really, do we? No-one's proven it either way."

"Well, that depends on who you talk to and what you consider 'proof'," she said with a smile. "How else would you explain what you experienced?"

She held my gaze, and I squirmed a little, but there was no way to avoid that question. "I can't explain it," I muttered when the silence grew too intense. "Even before tonight, when I felt things, when I thought I saw things, I didn't know what was going on. But I didn't want to believe it was ghosts, or poltergeists, or anything... supernatural."

"Supernatural is just another word for something we can't explain yet. But that doesn't mean you have to accept other people's theories about the phenomena."

"What do you mean?"

She took a slow drink from a water bottle, and it reminded me of how thirsty I was after my vision, or whatever it was. "Ghosts don't exist, and I don't think those men exist anymore. I don't think they are ghosts, or spirits waiting to 'move on'. There's something else going on here."

"Like what?"

"I've seen no evidence for the concept of 'ghost' that pervades superstition and popular culture," she said, glancing idly at a passing group of noisy teenagers and not answering my question. "But that doesn't mean remnants of previous lives do not linger."

"I don't understand. What's the difference?"

"Sentience, mostly. I have yet to encounter any phenomena that show the ability or inclination to interact with me or anyone else. It's the difference between watching live music and listening to the radio."

"I'm a Spotify man myself," I said before I could stop myself. Rosalind pursed her lips, and I hadn't been out of school so long that I failed to recognize what that look meant. "So, are you saying what I saw, what I felt in Colton's place, was some kind of recording?"

"Perhaps," she said. "Maybe 'memory' is a better word, imprinted somehow. The sensations are localized, sometimes to the building, sometimes to a single room."

"But wouldn't memory imply sentience?"

She laughed suddenly, and it was as if a beam of sunlight had pierced the long overcast day.

"Very good, D! Yes, it would, and the implications for that are terrifying. I cannot give you the perfect term for what I have experienced. I don't have all the answers, I'm afraid."

How about some answers? I thought, but didn't say. I'd told her what she wanted to know, but all I was getting in return was what wasn't going on and vague conjecture.

A shrill wail startled me, and I jerked around to see a young man wrestling a toddler into a stroller. Behind him stood a pretty slip of a girl watching, her face weary.

"If you won't walk, you have to ride," the man told the toddler, who bawled even louder in return. I don't know how parents of young children make it through the day; they scare me more than any ghost.

I turned back to Rosalind and surprised a curious look on her face as she watched the young family, somewhere between amusement, irritation and sadness. As soon as she noticed my attention, her expression hardened. I coughed, embarrassed, although I couldn't explain why, and marshaled my thoughts. "So," I said, drawing the word out, "whatever these things are, memories or recordings or something to be named later, how often do they occur? And where do you come in? You say they're not ghosts, so you're not an exorcist then?"

"Not at all," she said, then frowned. "Although I suppose it amounts to the same thing, from a practical perspective. I try to erase that imprinted memory. It's almost like a therapy session. I listen to the room, to the building, and I... open myself to it, allow myself to be a conduit for the trauma to dissipate."

"If I said I didn't understand again, would that irritate you?"

She sighed. "Only mildly. I have never had to explain this to anyone else before, and my skill as a teacher only helps me so much. You are the first person I have met in seven years that possesses the same, shall we say, sensitivity."

I let that pass. "You've been doing this for seven years? How come no-one else knows? I would've thought it'd be all over the news by now." Or at least some disreputable paranormal cable TV show.

"It's hardly in my clients' interest to publicize what I do," Rosalind said, her hazel eyes crinkling in not quite laughter. "They are happy to call on me when needed, which is often enough to keep me in practice, but not to be a burden. Not yet anyway. And no, I don't have business cards. It's all word of mouth, and I end up working with many of the same people familiar with my skills." She settled back on the bench as I tried to absorb this. "So, have I answered at least some of your questions? Do you want to learn more? What do you want out of this?"

What did I want? As I considered my answer, I watched a crowd gather by the sea lion enclosure, perhaps expecting one of the public feedings. My hackles rose; this was not the best place for deep thought. "I don't want to freak out every time I come across one of these ghosts, or imprinted memories, or whatever they are. And I don't want to have to avoid places, to tell my girlfriend I can't eat at a restaurant she likes, because I'm afraid of reacting to something weird and turning a table over. I don't—" I took a deep breath, felt the circle of leather under my fingertips. "All I want is a steady job, to make an honest living and live in peace. I want someone to share it with. I want a normal life. And I can't do that if I can't control myself, if I don't know what I'm up against."

I slumped against the back of the bench and eyed the growing sea lion crowd warily. When I could bring myself to turn back to Rosalind, she was staring at her hands clasped in her lap.

"It gets better," she murmured, then looked up at me with a sympathetic smile. "At least I think it will if you let me help you, and you'll be helping me too."

I couldn't prevent the bark of a humorless laugh from escaping. "I can't imagine I could be much help to anyone," I said, and hated my self-pity.

"Perhaps not, not yet. But in time..." She shook her head abruptly and narrowed her eyes. "Are you alright, D?"

I managed a nervous laugh. "I'm not a fan of crowds, that's all."

"Fair enough," she said, and stood. "I need to head home anyway. These essays won't grade themselves, more's the pity."

She headed for the exit, and I followed her, grateful to leave the crowd behind. I wasn't sure how to respond to what she had told me. Maybe we both had more questions than answers. The biggest question for me was: what do I do next?

We passed through the exit into Forest Park proper, before she spoke again. Forbidding ranks of trees marched along the road outside the zoo; this was in the exact opposite direction to my apartment. The moment of disorientation passed before I realized she had spoken, but I hadn't heard a word, and had to apologize.

"I said, I think you should accompany me on my next job," she repeated, gazing at me. "If you want to master yourself, to live your life without fear of these phenomena, I can try to teach you how to deal with them. Think about it. I'll be in touch."

I wasn't sure whether to shake her hand, or say "Yes, miss", and settled for a mumbled "Okay". She smiled, then turned on her heel and strode off into the trees.

Excerpt of email recovered from closed account, owner untraceable. Destination account also closed and untraceable.

From: (address withheld)
To: (address withheld)
Subject: St. Louis 2023-04
Sent: 2023-04-14 22:43:07 UTC

...an uneasy partnership, perhaps, but since I've been stuck here much longer than anticipated, I am grateful for the help.

Although, I miss the resources at Cambridge, or even Ithaca. My second student continues to make progress, but far slower than I would like. Still, better that than the alternative. They're like children in a way; they simply don't know what they're up against, and it's my job to shield them from the real peril.

The recent intrusion profile in St. Louis matches predictions much more closely. If you can find a replacement - Gomez, perhaps? I heard she was coming out of Mexico City - I think my talents may be better served elsewhere. The remaining freelancer is still active, but I hope to have that situation in hand before midsummer. I'm not entirely sure I can deal with weeks of heat and humidity like last year's.

Speaking of Gomez...

CHAPTER FOUR

CAN I GO HOME NOW?

Hickory wasn't a big place, although it spilled a handful of tables onto the sidewalk during the summer months to complement the tree-shadowed patio out back. We weren't there yet, however, and the mercurial Spring weather took another nosedive to freezing overnight temperatures later that week. People still want their barbecue, and our modest dining room was loud and crowded as the weekend began. Two or three servers, depending on the shift, shuttled endlessly between it and the kitchen, squeezing past each other in the narrow joining corridor. The kitchen itself was just large enough for me and my two line cooks to work, and there was a tiny break room by the back door that contained a wobbly trestle table, a chair, and a row of shallow lockers along one wall, just big enough for a coat in the winter, and personal belongings like car keys and phones. It was in the break room on Friday night that I found TJ.

"Hey man!" he cried, as I popped in to check my phone in case Jess had messaged about coming over later. He offered his left fist for a bump, which I duly gave him as I took in the plaster cast covering his lower right arm, and hung suspended from a shoulder sling under his Billikens jacket.

"Hey TJ. How's the arm doing?"

"Hurts like a motherfucker," he grimaced, then grinned, exposing his crooked teeth. "Gets me sympathy from the ladies though."

"I bet." Tall, dark, lean, with stylish dreads, TJ fancied himself a bit of a player, and the one night we had grabbed beers after work, he'd spent most of the time chatting up any girl who came near. And to be fair, they had kept coming. I looked carefully, but could see little evidence of any broken nose from his car wreck, so that wouldn't harm his chances.

"Anyway, how you doing? I know Mike's got you working crazy hours. Sorry, man."

I shrugged. "Not your fault. What happened to you sucks. I'm just glad it didn't hurt you worse."

"Thanks. Car got totaled though. Good thing I had insurance. When I get out of this thing, I gotta go shopping."

"Cool. What are you looking at?"

Before he could answer, our boss, Mike, appeared in the doorway. Shorter than both of us, but solidly built, he commanded respect, and I couldn't help but start guiltily even though I'd been away from my duties for less than two minutes.

"Candace just walked out," he announced in a growling baritone. "Threw a plate of ribs at a customer and left through the front. D, I'm gonna need some re-plates."

"On it," I said.

"Ain't her coat in here?" asked TJ, eyes scanning the rack on the far wall, then lifting out a gray faux-fur jacket. "Want me to go talk to her?"

Mike threw his hands up. "If you want. And if you can find her."

I hurried back to the kitchen while TJ hustled out carrying Candace's coat. Mike hovered for a minute, scratching absently at his silvering buzz cut, before I realized he was probably waiting to take these plates out personally.

"Are they pissed?" I asked as I scooped mounds of pulled pork onto two plates, and laid generous slices of brisket on another.

"The guy covered with brisket and potato salad is," said Mike, frowning and adjusting his eye patch. I refocused on my plating. "His buddies seemed to think he deserved it and found the whole thing hilarious, which is why I'm just giving them free food and not calling in the riot police."

"Sorry, boss," I said, finishing up. "Guess that's been brewing for a while. You gonna take her back?"

"That depends," he said, gathering up the plates with a practiced hand. "We'll see what TJ can do with her."

I sighed. I liked Candace. She showed up on time, worked hard, and rarely messed up an order. But she did have a temper, and I knew what that was like. Mike prided himself on giving second chances, but the well wasn't inexhaustible.

I was on edge the rest of the night, narrowly catching more than one of my own errors before food went out. TJ never returned, so I had no idea if he'd caught up with Candace or not, and we had no more trouble as 9pm approached. I just don't like the attention, none of us do. Sure enough, as I slipped out onto Cherokee before Mike locked the doors, heading west toward where I had parked my car, I noticed the St. Louis City Police cruiser immediately. Cursing under my breath, I stared down at my feet and tried to look inconspicuous as I passed by.

"Rodriguez! Walking home tonight?"

Shit. "Officer Kennedy." I nodded at the cop behind the wheel, a pale, middle-aged man with an ugly scar on his left cheek that twisted his grin into a leer. Despite the chill breeze and fitful drizzle, I also took my hands out of my jacket pockets, allowing my arms to hang in a neutral position.

"Heard there was a bit of a fracas at your place tonight," he drawled. "Care to share what happened?"

"Is that an official question?"

"Not yet. You weren't involved, were you?"

"I didn't see what happened. Too busy."

"Of course, of course. You're a hard-working guy, aren't you Rodriguez?"

I ground my teeth and peered at the figure in the passenger seat. Kennedy's partner was a young white woman who studiously avoided looking in my direction. No help there then.

"I am and I'm tired and cold. Can I go home now?"

Kennedy stared at me in silence for a while, the ghost of a smile on his lips, then sniffed. "Go home. And be careful."

I turned and resumed the walk to my car, forcing myself to maintain the same easy pace as any other night. It was parked just around a corner, and as soon as I slumped into the driver's seat, I locked my doors, gripped the steering wheel, and let out a long shaky breath. I didn't start the engine until my knuckles regained their normal color.

Much to my surprise, Jess texted while I was driving home and asked if she could come over. Even though she was a night owl, this was late for her to stop by. Perhaps it was convention stress. Whatever the reason, I wasn't one to look a gift horse in the mouth, especially after the evening I'd had.

It was closer to 11 by the time she arrived. She shrugged off her raincoat, and, in the same fluid motion, fell into my arms. For some time we simply stood there, wrapped up in a silent hug. I realized she was trembling, which for some women might have foreshadowed tears, but for Jess more likely meant barely suppressed fury.

"What's the matter?" I asked at last in my most soothing voice.

"Stupid immature assholes," she replied, and clapped me on both shoulders as she withdrew from my embrace and strode to the fridge. She scowled as she rummaged inside, tossing her long black hair over her shoulder, then yanked out a bottle of cheap Sauvignon Blanc that I kept for emergencies. I already had the corkscrew ready and poured her a glass. She drained half of it, then thrust it toward me for a refill.

"I get teenage boys like gaming, but they aren't the only ones. And teenage boys old enough to be my father are really tough to take, especially when they're leering at me the whole time."

"Did any do worse than leer?" I felt the beast stir, its protective urges aroused.

"Oh sure, one even wondered why a girl with my skin color would be interested in gaming. I can take the flirts and the creepers, but the racists are something else." She drained her glass and tossed it into the sink. Fortunately, it was plastic, not actual glass, and didn't shatter, although I'm not sure she cared right then.

I realized I was fiddling with the leather bracelet I wore around my right wrist and made myself stop.

"You didn't throw anything at anyone, did you?"

"No, but I so wanted to. It's times like this I hate being a bartender."

I reached out and drew her back towards me. She sighed and threw her arms around my neck, imprisoning me with those dazzling eyes.

"Well, that's why you started doing this coding thing, right?"

"Shift_Dev? Yeah, one of the reasons. Getting a job working with other professionals and not the public is definitely a plus. And it's fun."

"First class went okay then?"

"Yeah, just a bunch of setup stuff mostly. I hope it's all that easy."

"You'll do great."

She squinted at me, then grinned. "Thanks. I hope you're right, and that I can make it through six more months of dealing with assholes."

"You want me to stop by between shifts tomorrow, set the record straight for those guys?"

"Hell no. I still need that job. You already cost me one of those."

"I never got you fired!"

"No, you just scared the crap out of one of my customers, and my boss asked me to tell you to stay away. I pretty much had to quit."

She cuffed me lightly on the side of my head, but she was grinning now.

"Well, if I can't help you with my intimidating presence tomorrow afternoon, what can I do for you?"

She kissed me then, suddenly and fiercely, her body pressed close against mine, and when she stopped and we opened our eyes again, there was a fire in hers. "You can take me to your bedroom," she whispered. "And make me forget about everything else."

Afterward, we lay naked on top of the sheets for a while, the remaining covers strewn around the floor. I lay staring at the single window, at the streetlight leaking around the edges of the blinds. Jess nestled behind me, breasts and stomach against my back, knees in the crook of mine, one arm around my chest, her caramel against my light copper. My fingertips drifted idly over the lines of her half-sleeve dragon tattoo while she softly kissed the ankh at the back of my neck, nuzzling my ponytail aside. I've never trusted another human being to touch my neck, and she knew it.

If I'd successfully driven away her frustration about her night at work, she had done the same for me. My thoughts turned again to my conversation with Rosalind at the zoo, as they had done almost every idle moment since Tuesday, worrying over it like an aching tooth. I would have to tell Jess about it, tell her about Rosalind soon, but now didn't seem like the best time. Still...

"Let me ask you something," I said suddenly, almost surprising myself.

"Mmm?"

"Have you ever seen a ghost? Or something that seemed or felt like a ghost, like someone else's memory?"

"Really? You want me to answer a question like that, or do you want me to keep kissing you?"

"I want you to answer that question, and then go back to kissing me."

She punched me in the small of my back, but at least she didn't bite anything. "You're weird sometimes."

"Oh, I'm just getting started."

"Well," she said after a pause long enough that I almost turned over, "My Gramma's farm was supposed to be haunted, according to Kirksville tradition anyway. I was out in the barn by myself one night. Let's see, I was in junior high, so twelve or thirteen I guess, and I got spooked. Thought I saw shapes in the shadows, ran back to the farmhouse and wouldn't go back without company. Probably just bats or something."

"Probably," I murmured. "I wonder how common it is."

"How common what is?" Jess's hand clawed at my chest. "Can I go back to kissing your neck now?"

"Sure." I squeezed her hand, but she shook it off. I tried to relax.

You are the first person I have met in seven years that possesses the same sensitivity. Could that be true? Even if it was, so what? How many people would choose to admit such a thing, other than the genius that is yours truly? I didn't want to stand out. I was doing my damnedest to blend in, to become just another barely functioning member of this great American society. I didn't need it, and I didn't want it. Did I?

"You still with me, D?" I felt the soft touch of Jess's lips as she breathed in my ear.

"Always," I whispered back.

"Good," she said, and her hand drifted down over my stomach.

CHAPTER FIVE

LISTEN

Jess was gone almost before I knew it was morning.

"I'm late," she called over her shoulder after her hurried kiss woke me.

"Don't murder anyone!" I replied, but the apartment door closed halfway through. Perhaps "I love you" would have been better, so I whispered it anyway. For what it was worth.

I had to get ready for work, so I rushed a shower and grabbed a granola bar on my way out. Foul things, but I told myself they were good for me, and I believed myself just enough to force them down.

The lunch service was quiet, but then the sun dispersed the lingering cloud cover and the dinner rush came early. The buzz around the kitchen was that Candace had quit for good, and Mike was already talking to New Hope about a potential replacement. I was sorry to see her go, but before long, I was too busy to give her much thought. Sunday was busy too, and soon I was back in the rhythm, seasoning meats, preparing sauces, and barking at the rest of my crew just enough to keep the kitchen focused. I loved this job, loved the routine and attention to detail, loved the satisfaction of putting out a great plate of food, and I loved how comfortingly normal it was. I belonged here, and I was making people happy, or at least a lot less hungry. Jess texted me Sunday evening to say she had finished out the convention without incurring a body count, and, after some raunchy back and forth, told me she'd see me on Tuesday. Life was back to normal.

For another day or two, I wondered if I would hear from Rosalind again, and told myself I wasn't disappointed when I didn't. Two weeks passed. In retrospect, I wish I had enjoyed the time more, but that and a dollar will get you up a cup of coffee, or at least it would somewhere they instantly forget your order.

Rosalind called around 4pm on a Thursday, just as preparations for the dinner service were underway. I usually let the rare phone calls I receive at that time go to voice mail, but Greg, my younger line cook, was getting on my nerves again and I needed the distraction. I still hesitated after I saw who was calling, but answered as I stepped out onto the world's tiniest deck overlooking the back patio.

"D? I hope I'm not interrupting anything."

"I'm at work, but I can spare a minute. What's up?" Like I didn't know why she was calling.

"Very well, I'll be brief. Are you free either afternoon this weekend?"

If I had said no, would that have been the end of it? I'll never know, because I told her I had Saturday lunchtime off work.

"Excellent. Are you up for a field trip?"

"Where to? I have to be at work by three."

"To the exotic suburb of Crestwood. We can have you home by three."

"At work by three," I corrected, and she chuckled. Teasing then. Great, glad you're having fun.

"We should arrive together. Can you meet me in the parking lot by the Starbucks, opposite the old mall? Say around noon?"

I said I could, mostly because Greg was waving frantically at me through the window and I needed to avert the impending culinary disaster. It occurred to me several hours later, during a blissful pause in the evening rush, that I knew nothing about what this field trip was, beyond a vague idea it must have something to do with a haunting-but-not-by-a-ghost.

Crestwood is one of the last suburbs you pass through as you take Interstate 44 south-west from downtown St. Louis, and before you cross Interstate 270, the Missouri half of the ring road around the metro area. Watson Road, once a stretch of the legendary Route 66, runs parallel to 44 and bisects Crestwood, before giving up at its western border and joining that mighty highway as it forges onward into the heart of the state. Further east, especially before you cross the River Des Peres and enter St. Louis City itself, somewhat shabby motels, diners and other remnants of Route 66 iconography still flank the road. By the time it reaches Crestwood, however, it has surrendered to the strip mall architecture of Everytown USA, except what once was Crestwood Mall, "where St. Louis goes to shop", a former open air shopping center hurriedly covered over in the 1980s. Vibrant for a time - hell, I still remember a family outing there in the early 90s, where my wish to sit on Santa's lap was indulged for the one and only time - infrastructure and foot traffic decayed until stores began closing for good in the mid

00s. Futile attempts to keep at least the cinema open continued for a few more years until everyone gave up and they demolished the entire thing in the mid 10s. Now the site was mounds of dirt covered by prairie scrub, forlornly awaiting the attention of the next developer to propose a viable plan.

Across from the old mall site - dubbed Mount Crestwood by locals - was a nondescript strip mall with a Starbucks and a Mexican restaurant. The first weekend in May was making a statement of intent with seventy degree weather, part of the region's annual headlong rush from freezing cold winter to hot and humid summer. Consequently, both patios were spilling over with customers, and I abandoned my plan to grab an overpriced coffee-related beverage. It turned out there was no need, because as I parked my ten-year-old Elantra as far from the crowds as possible, I spied Rosalind standing next to a royal blue Mini Clubman a few spaces away, holding a paper cup in each hand.

"Just coffee, black," she called as I approached, locking my car with the remote. Music was blaring from the Mini's open window, New Order's *Age of Consent*, if I had my 80s British music scene right.

"Sorry, I'll turn this off. Or down at least." She grinned and suddenly seemed much younger than the mid-forties I had guessed her to be. Shorter too, and in the bright sunshine, her light tan dress suit rendered her almost insubstantial. I hadn't really looked at her before, having had other things on my mind in our prior meetings, but I did so now, as surreptitiously as possible. Her chestnut, shoulder-length brown hair was just starting toward gray, but the pale oval face it framed was smooth and unlined, and her hazel eyes were clear. She was slim, not as curvy as I tend to like, but I realized she was still a very attractive woman and that it was probably time for me to speak.

"I feel underdressed," I offered as I accepted a coffee, and gestured at my jeans and plain black t-shirt. "I just wore what I wear to work."

"Where is that?" she asked, sipping her coffee and smiling.

I suspected I might be staring and tried to pull myself together. "Hickory. It's a BBQ joint in South City. I'm one of the cooks."

"Good for you. I admire a man who can cook. My husband's repertoire begins and ends with frozen pizza, I'm afraid."

"So, where are we going?" I asked, trying to find more comfortable territory.

"Yes, let's get to work," she said, and suddenly her manner was all business. "Why don't you get in, and I'll explain on the way."

I squeezed myself into the passenger seat - I swear the car was actually smaller on the inside - and she pulled out of the parking lot, pausing only to key an address into the navigation system.

"We're going to a normal-looking house on a typical suburban street," she said, gunning the Clubman and barely making the left-turn light at the intersection. "There, we'll meet a realtor friend of mine, and possibly the family too. According to him, one of their young boys has been having a terrible time since the family moved in three months ago, and it appears related to something in his bedroom. Something that my friend believes may be in my neck of the woods."

"Your neck of the woods?"

"Mark uses the expression all the time. My realtor friend. You'll hear it more than once. Count on it. I do not think it means what he thinks it means."

She chuckled as she turned down a quiet side street at the navigation system's urgent behest. Residential expansion in Crestwood had mostly been in the 1960s and 70s, before subdivisions and limited choice of build plans. Houses here were all shapes, although much the same size, variations on the three bedroom two bath theme, with opportunities to finish the basement. Two stories, split-levels, and ranches sat back a modest distance from the road, most with garages, their front yards sprinkled with fresh blooming flowers, and mature trees sporting their height of spring finery. Children rode bikes, scrawled on driveways with sidewalk chalk, and some stared as we drove slowly by. It all looked gloriously middle-class America, or what I imagined that should be.

"You have reached your destination," the navigation system told us in a smug tone, as we stopped outside a smart-looking two-story house, its lower half red brick with clean white siding enfolding the upper level. The roof looked new, as did the windows, and the landscaping looked well designed and maintained. It was a far cry from Colton's apartment in the city. Two cars stood in the driveway, a blue minivan in front and what looked like a black Lexus SUV behind it. Next to the Lexus stood two men, the thin one with the shock of blond hair wearing a shirt and tie, presumably the realtor and Lexus owner. The other was a stocky black guy wearing an old Ray Lewis Baltimore Ravens jersey, and I pegged him as the father of the house. Both watched in silence as Rosalind and I got out of her car, she with considerably more grace than I.

"Rosalind, I'm glad you could come on a Saturday," said Shirt and Tie, with a professional smile. He shook her hand, then glanced at me, curiosity plastered across his face.

"No problem, Mark," said Rosalind. "This is D. You can think of him as my trainee if you like. D, this is Mark Zellers of Hostetler Realty. His daughter is at Holy Cross."

I shook Mark's hand as he sighed. "Not for much longer. One more year and then college. Unbelievable. Ah yes. Rosalind, uh... D, this is Dre Adams. Dre and his family moved in earlier this spring, March, or somewhere in that neck of the woods." I fought to keep my expression neutral.

"Hello, Mr. Adams." Rosalind said, extending her hand for the father to shake. His response was awkward, and his eyes flickered over our shoulders. Not too comfortable with the attention, I guessed. I didn't know the demographic makeup of Crestwood, but I hadn't seen another person of color since leaving the Starbucks parking lot. I shook his hand firmly and earnestly; he stared at me, then turned back to Rosalind.

"I wanted to talk to you out here first," he said, his voice low and soft. "Sierra and the boys took a walk to the park. I'm hoping we can take care of this before they get home."

"We'll see what we can do," said Rosalind, her tone gentle. "Mark told me a little about what has been happening, so I won't ask you to repeat it. Is there anything else you can share before we go inside?"

Dre chewed his lip for a moment. "It's getting worse every day," he said at last. "Xavier, my son, he won't go into his room anymore, even with me or Sierra. He's sleeping with her in my bed, and I'm on the couch. We have to fetch clothes and stuff for him. We just moved in, and we can't afford to look for another house." He gave a helpless shrug and glanced at me. I tried not to look helpless back.

"Have you considered switching his bedroom with your other son?"

"He's got Derrick all spooked too, even though he don't seem to notice anything wrong. None of us do, except Xavier."

"I see. Well, let's use our time wisely then. I don't know how Mark explained what I do, but let's just say I may be able to help, although there are no guarantees."

"Okay, I got it." Dre looked resigned and a little defiant, like he didn't relish asking for any kind of help, especially the kind he didn't understand. I couldn't blame him.

We were walking in single file up the narrow concrete path to the front door when I remembered to be nervous. That sounds stupid, I know. But I was out of my element, stuck in suburbia with a woman I barely knew, and listening to someone else's problems. And soon I had problems of my own.

As the door opened, I sensed it, and it was much worse after I stepped through into what looked like the living room. I had a vague sense of untidiness, of gray and beige furniture, and a large black TV screen dominating the wall to my right, but the wave of heat almost knocked me over. I stopped and Mark the Realtor stumbled into me. He apologized, although it was my fault, and I gestured dismissively. How could anyone breathe in here? It was so hot and there was no air, just a reek of smoke, of things burning that shouldn't be. I wanted to leave, needed to leave, I—

"Breathe."

I glanced up and Rosalind had paused a few steps ahead, gazing back at me with a placid expression. No, not placid, controlled, her arms oddly stiff at her side as if she were trying too hard to act casual. She felt it too, or felt something, she was just better at dealing with it. Come on, D, you can master this. You *need* to master this.

In. The air was too thin. Out. In. Slower now. Breathe. It's not real. It just feels real.

"Okay." I nodded to Rosalind and glanced at Dre, who was staring at me and likely having second thoughts about inviting me into his home.

"D does not yet have the experience I do, Mr. Adams," Rosalind said in calming tones. "We are experiencing what your son senses in this house. He'll be fine." She smiled. "Now, you may show us to your son's room or direct us, but once there, we'll need time and space to concentrate."

"Up the stairs, only door to your left," said Dre without pause. "Do you, uh, need anything?"

"No, thank you. We'll be back down as soon as we're done."

She headed for the stairs, and I forced myself to follow. The heat grew more oppressive with each step up the carpeted staircase, and the "otherness", for which I knew no adequate words, was palpable. I made it to the narrow upstairs hallway, trembling and breathless. Rosalind had paused outside the closed door to Xavier's bedroom, eyes shut and head cocked as if listening. Fine lines etched her forehead as she concentrated, but there was no hint of flushing or perspiration. I blinked sweat out of my eyes and tried not to touch the walls. I could have sworn the house was burning down around us.

"We must go into this room," she whispered, and opened her eyes to consider me. "I neither expect nor want you to do anything but observe me. Remember what I told you at the Zoo: I am going to open myself up to whatever memory has imprinted itself here, whatever is traumatizing this child, and erase it, allow it to flow through me and away. I'm not sure you perceive this quite as I do, but the principle should be the same.

There is a certain state of mind required, and then, well, intent is the best word I can think of. You can achieve the former, and learn the latter."

My head spun. "Achieve it how?"

"Listen. Imagine you are listening for the quietest voice in a classroom full of young children heading out to recess."

"I don't understand."

"Listen!"

And with that, Rosalind opened the door. My ears popped, but I barely noticed. The room was on fire.

I don't mean that metaphorically. Flames covered the walls to the left, consuming the tattered remnants of the curtains as I watched, the window behind them inaccessible. Thick, black smoke billowed throughout the top half of the room, pungent tendrils stretching toward me, and I coughed so hard I had to grip the doorframe for support. The twin bed against the far wall had just caught alight, its pillows aflame and blankets smoldering. I just had time to register the HR Puff N Stuff comforter when I saw the little girl.

She sat on the floor in the far right corner of the room, wedged between a free-standing wardrobe and a chest of drawers. I guessed she was nine or ten years old, with curly blonde hair that spilled over a pink t-shirt. She had drawn her knees up to her chest, her arms covering her head, and was clearly screaming her lungs out, although I could hear nothing. I froze. I couldn't watch this. She was too young, far too young! But what could I do? This wasn't real. At least, it wasn't happening now, not in the world outside this bedroom. But whatever was in this room clearly had other ideas.

Screw it. I couldn't just watch. I had to do something. There was still time to get her out! I took a step toward her.

Rosalind put out an arm to bar my way. She stood still, feet apart as if poised for combat, eyes closed and mouth working silently.

Call me stubborn, accuse me of panicking, but I didn't know what she was doing. All I knew was that the smoke was thickening while the flames crept closer to the poor child huddling in the corner. I took another step.

Rosalind's eyes flew open, and she shot me an almost murderous glare. "Listen!" she hissed. "Don't interfere."

Few people have ever intimidated me the way she did then, wide eyes boring into mine. I stopped, and even took a half-step backwards, before she closed her eyes again and turned back toward the burning room. She had to be a terror in the classroom.

Which, in a sense, this was. She was trying to teach me, and just because I didn't understand what was going on, or what she was doing, didn't mean I couldn't learn anything.

So. Deep, shaky breath. There was a girl in mortal danger just ten feet, but likely several decades away. On the long list of things I didn't know was what would happen if I tried to reach her physically. Would I burn? Would the smoke overcome me? Or, most likely, would nothing happen at all?

Perhaps I should listen to Rosalind. What was it she had said?

Listen to the quietest voice in the room.

I closed my eyes, trying to ignore my body screaming at me that the room was on fucking fire, and I needed to grab that little girl and get out. She was still there, which helped convince me that this was happening inside my head, my normal eyesight irrelevant. The smoke billowed, growing thicker and settled lower, obscuring the flames whose intense heat I could still feel beating against me in waves. I didn't want to see this, but I forced myself to focus. The girl's mouth was moving now, as if she was talking instead of screaming.

Listen.

"Make it stop. Make it go away."

It was the merest hint of an echo, like someone calling from the bottom of a deep well. I screwed my eyelids tight.

"Don't worry, sweetheart, I will," replied another voice, louder but still indistinct. I guessed it belonged to an adult, although I couldn't tell if it was male or female. "But you need to help me. Can you do that?"

"Make it stop."

"Take my hand. Take my hand, and it can stop."

The smoke almost entirely obscured the room now. All I could see was writhing and black. My flesh burned.

"Make it go away?"

"Far away."

"Please."

A sudden rush of furious wind and smoke raced past me. I coughed so hard this time that I doubled over and then sank to my knees. As I did, shadows blurred, as if figures rushed past me in both directions. I recoiled, gripping the carpet beneath me like a man clutching a water-slick rock amidst the deadly pull of rapids. Dizziness almost overcame me, and I rested my forehead on the floor.

Breathe. Just breathe.

The fit passed. I realized the heat was fading and the air no longer reeked of burning fabric. Hesitantly, I raised my head and wiped the lingering sweat from my eyes.

It was a normal child's bedroom with a twin bed to my right. The furniture was all different, surrounded by walls painted in royal blue. And, more to the point, there was not so much as a candle flame in sight.

Rosalind stood above me, panting and sweating, but smiling and offering me her hand.

"Let's go find some water, D. I suspect you could use it. I know I can."

CHAPTER SIX

TELL ME WHAT YOU REMEMBER

We found the entire family waiting for us downstairs, sitting on their taupe leather living room sofa. Dre hugged the smaller, scrawnier, and presumably younger boy, while his other son buried his face in his wife's neck. The hope on her face was almost painful to see.

"This is my wife, Sierra, and my boys Derrick and Xavier," said Dre, his voice carefully flat. "They came home while you were, uh... busy, so we came inside to wait."

How long had we been up there? It couldn't have been more than a few minutes, surely.

"Hello, Mrs. Adams," said Rosalind with a smile. "Hello Derrick, hello Xavier."

Derrick stared at her with wide eyes, but Xavier made no move.

"Can you help us?" asked Sierra. Her voice had a rural twang. Not quite Southern, maybe Ozarks. She was white with a natural blonde pixie cut, her athletic figure accented by a bright pink tank top and gray shorts. The boys' skin color and hair took more after their father, and I felt a sudden empathy for them as I thought of Jess.

"I believe we have," Rosalind assured her, then turned to Dre. "Mr. Adams, could I trouble you for some water for D and myself?"

"Sure." Dre stood and stepped into the kitchen. After a moment's hesitation, Derrick scampered after him.

Rosalind walked slowly to the end of the couch and kneeled down so that she was level with the older boy's face. Sierra watched her carefully, but said nothing.

"Xavier?"

The boy twitched, and his mother drew him fractionally closer. I guessed he was maybe nine or ten years old. About the same age as the girl in the burning room.

"Xavier, my name is Rosalind. Your parents asked me to look at your room. I know it's been upsetting you. I understand why."

He peered at her from under his mother's chin, but said nothing.

"What did you see?" Dre had returned with two bottles of off-brand spring water, one of which he handed to Rosalind and one to me. His eyes searched mine as he did so, and I wanted to reassure him, but I didn't want to interrupt Rosalind, so I smiled and nodded, hoping that would be enough.

"I saw the fire."

Xavier's eyes widened. "You did?"

"I did, and so did my friend D here."

He turned to look at me. I smiled and nodded again. I was getting good at that.

"Xavier, I want you to know that we put the fire out. I don't think you'll see it anymore."

"You sure?"

"As sure as I can be. I can show you, if you like."

He shrank against his mother, but held Rosalind's gaze.

"Your mother can come too. I promise it will be okay." She glanced at Sierra, who bit her lip and then looked down at her son.

"Come on, Xavi, let's check it out." She stood, and after a moment's resistance, he did too. Rosalind pushed herself up using the couch's arm and grimaced, then led them upstairs. Xavier halted after a few steps, clearly fearful, but his mother bent down and whispered in his ear, and he allowed himself to be coaxed upwards.

"So did you like do an exorcism or something?" Dre asked me when we heard them reach the top of the stairs.

"Honestly, Mr. Adams, I have no idea what we did. I'm very new at this."

He grimaced. "Call me Dre. I can take being called 'Mr. Adams' by a cute British lady, but not by anyone else."

I laughed before I could stop myself. "I hear that, Dre."

He looked toward the stairs and cocked his head. We could hear low, muffled voices, too indistinct to catch any words, but that was for the best.

"You know, if you have stopped whatever it was from happening, I don't know if I can ever thank you enough. It would be a miracle."

"Thank Rosalind," I said firmly. "If any miracles happened here today, she's the miracle worker."

I'm guessing we had been in Xavier's bedroom for almost a quarter of an hour, based on the time we arrived and the time we left, just shy of half-past one. How we could have been up there so long when it seemed like only five minutes was one of a long list of questions I had about the experience.

We took our leave of the family as soon as seemed polite. They were hesitantly grateful, but clearly needed their privacy. Rosalind told them to contact Mark if they had any more problems. The realtor grimaced when the family weren't looking, handing Rosalind a white envelope which she stuffed discretely inside her purse.

"Do you think they'll have any?" I asked her as she drove me back to my car. "Is it over?"

She sighed. "It's hard to say. I think so. Most of the time, I can deal with these things in one go." She glanced at me while we waited at a red light. "I know you have more questions. Are you hungry? If you have time, that Mexican restaurant by the Starbucks is not a bad place for lunch. I'm famished."

I did have questions, and I had time. And I was hungry too.

The restaurant's lunch rush was over, and we easily got an outside table away from most other diners at the end of a modest patio alongside the building. A man and a woman, both blonde, white and about my age, were paying their check at the next table, glancing at us from behind identical black sunglasses as we sat down. I wondered what they thought they were looking at, and forced myself not to return their gaze. The wait staff plied us with tortilla chips and salsa, and Rosalind ordered a frozen margarita, claiming they were some of the best in the city. I contented myself with hogging the pitcher of water. We ordered our meals - I'm no connoisseur of Mexican food, but I like a chimichanga as much as the next guy - and the waiter left us to it.

"Can I ask you a question before you ask yours?" Rosalind said, snapping a chip in two, before stabbing her dish of salsa with it.

"Sure."

"Why 'D'?"

"Why what?"

"Your name. Is it a nickname? I learn dozens of new student names each year, and they always fascinate me. Or I'm just nosy, if you prefer."

I shrugged. I get the question often enough. "Well, I never really liked my name. It's easier to just go by the initial."

"What about your middle name?"

"I never liked that either."

She chuckled. When she laughed, the lines at the corner of her eyes and the dimples in her cheeks deepened, but were both eclipsed by the merriment in her eyes. "Fair enough! Alright then, D. Ask away."

The door to the restaurant opened, and the waiter appeared with our food. As he set the plates down in front of us, I marshaled my thoughts. Strangely, I thought I heard my name from somewhere behind me, but when I glanced over my shoulder, I saw that the couple at the adjacent table had left, and a group of young women at another nearby table were leaving, rounding the corner of the patio and heading toward the parking lot. I frowned, then shook my head to rid myself of the distraction.

"You told me before that these, uh, experiences were like memories. That implies we both saw the same thing. But what I saw can't have lasted fifteen minutes. Did I miss something?"

She frowned. "Tell me what you remember."

I did, in as much detail as I could, except for the part that bothered me most.

"That seems consistent with what I saw, although not as complete. You didn't see the girl playing with matches, then?" I shook my head.

"The room shared its memory with us, or rather, we both viewed the memory independently. It's possible we received different versions of that memory. It's also possible I am more sensitive, but likelier that I have developed more skill at 'listening'. I hear more. I feel more. And right now, I can do more."

She shivered, then raised a forkful of shrimp and rice to her mouth.

"I guess that makes sense. So are you saying that anyone affected by these memories, like me or Colton or even the boy Xavier, can learn this skill? With enough practice, we could learn to do what you do."

She chewed thoughtfully, then shook her head. "I'm not an expert, but I don't think so. Just because you're affected doesn't mean you can do anything about it. It's a matter of sensitivity. Neither Colton nor Xavier seemed affected beyond their rooms, other than their fear of what they sensed there. I could tell it affected you as soon as I saw you walk out of that elevator all the way down the hall from Colton's apartment. It was the first time I had seen that in anyone but me. I knew you could do it, or learn to do so."

"I doubt I can do anything yet," I replied, trying to decide if I was pleased or intimidated by her statement. "Even if I understood half of what was going on."

"You'd be surprised, both at what you understand and what you could do if you had to. A lot of this is a natural reaction to the experience."

I laughed, and she paused with her fork in midair. I raised my hand, palm facing out. "Sorry, but the idea of a natural reaction to something like this is..." I dropped my hand back down to my lap and glanced away for a moment. "I mean, we're watching people die here."

"Not always," she said. "Every memory I have seen was traumatic, or perhaps 'emotional' is a better word. Some involve death, by direct or indirect means, but most do not. That little girl in the burning house didn't die. She wasn't even burned. She escaped with smoke inhalation and a very guilty conscience, which I imagine was severe enough. I believe she still lives in the area."

"You saw all that?"

"No, I read about it. Contemporary newspaper articles stored on microfiche at the St. Louis Library. You know what microfiche is, I assume."

"Like plankton, you mean?"

She threw a shrimp at me. I caught and ate it, and she grinned.

"I do my research, D. I never walk in unprepared, or at least as prepared as I can be. Mark called me about this house on Monday. I spent two evenings in the main library downtown hunting down every scrap of information I could find on this house. Not everything is online, before you ask. I wanted to know what I was dealing with, especially if I was going to invite you along. A memory's potency is not necessarily proportional to the size of the building. And the only thing I could find was a report of a house fire in 1978, started by a seven-year-old girl playing with matches in her bedroom. I thought it would be less traumatic than what you saw at your friend's apartment, and probably more instructive. I think I've been proven right so far."

She drained her frozen margarita and set her glass down regretfully. The waiter reappeared as if by magic and asked if she wanted a refill, but she told him no, just the check, please.

"I know you have to leave for work soon," she said, also regretfully. And as strange and disturbing as my brief relationship with her had been, I wasn't in a hurry to leave either.

"I have a few more minutes. You said 1978? If the memory is that old, how come this is the first time it's surfaced?"

"Oh, I don't think it is. The house has been sold seven times since then, the first time only a few months later. The damage was reparable, evidently. But two of those seven buyers stayed a year or less before selling again, and that excludes the Adamses. That could be coincidence, but I think at least one or two others who have lived in that house were sensitive enough to experience the memory to some extent."

I pondered this while Rosalind paid the bill, brushing aside my attempts to pay for my share by insisting it was a business expense, reminding me of something else I wanted to ask about later. But I suddenly thought about Jess's story of the barn at her grandmother's farm.

"One last question," I said, glancing at the time on my phone. I could still make it. "Towards the end, at least of what I remember, I thought I heard a conversation. One voice asking for it to stop, another telling it to 'take my hand and it will', something like that. At the time, I thought the first voice was the girl, and the other was an adult, a parent or a firefighter, maybe. But now I'm not so sure. Would it be possible that I heard you talking to the little girl? Or maybe even to the room?"

Rosalind stared at me for a full ten seconds before replying. It was one part the stare of a teacher considering how to answer a precocious student, and one part the haunted look of someone who knows or suspects an answer they are unwilling to give.

"I think you heard the girl and her rescuer," she said at last. "That seems the most likely explanation." But her eyes didn't quite meet mine.

Excerpt of email recovered from closed account, owner untraceable. Destination account also closed and untraceable.

From: (address withheld)
To: (address withheld)
Subject: St. Louis 2023-05 #2
Sent: 2023-05-12 03:11:39 UTC

...and while I understand that we need expertise in Seattle, and Gomez has valuable connections there, a rotation out of St. Louis would have been appreciated.

Enough said. Perhaps my frustration is fueled by three consecutive days of 95 degree temperatures - in May! Even the locals are grumbling, when they're not gushing over their beloved Cardinals' start to the season. Or maybe our business partner is the source of my discontent, for he continues to exercise what he considers his prerogative in directing my activities. If our very different motivations did not so neatly coincide for our mutual short-term gain, I would be more than happy never to deal with the man again. As it is, he apparently has a familial connection to the second freelancer, which complicates my study of the first. This needn't become personal, and I will endeavor to curtail their activities with all the dispassion I can bring to bear.

That said, she is very, very good...

CHAPTER SEVEN

WE DON'T DO MODERATION

It was a lot to think about, but for a while that's all I had to do, and I barely had energy for that. The balmy late spring weather, for once enduring more than a week or two between winter's chill and summer's heat and humidity, brought St. Louis to the streets, to the parks and to the restaurants. Mike, in a stroke of genius, had spent April and early May refurbishing and expanding Hickory's modest back patio into a full-fledged beer garden, increasing our capacity by fifty percent. And we used every inch, most nights and through the weekends, as temperatures soared. It was all the kitchen could do to keep up, and if TJ hadn't returned to work with his arm healed, I'm not sure I would have survived. Rosalind called me mid-month "just to check in" and to tell me she was buried with preparing, giving, and grading end-of-year exams, so not to expect any more jobs until after Memorial Day. I was both relieved and frustrated, but I had little time to dwell on my latest brush with the paranormal. I wouldn't have thought on it at all, if it wasn't for something I heard while at New Hope.

Mike hired all his staff from New Hope and other re-entry facilities in the St. Louis area. Janelle, the new server hired to replace Candace, who had refused to return to work, was no exception. He also liked to cater events there on occasion and encouraged us to volunteer our time. I didn't mind, having a lot to thank New Hope for, having had nowhere else to go when I returned to free society eighteen months ago. I enjoyed seeing the staff, most of whom were still there, and I liked the chance to give a little encouragement to those going through the program, awaiting their own chances. The Sunday afternoon of the holiday weekend, I helped Janelle serve the food Mike and I had prepared earlier that day, smiling as both staff and residents congratulated her on her new job.

"It doesn't seem so long ago we were all wishing you well," said Toni, the matronly Director of Operations, coming to stand next to me as I began the takedown process. Toni always had a lot of time for the residents, and consequently I had a lot of time for her. I offered her the last two slices of brisket, and after a moment's hesitation, she accepted.

"Almost a year," I said with relish. "That was one of the best days of my life. Not that I wasn't sorry to say goodbye, though."

She gave a rather wistful smile. "The more we say goodbye, the better we're doing our job. It's hard sometimes, especially when things don't work out. I'm glad it did for you."

"Me too." I nodded, then paused. "I ran into Colton Lynn a while back."

"Oh yeah, how's he doing? He left not long after you did, if I remember right."

"I guess. He got a job as a courier. Bit of a change for him, but he seemed happy with the new start."

"Good. Didn't he get a place in one of those apartments on Washington?"

"Locust." I hoped she wouldn't ask me about it, but she just nodded and took another bite of brisket.

"Do you remember Trey? Trey McDonald? I think he started here before you left."

"Lanky white guy with a goatee?"

"That's him. He got an apartment on Locust. I wonder if it's the same building."

"How's he doing?" I asked. I only just remembered Trey, but I was happy to steer the conversation away from those apartments.

"Well, I think," said Toni, then frowned. "He got a job as a janitor at Chouteau Village, those upmarket condos a couple blocks from here. He was pretty happy with it, but I hear they've been having some problems with that building. I hope he lands on his feet."

"Yeah, I hope so," I said, frowning myself as I tried to remember where I'd heard the name "Chouteau Village". It wasn't until I was driving home that it popped into my head: a passing comment between Rosalind and Nicole, the property manager at 1500 Locust, after Rosalind erased the memory in Colton's apartment. I wondered if those were the kinds of problems Toni was talking about, but I didn't wonder for long, because soon I had more pressing problems of my own.

Jess had been warning me about "Kenya Day", as she called it, for weeks. I had only met all her family together twice, starting with last Christmas Day. It wasn't long after we'd started dating, and I'm not sure whose eyes it had opened more, theirs or mine. I half-believed Jess had hooked up with me for the express purpose of grandstanding the event, but she assured me that wasn't the case. It was just a bonus.

"Anyway, last Kenya Day I brought Nina," Jess said, laughing afterwards. "I thought Dad was gonna explode! You were definitely a step up in his book."

So, as June 1st approached and Jess reminded me she expected me to accompany her to "fucking Kenya Day", I was as unexcited as I could possibly be about the prospect of spending an evening with her. The best thing I could say about her family gatherings was that they were not my family gatherings. And since I never went to any of those, this was not shaping up to be one of the year's high points.

June 1st is officially known as Madaraka Day in Kenya, celebrating the nation's attainment of self rule in 1963 after being a British colony since 1920. At least, that's what it said on Wikipedia. Jess's mother, Zawida, was three years old when her parents left Nairobi in the mid-seventies, taking her and an older brother to a new life in the unimaginable and exotic American Midwest. Chicago, to be precise. Determined to assimilate, Gathii and Atieno Maina allowed many of their traditions to lapse and were filled with genuine happiness when their nursing student daughter brought home a fine, upstanding white boy from Evanston. They didn't even mind too much when the newlyweds Calvin and Zawida Evans moved five hours due south to St. Louis, to live the American dream in the Gateway city to the West. Yet the one tradition they always preserved, and which they instilled in Zawida for life, was to celebrate that day of independence, of freedom from the oppressor, and of opportunity. Zawida insisted Jess and her two older brothers join that celebration every year, no matter what, on pain of banishment from the family. Or so Jess said. She also said banishment had tempted her more than once, but she hadn't missed Madaraka Day in the Evans household yet.

I was a little late picking her up after one of Mike's "heart to hearts" followed a chaotic lunch service, during which he alternated between yelling at us and apologizing for yelling at us. I had rushed home, showered, and dressed up in the smartest clothes I owned: a white button-down shirt, sober blue tie, black pants and dress shoes, great for weddings, court hearings, and funerals. And Kenya Day - no, Madaraka Day, don't call it Kenya Day in front of Jess's family, you moron. Jess was irritable, but I expected that. She didn't laugh at my jokes, snapped at me for almost running a red light, then again when I apologized a second time for being late. So, we spent much of the drive through Forest Park in silence, and I resigned myself to an evening of damage control.

Despite a valiant and near-blinding appearance as I drove west out of the city, the sun soon submerged under a menacing line of advancing thundercloud. By the time we reached the Evans family home, an elegant four-bedroom townhouse a mile northwest of Forest Park, it was dark enough for the street lamps to flicker reluctantly to life. I sighed, inwardly I think. Calvin and Zawida Evans's back yard was expansive and immaculate, with plenty of room for a large dining area on the patio. Instead, eight adults and five young children were likely to be squeezed inside the modest dining room and overflowing into the kitchen while the storm rolled through. And yes, that does add up to thirteen people for those of you keeping score at home.

I had never run on these streets. The closest I ever got was the fringes of Delmar Loop in University City to the east, which is about as diverse as St. Louis gets. My lower middle-class feet had never so much as touched the pristine asphalt of a Clayton residential street until last Christmas. I still felt conspicuous stepping out of the car despite, or perhaps because of, my relatively smart attire. Part of me was waiting for the Neighborhood Watch to spring out from behind a well-groomed bush like Monty Python's Spanish Inquisition and haul me off to somewhere more within my reach, perhaps Brentwood. Jess surprised me, given our journey there, by grabbing my arm and propelling me along the path to the boxy porch and front door. I offered her a reassuring smile, and she rolled her eyes before stabbing the doorbell.

"Take your shoes off!" she hissed, as she slipped off her sandals, kicking them along the porch until they came to rest against a line of other shoes. Most were other sandals, but also included two pairs of smaller flip flops. Looked like brother Kioko and his family were here already. I bit my lip as I struggled to unlace my shoes before someone answered the door, hopping in a rather graceless fashion on one foot. I always forgot about this custom, so I could have just worn sneakers for all the difference it had made.

"Jessica! Give your mother a hug!"

Zawida Evans was shorter and plumper than her daughter, her graying hair cut short, benevolent eyes shining from her dark face. Her dress was a riot of color, shades of blue, green, and yellow entwining her from shoulder to calf. She beamed as Jess embraced her, then peered around her daughter's shoulder at me.

"Hello, D. Thank you for coming."

"I wouldn't miss it, Mrs. Evans." Which was true; Jess would kill me.

"Still calling me Mrs. Evans!" she chortled, and backed up into the house so we could enter. The smoky tang of singed meat and exotic spices wafted from the kitchen. Distant thunder rumbled as she closed the door behind us. Or perhaps that was my stomach. "You call me Zawida! Or did you forget my name?"

"He's just scared of you, mom," said Jess, with a hint of impatience. "Where are Kioko and the kids?"

"In the living room. Your father is acting the fool for them."

"Great. I'll go say my hellos."

Jess slipped through the doorway on our right, through which I could hear children's laughter. To the left was the dining room, table already set for eight at close quarters, while ahead the short hallway bypassed the stairs to the upper level on its way to the kitchen. The home was clean, well-appointed, its off-white walls accented with dark wood moldings. It just seemed a little on the small side for a couple to have raised three children.

"Oh no, you're coming with me!" Zawida said as I made to follow Jess, and for emphasis grabbed my arm and led me along the hall into the kitchen. "I need another cook's opinion!"

Having learned of my profession, Zawida made a great show of seeking my blessing, if not advice, on every dish she prepared for these family gatherings. I was flattered, although my culinary skills were limited to Hickory's BBQ menu and the variety of uninspiring fare I had helped prepare during my time at Missouri Eastern Correctional and New Hope. I knew enough about flavor and technique to understand another's recipe, and how to recover from most mistakes, but I seldom attempted anything of my own.

However, I appreciated the quality of someone's cooking and the kitchen in which they did it. Zawida's kitchen was state-of-the-art, nothing but the best and no expense spared, from the smallest stainless steel measuring spoon to the industrial-strength gas range and oven. And she knew how to use it. Her pride was unmistakable, as she led me to sample one dish after another: from chapatis and vegetable samosas, to collard greens and *irio* (mashed peas, potatoes and corn, which is way better than you might think), to a spicy chicken stew and the *nyama chola*, which is essentially singed roast beef. I was half-full even before the family sat down to eat.

"Jessica is happy with you," Zawida declared with satisfaction, as I swallowed the last of my beef.

"I think so," I said. "Most days anyway. She's mad at me today, because I was late."

"Pssh. She is mad because I make her come here to see the rest of her family. She never enjoyed being the youngest child, but like I told her, what can I do about that?"

"Nothing," I said after an awkward pause, in which I realized the question wasn't rhetorical.

She sighed. "No, you're right. Well, help me get this food on the table. Where is Jonathan? That fool better not be late!"

Right on cue, Jonathan, the eldest of the three Evans siblings, whose buzz cut and light skin most favored their father, and who had just joined me at thirty-five, arrived with his wife, Nicole, and their three daughters. Don't ask me their names, I don't remember, although I'm pretty sure one of them is Marianne. The youngest was asleep in a car seat, while the others looked shellshocked at being deprived of their iPads. Kioko's boys screamed with glee in the living room, and were the same age as the older girls, but he and his wife Sharelle had sworn off any further additions. Zawida looked with little hope to Jess for providing more grandchildren.

With the food on the table, the extended family milled around, hugging, kissing, or shaking hands. Only Sharelle greeted me with anything approaching warmth, throwing me a conspiratorial wink, as her husband just about managed a stiff nod to me on his way to the dining room. She joined Nicole and daughters in the kitchen, while her sons took seats at the adults' table. Calvin, who at least shook my hand and offered me a wry smile, sat at the head, his sons flanking him, followed by the two boys, Jess and I, and Zawida at the other end. This mattered, as in true Kenyan tradition, Zawida served the men first, starting with her husband and ending with me. I could sense Jess fuming without looking at her, although she accepted her food with good grace before Zawida began taking plates to her daughters-in-law and granddaughters in the kitchen. Jess had instructed me earlier to eat with my right hand only, and to use slices of cornmeal cake to scoop up my stew. The resulting mess at least amused the boys.

I hadn't expected a lot of conversation in my direction, and I wasn't disappointed. Jonathan, a heart surgeon at Barnes Jewish Hospital, spent considerable time debating the merits of a new cholesterol drug with his father, a primary care physician, most of which was incomprehensible to the rest of us. Kioko, the darkest of the siblings in skin color and often in mood, made several unsuccessful attempts to steer the discussion to his sons' notable achievements in pre-school, before lapsing into a sullen silence. Jess was already there, picking at her food and avoiding looking at me. At one point, her mother put a hand on her arm and asked quietly if she was alright, but Jess shook her off. I sensed an explosion coming, and it wasn't the wall-shaking thunderclap that almost immediately followed.

"D, you must have an opinion on this," Jonathan said out of nowhere, interrupting my contemplation of my now empty plate. I glanced up to see the three men looking at me expectantly, as my teachers often had when I woolgathered in class. Somehow, none of them were as intimidating as Rosalind.

"I'm sorry, about what?" I smiled apologetically, as one of the boys flicked a whole pea across the table at his brother, earning a furious glare from Kioko.

"Cholesterol warnings on menus, the ordinance they just passed in the county. You had one in the city last year, right? Did it hurt your restaurant's business?"

I shrugged. "Not that I could tell, but I'd only just started working there. I don't know how many people understand enough about that kind of thing to care."

"Exactly," smirked Kioko. "Especially people who eat at chain restaurants. I mean, who bothers counting calories if you eat at McDonald's every day?"

"I like to think we're a little more refined than McDonald's," I said, my tone somewhat cool. Kioko waved his hand, dismissing my comment, and I resisted the urge to grab it and give him a few choice words.

"You'd be surprised," Calvin said, with a frown in his son's direction. "I have many patients who eat fast food and worry about their fat intake, and count calories, and worry if I tell them they have high cholesterol. But they need education to understand what they eat, not some bureaucrat scaring them away from eating so-called 'junk food' in moderation."

"Dad, this is America," said Jonathan. "We don't do moderation. You haven't seen what I've seen. And if we scare a few customers away, that will encourage restaurants and bars to offer healthier fare. Cracking down on drunk drivers didn't scare people away from bars, it just made them adapt, right Jess?"

"Oh, are the women allowed to talk now?"

The men stared at her while Zawida squirmed in her chair.

"Now Jess..." Calvin began.

"No, dad, don't 'now Jess' me! It's the same every year, every meal, every time we get together. You pay attention to Mom because she feeds you, but none of you care less about how I am, what I'm doing, or what my opinion is about anything. I'm just here to make up the numbers. And you wonder why I don't want to come," she finished, looking at her mother with fierce eyes.

"That's a little unfair, Jess," admonished Calvin in what he must have thought was a reasonable tone of voice. I eyed the exit. "Of course, you're welcome to join the conversation."

"Oh sure, I can comment on whatever the men are discussing - the ordinance is stupid, by the way - but no-one ever thinks to ask me. And you never ask me about me, about my job, or Shift_Dev, or D."

"I'm sure Sharelle and Nicole would be interested," said Kioko. "You can talk to them after dinner."

"Jesus, Kioko, can you be any more patronizing?"

Jonathan shook his head, but he still said nothing to Jess. She looked right at me for the first time since we'd entered the house. "I'm done. Take me home, D."

I got up while her parents protested, and her brothers bickered. While it was refreshing to see that dysfunction extended to other families, I wasn't unhappy to leave. I thanked Zawida for a wonderful meal, and she gave me a tearful smile of gratitude. But I was out the door ahead of Jess, fishing our shoes out of what was now a jumbled wet mass. The rain was almost torrential, but I didn't care. I knew Jess needed to get out of there. I recognized the signs even if her family didn't.

She snatched her sandals from me, and we splashed our way to the car. We buckled up, and she sat hugging herself, staring straight ahead as I pulled out and tried to remember how to get back to Forest Park Boulevard. I knew platitudes wouldn't work and waited for her to speak. When she did, the question surprised me.

"What's in Crestwood?"

"What?"

"Crestwood. I saw Nina yesterday, and she told me she saw you having lunch in Crestwood a few weeks back."

I hesitated. Partly because it took me a moment to realize what she was asking about, and also because I wasn't sure what to say. I'd never lied to Jess. I try never to lie to anyone, but especially not to her. But I wasn't sure I was ready to talk about Rosalind and the strange things she was getting me into.

"I didn't know you still saw Nina," I said, trying to buy time. Jess wasn't having it.

"We're still friends, D. She's not the only one of my exes I hang out with sometimes. Crestwood. A Mexican restaurant. A pretty woman. Ringing any bells?"

"I'm not sure how to tell you about that."

The temperature in the car chilled. In retrospect, there may have been worse things I could have said, but nothing springs to mind.

"I see. Well, if you figure that out, text me and I'll decide if I want to listen."

She stared out of the passenger-side window the rest of the way back to her apartment in silence.

Fucking Kenya Day.

CHAPTER EIGHT

TAKE THE LEAD ON THIS ONE

Jess didn't answer my texts either of the next two nights, although, to be fair, they were of the "miss you" variety, and didn't address the divide that had opened up between us. I felt lost, knowing I needed to bridge that gap, but I didn't know how. I no longer had any other close friends. Those I would have called so once had either helped me down a path towards twelve years in prison, or had kept their distance since. Since my release, I'd kept to myself. Jess had enough friends for both of us, but that didn't help me now.

I considered asking Rosalind for advice, but something held me back. *You don't really know her at all*, I told myself. And part of me blamed her for landing me in this mess.

So that left me Fiona, my younger half-sister and the only family member with whom I was on speaking terms.

"Hey, D, how are you?" she said when we finally stopped playing phone tag. I could hear a sobbing baby in the background, and the low consoling baritone of her husband Eric.

"Not great," I told her. "I mean, work is fine and all that, but I've had a fight with Jess and I'm not sure how to fix it."

"Well, don't have babies with her, I can tell you that. Eric, she needs a bath. I know you're capable of giving her one." I waited, feeling awkward, as I cradled my phone while the couple bickered and wondered whether this was the best source of advice for my current problem.

"Sorry about that," Fiona said at last, "we've both had rough days at work, and now RSV is going around the daycare again, so, in all likelihood, we're all going to get sick. And every time we get sick..."

She left the thought unfinished, but I knew where she was going.

"How's Mary doing?" I asked.

She sighed.

"Not great, to be honest. She still insists she wants to stay in the house, even though she can't take care of it by herself. Her kids keep her busier than mine keep me. And she's still so sad. Mom and I talk to her when we can, but it's not enough, and she still refuses to go to any kind of therapy."

"Did she and her kids get vaccinated yet?"

"No. I don't understand it, and she knows I won't visit her until they do. Mom does, and that worries me enough." She paused. "I know you haven't seen or talked to them in years, but I think Mary might be ready."

I stifled a bitter laugh. Just because Fiona had seen past our different fathers, and our mother's increasing disdain for me growing up, didn't mean her big sister had. Fiona was the most genuinely good person I knew, at once forgiving my transgressions while also holding me accountable, and the only family member to have ever visited me in prison. Mary and I had always loathed each other. If Mary was ready for anything, it was to yell and scream at me.

Fiona and I talked for a few more minutes, but it was evening and I sensed she wanted to get her kids ready for bed. She gave me some general advice about Jess, which boiled down to "just tell her the truth, in person, if possible." It wasn't anything I hadn't already thought of, but didn't help me make it happen. "That's up to you," she said. "If you can't figure that out, why are you in that relationship?" Harsh, but fair. Our conversation still cheered me up. I didn't ask about Mom.

Over the next few days, I fell back on those things that had kept me sane during my time at Missouri Eastern Correctional: I cooked and worked out. Obviously, I cooked at my day job, but I began experimenting at home too, nothing too fancy, just playing with different ingredients and flavors. I owned some cheap free weights, bought from a former line cook who had moved out of state, and as the long hot days of summer arrived, I made it a point to get up with the dawn and run in nearby Tower Grove Park. Soon, I developed a new daily rhythm: run, work, cook. I just didn't care for it as much.

I had almost screwed myself to the point of stopping by wherever Jess was working and trying to explain everything to her, while trying not to sound crazy, when Rosalind called to say we had another 'job' and asked when I was next free. I told her Saturday morning would work. This time, I was grateful for the distraction, and realized I was looking forward to whatever weird experience fate had in store for me. It just goes to show you need to treat fate with a little more respect.

This one was also in my neighborhood, a hardware store called Stengel and Sons on South Grand, a few blocks south of the park. It nestled among a crowd of family-owned restaurants of every imaginable ethnicity, in a building that was a holdover from the area's first glory days of the 1920s. It had started life as a pharmacy, survived the suburban flight of the 1960s, only to close in 1973. Saving it from the fate of unluckier neighbors, Joseph Stengel Sr. acquired the premises three years later and opened his hardware store, a lifelong dream. It survived still, filling a niche in the now-rejuvenated district for those unwilling or unable to make the trek to the nearest Home Depot or Lowe's.

I knew all this because Rosalind had printed out a five-page document containing the results of her research into the property. She thrust it into my hand as soon as I met her at a table outside a coffee shop one block north of the store. Her concession to the heat, already pushing ninety degrees at 9:30am, was a lighter colored blouse and a shorter suit skirt. I glanced around in a fruitless and pointless attempt to spot any of Jess's friends who might be in the vicinity. Teenagers or young couples occupied most of the half-dozen tables, except for one where an older black guy huddled over a laptop. I sighed and sat down.

"Read it," said Rosalind. "I would have ordered you a coffee, but they have about twenty kinds here. It's worse than Starbucks."

"Oh, you don't even know," I muttered, as I flagged down the server. This coffee shop had a great reputation, but I avoided it. I had never been inside after my first experience, the sticky warmth, the stench of bleach, and the "otherness" that no-one else seemed to notice. I considered mentioning this to Rosalind, then decided not to head down that rabbit hole.

After reading through her document, I waited for my Thai iced coffee, but I took little in after the second page, which was unfortunate as it turned out. But I did notice the handwritten "CV - Aug?" at the end, and frowned.

"You seem distracted," Rosalind said, peering over the rim of what looked like a bone china teacup. I wondered if it was the coffee house's or if she carried one around in case of emergencies. I stared back at her for a few long seconds before I registered what she said.

"Yeah, well, I've had better weeks."

"Trouble at work?"

"No, work's good. It's... well, it's personal."

She offered me a grim smile. "Sorry, D. I didn't mean to pry. What we do requires concentration and attention to detail. I want to make sure you're up to the task."

Was I? I felt my enthusiasm start to fade.

"My girlfriend broke up with me," I blurted, surprising myself. Rosalind didn't react, just continued to watch me as if I were a student fumbling over a question in class. "At least she's not talking to me. And it's my fault. Someone saw us in that Mexican place in Crestwood, and I didn't know how to explain and..." I tailed off in horror. What was I saying?

She raised an eyebrow and smiled.

"Why, how flattering. I take it she reached the wrong conclusion?"

I shrugged and looked away. A pair of teenage girls at the next table giggled as my gaze passed over them, and I turned back to Rosalind.

"Truth is, I don't know what she thought. Or thinks. But I didn't want to lie, and I didn't know how to tell her about..." I gestured at nothing in particular.

"I see. And you care for her?"

"Yes." *I love her.* "Yes, she means the world to me."

Rosalind nodded and set her teacup down on its saucer. "Very well. After we're done here, I suggest you call her and tell her my husband and I have invited the two of you over for dinner the next night you're both free, when all will be explained. To be honest, it's about time Martin met you, too. He's getting rather nosy about my new protégé."

"Really? I... well, I need to check my work schedule. And Jess's if she's game."

"Naturally. Check away. We'll find an evening to make it work. I think some clearing of the air will do us all good."

"Yes, thank you. I'll ask her."

"Good. Now, that said, do you believe you can focus on our task at hand?"

I took a deep breath. Sure, I could pull myself together. I nodded.

"Excellent. Because I want you to take the lead on this one."

I stared at her. She returned my gaze; she was serious. And now I wasn't so sure.

"But I can't - I don't know what to do!"

"Yes you do. You've shared the experience twice now, even if you didn't understand what was happening the first time. You know how it will affect you, and you understand how to listen. I've given you the research, so now you know as much as I do. The rest will come naturally."

My skepticism must have shown in my expression, because she leaned forward and took one of my hands in hers. They were tiny, and they were freezing; how was it possible to survive with hands that cold?

"You can do it, D. I know you don't think you can, but I do." Her voice was low and earnest as her eyes searched mine.

"How can you be so sure?"

"Because I knew nothing more than you now, when I started. I had to rely on instinct. I'm not saying it was easy, but I managed. And I didn't have anyone to help me. You do."

I heard a snicker from one of the teenage girls at the adjacent table, and became conscious of Rosalind's hands holding mine. I slowly withdrew my hand and adjusted my ponytail as pretext. She gave me a thin smile.

"How did you get involved in all this, then?" I asked. She sighed.

"I'm afraid that story must wait," she said, extracting her wallet from her purse. "We don't want to be late meeting our client."

"That's mine," I told her, whipping out my billfold and throwing a ten-dollar bill onto the check. "You paid last time."

She laughed and thanked me, then we rose and pushed our chairs back under the table. I was careful to avoid looking at the teenagers as we slipped through the cluster of tables and headed south down Grand.

The day was already hot enough that I was sweating, and Rosalind's cheeks were flushed as we arrived at the squat brick art déco trimmed building that housed the hardware store. A "CLOSED" sign hung on the door, which opened from the inside before we could knock. The interior was dark and shadowed after the bright glare of the day, and the proprietor apologized as we stepped inside, blinking furiously.

"I don't want to attract attention," he explained in a quiet, gravelly voice, closing the door behind us. He was a balding, middle-aged white guy, not much taller than Rosalind, with a scrubby, gray-flecked beard. Despite the season and the straining air-conditioning, he wore a shop coat that did little to disguise his paunch. I frowned. I couldn't feel anything out of the ordinary.

"Tom Wurzburger," he announced, holding out his hand to me, then Rosalind, to shake. "Thank you both for coming so early. I was hoping to be done before opening at eleven, you see."

Rosalind smiled, but said nothing, and I realized she was deferring to me. No pressure then.

"Not a problem," I said, more loudly than I had intended. "Coming early, I mean. We, uh, know a little of this building's history, but perhaps you could tell us what seems to be the problem."

I shut my mouth before I could add the word "squire".

"It's hard to explain," said Tom, and then gave a rambling account of occasional 'creepy feelings' and 'wild temperature swings' in the stock room at the rear of the property. "One of my assistants quit over it, said he felt like he was being watched all the time he was back there. I don't get that, but there's something weird going on. My buddy Danny said you might be able to help." He shrugged like this was all a little foolish.

"I know Danny," said Rosalind. Her head cocked as if listening or waiting to hear something. "Why don't you take us to the stock room?"

The store was deep, but packed with shelves and an occasional free-standing display. I had to concentrate on not knocking anything over, and I didn't recognize the chill until we had almost reached the counter at the back, which was empty except for the digital cash register. Behind the counter was a door, painted gunmetal gray, and I didn't have to guess that the stock room lay beyond. Doors don't have eyes, but something in or behind it was watching me.

As Tom opened the door, I tried to remember what was in the research Rosalind had given me. I knew that the last owner of the pharmacy back in the 1970s had tried and failed to hang himself back here. Nothing else had stood out, but I realized I had skipped through, and over, several paragraphs. I felt too embarrassed to consult it again now.

The familiar sense of otherness and a metallic tang wafted out of the stock room, along with the chill. Yet, the sensations weren't as strong as those in Colton's apartment or the house in Crestwood. Tom let me and Rosalind pass inside and muttered that he would stay in the main store if we needed anything.

I stood and peered at the stacks and shelves obscured by the gloom. Rosalind had the presence of mind to turn on the light, an erratic flickering fluorescent strip in the middle of the ceiling. Stacks of boxes punctuated the almost cubic space, while narrow wire mesh shelves lined the walls to either side, cluttered with more boxes and occasional loose items. A heavy-looking black door, that looked like it led to the outside, drew my gaze. And it screamed at me.

I don't know how else to express it. I have tried to describe, to myself, what I think of as a "presence" at the heart of the unsettling sensations that have afflicted me in the past, wondering if I was projecting a personality onto something that just wasn't there. This was there. A scream of rage and pain, and I flinched.

"Remember what I told you last time," said Rosalind.

"Listen for the quietest voice."

"Exactly. Focus on that, and use it to drain away the memory."

Easy for her to say. It made no sound in the real world, but what lay beyond the door was deafening. How could I hear anything but that?

One way to find out. Come on, D. Rosalind believes in you, why can't you?

I took a deep breath, half-expecting to exhale a cloud of condensate, it was so cold. Then I strode forward, grasped the handle, and tried to push open the door, fighting all the while to drown out the screaming.

In an instant, I was outside, in a dark, ill-lit alleyway. The transition was so fast it was nauseating, and my vision blurred for a moment. It was dark because it was night, or so said the black sky enshrouding the scene before me. The alley was just wide enough for a vehicle to thread in-between a tall wooden fence on the far side and a series of skips, trash cans, and other unidentifiable debris that marked the rear entrances of other buildings on the block. The only light of note came from a single street lamp a few doors down to my left.

That was all the detail I could take in before I saw the two men confronting each other just to my right in the midst of an argument. A white guy wearing a dark-colored hoodie pointed, with obvious anger, toward a black guy in a jacket and backward-facing baseball cap. Both men's jaws worked nonstop, but I could hear nothing. Or I realized the scream I'd heard on seeing the stock room door was still there, filling my head and drowning out everything else. I tried to concentrate, watching their mouths move and listening for sounds that matched. I began to hear fragments, words or syllables, but nothing coherent, and I tried to push the scream away and focus. And that's when all hell broke loose.

The man in the hoodie made a grab for Baseball Cap, who twisted from his grip and took a few steps back. Next thing, he was brandishing a knife, and Hoodie raised his hands in placation. I watched in horror, the focus I needed to attempt whatever Rosalind did to "drain" this memory slipping away. Baseball Cap turned to run, but managed only a step before Hoodie lunged and grabbed him by the arm. The wrong arm. Pivoting in place, Baseball Cap used his assailant's momentum against him, and the knife sliced through the fabric of the hoodie and between the ribs underneath. I caught a vivid glimpse of the dying man's face as realization struck - he was so young! - and then he slumped to his knees, clutching his chest while Baseball Cap backed away, mouth agape in shock or horror, before turning to flee. I felt powerless, horrified. I wanted to close my eyes and shut it out, but that didn't seem to work here.

A shift. A sickening lurch, like an earthquake or sudden unexpected plunge on a roller coaster. Again, my vision blurred, and then I saw two men, one in a hoodie and one in a baseball cap, facing each other and arguing. And it started all over again.

The cowering, rational part of my mind knew this wasn't good, pleaded with me to do something, anything, while the scream in my ears became a roar. I couldn't hear anything, but I could see everything. Oh, make it stop, please, make it stop. I don't want to watch this again. I can't watch it again, not the knife. No, Jesus, not the knife, don't do it. He's so young. Please God, you'll regret this the rest of your life. Make it stop, the screaming, oh the screaming, MAKE IT STOP!

Something else. There was something other than the screaming and the two young men and the knife, something my reeling brain perceived but couldn't identify. I reached toward it by instinct, but it brushed me aside, and then, mercifully, I knew no more.

CHAPTER NINE

THERE'S SOMETHING YOU SHOULD KNOW

I opened my eyes and immediately wished I hadn't. Light blinded me and my instinctive recoil sent bolts of pain ricocheting around my skull. I squeezed my eyes shut again and forced myself still, enduring the pain until it ebbed enough for me to think straight.

I was sitting down on a hard surface, maybe concrete. My back rested against a wall, jagged and lined, brickwork of some sort. My legs stretched out ahead of me, and my shins felt warmer than the rest of my body. Outside then?

Cracking my eyelids open, I confirmed that self-assessment. I was in an alleyway - perhaps *the* alleyway - along which the hot summer sun had penetrated just enough to reach the ground where my lower legs splayed. I dragged my ankles back into the shadows and let my eyes adjust.

Why was I outside? What had happened in there? Where was Rosalind?

As if on cue, she emerged from the doorway to my left and squatted down beside me, proffering a liter-sized bottle of cold water with one hand and clutching her phone in the other.

"Don't drink too fast," she cautioned as I tore off the cap and raised the bottle to my lips. Good advice. I had a desperate craving for water, but my stomach cramped almost as soon as the liquid hit it and the resulting coughing fit set off another fusillade of agony inside my head. I forced myself to sip instead of gulp.

She sat down beside me, one hand solicitous on my upper arm. Sweat plastered her hair to her face and still trickled from her brow, and she stared at me with an expression I struggled to recognize. Concern? Fear?

"How are you feeling?" she asked once I'd paused about halfway through the bottle.

I let out a shaky breath. "Terrible. It feels like knives have been driven into my skull." Which was an unfortunate analogy in the circumstances. "I'm... I'm sorry. I know I failed you in there."

"Don't apologize," she said, tone fierce, her hand gripping me. "It should be me apologizing to you. I took for granted that your instincts and limited experience would suffice for you to handle the imprinted memory, but it was clearly stronger than I expected. I'm beginning to realize just how fortunate I was in my early days."

Her voice faded to a murmur, and she stared pensively at an orange tabby cat that sauntered heedlessly along the other side of the alley.

"It kept looping," I whispered. "I couldn't do anything to stop it. Was that you, at the end?"

She opened her mouth, then closed it again, pausing before answering. "Yes. Don't worry about it. There will be time to reflect later. I told the proprietor that we had dealt with the situation and I called my husband to help get you home."

"Your husband?"

She smiled tightly. "You're in no condition to walk, and I'm afraid I don't quite have the strength to haul you into my Mini."

Great. Meeting her husband for the first time in my current condition wasn't a thrilling proposition, but I was too weak to protest. I closed my eyes again and drank the rest of my water.

I must have dozed off because the next thing I remember was her voice calling my name and a sturdy pair of arms gripping me under my shoulders and hauling me to my feet. Coughing and parched again, I was too bleary-eyed to form much of an impression of the newcomer other than that he was almost of a height with me and sported a goatee that was more gray than black. He smelled of the beach. They bundled me into a black SUV, reclining the seat, and Rosalind buckled me in to prevent me from rolling over onto the back seat.

"D? We'll save proper introductions for another time, but this is my husband, Martin."

"Thank you," I rasped, as he climbed into the driver's seat. He nodded once but said nothing, and we drove in silence once I had provided my address to the GPS. I was determined to make it to my apartment under my own power, but they were having none of it, especially after I staggered off the sidewalk and almost face-planted into the linden tree in front of the building. Only once I was lying on top of my bed with a big plastic cup of ice-water on the nightstand were they willing to leave me alone.

"Get some rest, and call me later, whether you feel better or not. Especially if you don't," Rosalind said, drawing the blinds. I muttered my thanks and stared up at the ceiling fan, hypnotized by the methodical sweep of its blades. My bedroom was cool and dark and the ghosts of my past couldn't find me here.

"Mike? It's D. Look, I hate to let you down, but I got some sort of stomach flu or something. I can't make it in today, can barely make it out of bed, to be honest."

"Sorry to hear that, D. Doesn't sound like something you want to bring to my kitchen for sure. I'll call TJ. You need anything?"

"I need it to stop. I'll call you tomorrow morning."

"Sounds good. Feel better, my friend."

"Thanks."

I ended the call and dropped my phone back on the bedside table. Even that movement exhausted me, for all that I'd slept most of the afternoon. It's been a long time since I drank enough to have a hangover, but this reminded me of the worst of those: my head felt stuffed with fuzz, my stomach was cramping, probably from lack of food, and I still craved water even as I fought to keep it down. Stomach flu sounded better than 'hangover-like symptoms' when calling in sick, although I'm sure Mike's heard them all. It was the first time I hadn't been able to work my shift, so I hoped he would cut me some slack.

I lurched into the bathroom and urinated, then stared at myself in the bathroom mirror as I washed my hands and tried to decide if I had enough strength to take a shower. Dark eyes, a little bloodshot, gazed back at me from above the crooked, aquiline nose that had suffered two breaks. Patchy stubble covered my square jaw and hollow cheeks and black hair stuck up in tufts or wild cascades over my shoulders, having shaken free from its ponytail while I slept. In the stark bathroom light, I could pass for a rugged, well-tanned Caucasian, although anyone knowing my half-Irish heritage would immediately suspect such resistance to the sun. The Cuban half of my heritage for the win then, for ultraviolet light resistance if nothing else.

I heard my phone's cheerful ping at receipt of a new message and shuffled back into my bedroom. It was after five o'clock and I noticed there were several message notifications, some from Rosalind and one from Jess.

I looked at Jess's message first: '*You still alive?*' I stared at it for several minutes, trying to discern the sentiment behind it. Was she mad I hadn't apologized or otherwise tried to contact her? Was she worried about me? Did she need something? Did she need me? I started to reply twice but couldn't find the right words. She'd only sent it ten minutes ago; it was doubtless what had woken me up.

I read Rosalind's messages while my subconscious worked on inspiration for my reply to Jess. The first was '*How are you?*', followed by '*Hold thought on dinner*', and finally '*Call me when you can*' - so I did.

"D, I'm glad to hear from you," Rosalind said as soon as she picked up. "You had me worried there for a while."

"Yeah, I'm sorry," I said. See, apologies were easy. "It's been a rough afternoon, but I'm on my way back to the land of the living."

"Interesting choice of words," she replied after a pause.

"Oh. Yeah. I guess."

"I won't keep you long, but I wanted to make sure you were on the mend. Also, Martin suggested you bring your girlfriend to meet us at the Garden, tomorrow morning if you can both make it. He seemed to think it was more neutral territory than our humble abode."

"The Botanical Garden?"

"That's the one. Have you called her yet?"

"No, I'm trying to decide exactly what to say."

You can't hear a smile, but I'm certain that's what she did right then.

"I would keep it simple. Apologize and ask her to join us at the Garden tomorrow, or find out when she can. Tell her we'll try to answer every question she has. That's if you're up for taking relationship advice from an old married woman."

You're not old, I thought. *But you seem to have my back and I appreciate that.*

I promised I would text her back as soon as I talked to Jess and ended the call. I sat and stared at my phone for a moment, and wondered if I should take that shower first. Jess would know that I was working at this hour and wouldn't be able to respond to her straight away.

Except that I always had.

I made the call before I could procrastinate any longer and held my breath, half expecting to be shunted to her voice mail. She picked up after the second ring.

"Hi D."

"Hi Jess. Is this a good time?"

"I'm on break. Tiny Home Builders convention, in a big ass convention center. No joke."

I laughed and told her I missed her before I remembered how well those texts had gone down. "I'll try not to keep you long, then. Sorry, Jess. I know you were upset the other day. You know I would never lie to you, and I didn't. I just didn't know how to explain what I was doing in Crestwood. But I want to try. Not over the phone, though."

"Why not over the phone?"

"Because there's just too much. It's not at all what you might be thinking."

There was a pause, and I heard muffled voices in the background. "What do you think I'm thinking?"

"That I'm doing something behind your back with another woman and being a mysterious jerk about it?"

That got me a chuckle at least, if a little on the harsh side. "Something like that. And if I am getting the wrong idea, then you need to explain what's going on. I don't like being ignored."

"I know, and I'm sorry. Look, are you free tomorrow morning? Rosalind - that's the woman I had lunch with in Crestwood - and her husband invited us to meet them in the Garden. She promised to help me explain what's going on."

"You realize how creepy that sounds, right?"

"Jess."

"Fine. I'll hear you both out, as long as it's the truth."

"It will be - as strange as it might sound. I'll text you the timing. I love you."

Another pause, then, "See you tomorrow."

I spent my time in the shower analyzing the call. Could I have said anything better? It seemed positive overall. She had at least talked to me and agreed to meet. The pause at the end bothered me, and still would until I heard her say the words again.

I felt better after my shower, but didn't know what to do with myself. I exchanged texts with Rosalind and Jess to establish 10am as our meeting time at the Botanical Garden the next day, then I prowled my apartment, channel surfing, and explored my fridge, unable to make a decision. A usual Saturday night had me either working or seeing Jess. Now I was doing neither. I decided to go for a walk when another summer storm rolled in, and instead, I sat by my window and watched the roaring wind toss around sheets of torrential rain. It was hypnotic, and as the light faded, I felt myself doing the same. Party on, D.

They rightly tout the Missouri Botanical Garden as a St. Louis treasure. Opened in 1859 by a phenomenally successful businessman called Henry Shaw, who also gave his name to a nearby street and neighborhood. It's one of the oldest and largest such gardens in the country. The vast European estates he saw on his travels inspired Shaw and he determined to bring that beauty and grandeur to his adopted city. A botanist called George Engelmann persuaded him to go further, to emulate the world's finest biological institutions by building a library and a herbarium, and to establish a first-class scientific research facility. My elementary school science teacher had organized annual outings for students in every grade, and such had been her enthusiasm that we learned to love it for not just its considerable beauty, but for what it told us about the natural world beyond our city. The Garden is world-renowned, and since it's next to Tower Grove Park, it's right on my doorstep. Despite that, I hadn't visited since my teens and all I could remember was the Climatron, the huge domed greenhouse with a tropical rain forest inside.

I was nervous. Jess had said she would find her own way there, which wasn't unexpected. I arrived first and forced myself not to pace outside the entrance to the Visitor Center. The storm had brought cooler air

with it, yet I still sweated as I stood waiting for her and for the Hills.
Jess arrived first, climbing out of a friend's car and stretching, her black
Siamés t-shirt riding up above her jean shorts to expose the Mayan sun
tattoo on her back and the self-devouring serpent around her navel. She
saw me gazing enraptured and smiled as she walked up and kissed me
softly.

"I'm prepared to give you the benefit of the doubt," she murmured.
"Don't disappoint me."

I was still working out how to respond to that when I heard my name
and saw Rosalind approaching, clutching her husband's arm. Martin
was at least a foot taller than her, his thinning black hair as flecked
with gray as his goatee, but his tanned, fine-chiseled features were still
handsome in a James Bond movie villain kind of way. A pale blue polo
shirt and khaki cargo shorts failed to disguise an athletic, muscular frame,
and I wondered if he was a runner, a cyclist, or both. His dark eyes
glanced at Jess before fixing on me; the look wasn't unfriendly, but I
realized Jess wasn't the only one I had to convince of my good intentions.

"D, let me reintroduce you to my husband, Martin," said Rosalind
with a broad smile. She wore a riotous floral sun dress and a pair of
overlarge sunglasses for the occasion. Someone was enjoying herself.
"You weren't quite yourself when you met him yesterday. Martin, you
remember D, my reluctant protégé?"

I shook Martin's hand, expecting and receiving a firm grip.

"Glad to meet you again, D," he said, his voice a little higher than I'd
expected. "And that you've recovered from yesterday."

"Me too," I said, very much aware of Jess's eyes narrowed in curiosity.
"This is my girlfriend, Jess. Jess, this is Rosalind and Martin."

More hands shaken and hellos spoken. If Rosalind was aware of any
tension, she didn't show it.

"Let's go inside. The Garden will be spectacular after last night's
storm!"

Much of St. Louis appeared to agree with her. We waited in line for at
least ten minutes before Martin flashed his membership card, allowing
all four of us to enter, then we had to push our way politely through
the crowd that milled around inside the Visitor Center before emerging
into the Garden proper. The bright morning sun had teased apart the
post-dawn mists, revealing vivid and varied color, of flower and bush and
tree. For a while, the four of us walked together, passing comment on
whatever caught our eye. Neither Rosalind nor her husband appeared
to need signs to tell them what each plant or tree was, and it surprised
me how much I remembered from those long ago school outings.

Conversation was light and easy, and for a while I relaxed and allowed myself to forget why we were there.

We had passed the dome of the Climatron far to our right before I realized Martin was telling us an edited version of their life story, with Rosalind content to listen and, once again, hang onto his arm. They had met at university in a town called Bristol, which I had heard of but couldn't tell you where it was. He had grown up in London, in the suburb of Wimbledon, which just about everyone had heard of, including me. Rosalind came from a village in the west of England called Stow-in-the-Wold, which sounded like one of those pretend place names a Brit would use to tease us Americans. Before long, they were dating, and when Martin, an economics major, had landed a job at First American Bank in New York after graduating, they had a big decision to make.

"We both wanted him to take the job," Rosalind added, while Martin took a swig from his water bottle. "And neither of us wanted the trouble of a long-distance relationship. This was in the age before cell phones or widespread internet access."

"So I asked her to marry me before I took the job," said Martin, smiling fondly at her.

"Yes, it was very romantic," she laughed. "Will you marry me? Great! Now go pack your bags. It felt like we were eloping!"

Jess laughed too, then gave me a wicked grin I didn't know what to do with.

"Very close to it," Martin said. "The bank gave me three months to make the move, but they helped a lot, finding us our first apartment and greasing the wheels of the work visa process. Of course, it helped that I had family here: my grandfather was a GI from Mount Vernon, Illinois. Rosalind didn't really like New York, so when I got the chance to move to St. Louis, we took it."

After which Martin had continued to climb the ranks within the bank. Rosalind tried to parlay her History degree into a job at a museum or other cultural institution, but without success. With some reluctance, she began teaching, and after a few positions at a series of schools, had ended up at Gold Cross just over a decade ago.

"They love her there," Martin said, a proud smile plastered across his face. "They won't let her retire until long after I have!"

"That's cause you make almost ten times my salary, you oaf," she retorted, with a swift jab in the ribs, and they both grinned.

"How long have you been married?" Jess asked.

"It'll be thirty years next September," Rosalind said. She sounded happy about it, but for a moment I thought I caught something sad in her smile.

There was a pause in the conversation as we approached a building identified by a sign as the Sachs Museum. Sudden terror gripped me that either Martin or Rosalind would ask how long Jess and I had been dating, and about our backgrounds. Not that it wouldn't have to come out at some point, but I wasn't looking forward to it. By intention or otherwise, Jess saved me by claiming she needed to 'powder her nose'. Rosalind laughed.

"That's what my students say whenever they want to make fun of me," she said. "I hope that's not the case here." Her face assumed the Teacher's Look, and Jess blinked.

"I'm in an all-girl gamer forum, and some of my British girlfriends use that expression. Ma'am," she added, eyes twinkling.

"Perhaps I'll powder my nose too then," Rosalind said, smiling again. "As long as you promise never to call me Ma'am again. Why don't you boys walk on? We'll catch up with you in the Japanese Garden."

Martin raised an eyebrow that carried the full weight of his skepticism that the ladies could catch us up anywhere. She stuck out her tongue, and then took Jess's arm as they headed towards the restrooms. Martin looked at me.

"Let's take that walk, shall we?"

Our path led us through what claimed to be an English Woodland Garden, but I couldn't think of anything to say about it that wouldn't sound corny. Martin seemed content to walk in silence, so I followed suit.

"I always prefer the anti-clockwise circuit," he said at last, as we passed a path leading to the Japanese Garden. To our left was a decent sized lake, with at least one island in its midst, and paths around its perimeter. If I remembered right, there was a bridge where you could feed the fish. It had been one of my favorite parts of the Garden as a schoolboy, outside of the Climatron, of course. And I preferred it now, being in the open air.

"Rosalind is very grateful to you," Martin went on. "And so am I. I understand little about this talent she has, but I'm glad she has found someone else who shares it at last."

"I don't understand it either," I said. "And I don't seem to be very good at using it."

"She told me something about what happened yesterday. She worries about you, and I can see why. I've always maintained this is more dangerous than she thinks it is. I worried about her when she first tried to turn her talent into something that would help others. It wasn't easy on either of us."

"But you supported her."

"Of course. She's my wife. I may not share or understand what she does, but I know how important it is to her, and that is enough. And I will not see her hurt."

We turned into the Japanese Garden itself, and almost immediately he left the path and wandered across the grass toward the lakeside. I glanced at him, but his expression was unreadable. I had a pretty good sense of when another man wished me harm, and I saw none of that in him.

"To be honest, I'm not sure I can do it, or that I want to do what she does," I said, staring out at the sun-dappled water. "I have my own problems, and I just want a normal life and to stay out of trouble."

Martin gave a heavy sigh, but didn't reply for a while.

"Please don't misunderstand me, D. I'm very protective of my wife, but I'm not thumping my chest and telling you to back off. Quite the contrary. She needs someone to help her, and I'm here to encourage you to do so. Besides, a normal life is overrated, and a little trouble can be worth it."

He smiled at me, but I couldn't muster one in return. The moment was fast approaching; I was tied to the tracks with a freight train racing toward me at full speed.

"There's something you should know about me," I forced myself to say. "Although, I would prefer to tell you and Rosalind at the same time."

"Well, now may be your moment. For behold, the ladies have in fact caught up with us."

I turned, and sure enough, Jess and Rosalind were strolling toward us across the grass. Jess held my gaze, her expression quizzical until she stood before me, hands on hips.

"So I've heard both of you tell me what this is not, but I want to hear from you what it is," she demanded. I glanced at Rosalind, but she just raised her eyebrows before taking Martin's hand and drawing him a discrete distance away. This was on me then. Probably best that way.

I turned back to Jess, took a deep breath, and began. "Okay. So I ran into this old friend of mine getting my morning coffee..."

She heard me out, holding my eyes as I stumbled through, trying to explain everything that had happened since I had run into Colton Lynn and agreed to meet him for dinner. Only at the end, after I had recounted my failure at the hardware store, did she look at Rosalind, who nodded.

"I didn't know what I was expecting, but not that," Jess whispered. "I thought I was supposed to be the weird one in this relationship."

"The crazy one. There's a difference." She punched my arm.

"I'd be crazy to believe that, wouldn't I? But I have to admit, it's a good story."

I looked into her eyes, those spellbinding eyes, and willed her to believe it, or at least believe that I believed it. She didn't. Not yet, and I couldn't blame her.

"There's something you should know too," I said, turning to Rosalind. "If we're going to work together, you need to know. And you'll understand what happened yesterday." Another deep breath. "One night, when I was nineteen, I was walking home when another guy jumped me. He had fists, I had a knife. It was self-defense, but he died, throat cut." I swallowed. Everything had gotten so quiet, it was like no-one was even breathing. "Jury didn't see it that way. I got sent down for twelve years, voluntary manslaughter." Someone had to breathe, and it should be me. Jess took my hand in hers. "I've been out for a little over a year. Took me a while to get back on my feet, to find my place, something that could pass for a normal life. To find Jess. I don't want to give any of that up. I can't go back inside. I want to help you, Rosalind. I do, but you need to know who I am and what's at stake for me."

They all stared at me for a moment, then Rosalind stepped forward and took my other hand. She didn't have to say anything. She knew.

Excerpt of email recovered from closed account, owner untraceable. Destination account also closed and untraceable.

From: (address withheld)
To: (address withheld)
Subject: St. Louis 2023-06 #1
Sent: 2023-06-10 14:48:01 UTC

…which is ironic given that was precisely why he was sent there in the first place.

The St. Louis intrusion profile is stretching the model's 3-sigma predictions, most particularly and alarmingly in the one location. Astbury doesn't seem overly concerned; "that's what sigmas are for" was essentially her last response to me. Sometimes I feel like some time in the field would do her good.

I'm still not sure what to make of our freelancers. It is clearly as much a mentor-protégé relationship as that which I have with my own students. Equally clearly, they have little to no idea of the risks involved, and not just to themselves. The mentor's level of control is undeniably impressive, quite on a par with my own. However, I fear for the student.

Are you quite certain we shouldn't make a direct overture…

Chapter Ten

STOP

"You need to train before taking the lead again," Rosalind told me before we left the Garden. Her reaction, or lack thereof, to my big revelation still left me somewhat dazed. It wasn't something people usually took in their stride, not that I told more people than was strictly necessary. Martin had narrowed his eyes, but if it concerned him - and it had to, right? - he kept it to himself. For now, at least.

"Train how?"

"For one thing, you need to improve your focus and concentration, probably your endurance too. Do you have any experience in the martial arts?"

"What, like karate or jiu jitsu or something? No, I had a friend in high school who was obsessed with it, but he could never convince me to take it up."

"Pity. They've always helped me, and not just in dealing with these phenomena. I didn't have the easiest time growing up myself. It's never too late, and I think karate, judo, or something along those lines would be good for you."

"Okay," I said, my tone dubious.

She frowned. "I teach English and history to high school girls, D. I don't have a good name, much less a lesson plan for what I do. There isn't a guild, or even a Facebook group, and if there's a community somewhere on the dark web, I'm not about to go looking for it. All I have found in seven years of research is a handful of obscure references in occult literature, and I wouldn't credit most of them. There are always other things we can do to better prepare you for this journey."

It fascinated me that she even knew about the dark web, and I was curious about the "occult literature", but I had no time to pursue that line of inquiry. For one thing, I had called Mike and told him I was well enough to work my shift that evening, and I needed to get home to change. For another, Jess seemed intrigued, if still skeptical, and I wanted to take what little time I had to rebuild that bridge. She had to get ready for work too, but she let me drive her home and kissed me again before getting out of my car.

"I want to see one of these exorcisms for myself," she said before closing the passenger door.

"They're not exorcisms."

"They sound like exorcisms."

I shrugged. I didn't know what to call them either, but I hadn't seen Rosalind waving a cross around or heard her reciting bible passages. She described the phenomena as "imprinted memories" and I remembered her using the word "erase" at least once, but somehow that sounded too clinical to me.

"Whatever they are, is that okay with you? If I come along?"

"Sure," I said, although I would have agreed to just about anything at that moment. She grinned and told me to text her when I got home from work.

Although I had misgivings about Jess tagging along on my next non-exorcism - Erasure? - I saved that problem for another day. She had complained during the drive about how busy she was with Shift_Dev, doing her homework and finishing her first big assignment. Maybe she wouldn't have the time anyway. Regardless, after a long week and a rough Saturday, I now felt better about our relationship and, as a bonus, had come clean to Rosalind about being an ex-felon. I felt unburdened and may even have whistled as I worked at Hickory that night, at least until my line cooks told me to knock it off.

So it was only fair that Rosalind gave me homework the next day.

"I'm still thinking about a broader training program," she said when I returned her voice mail at a break in the evening service. "After you shared your past with me, I understand why you might have struggled with that particular memory at Stengel and Sons. It was almost designed to trouble you. One thing I learned early on was to distance my emotions, to be as dispassionate as possible in order to keep a clear head."

"Yeah, that's never been my strong suit," I muttered, cupping my phone close as a spirited discussion broke out in the kitchen over a messed up order.

"All the more reason to train," Rosalind insisted. "And I have other ideas, but I need to consider them more. However, one essential component of what I do, of what you will do, is researching the history of the building or site where the memory exists. You need to learn how to do this, and do it well. The more you understand about what could be happening, the less chance there is of being surprised. And, as I suspect you now know, surprises in this line of work tend to be unpleasant."

I grimaced. The notes she had given me to read at the coffee shop on Saturday morning had described a gang-related murder outside the hardware store in the mid-1990s, in sufficient detail that I might have anticipated, and so dealt better with, its memory. Forewarned is forearmed. Or at least don't skimp on the directions.

"If you're anything like me," she added, "you remember things better if you discover or work them out for yourself. So I want you to do a dry run, as it were. Find out everything you can about your apartment and the building it's in."

"Why? Did you sense something?" I failed to keep a note of alarm from my voice.

"Not at all. But that's not the point. Let's pretend something has been reported. You need to identify as many historical events that may be potential causes. I guarantee there will be something."

"That's not very comforting."

She gave a rather grim laugh. "There are dramatic elements in every building's history, just like there are in every person's. But very few, if any, appear to result in lingering trauma." There was a pause as we both pondered that statement.

"Why is that?" I asked before the pause grew awkward. "Now that I think about it, unless it's brand new, almost every building should have at least one such memory that needs... erasing."

"I have no idea," she replied, cheerful as ever. "As I said before, the documentation for these phenomena is thin on the ground. One task at a time, D. I'll send some web links to get you started, but I suggest you plan at least one trip to the St. Louis Library; they have resources that aren't accessible online. If you go to the Central branch, ask for Sophia: she's an ex-student of mine."

I had more questions, but my break time was up. Maybe I'd be able to find the answers to some of those questions myself. I was very conscious of the fact that despite my alarming experience in the hardware store - and we hadn't addressed what might have happened had Rosalind not been there to jump in and help - there was an unspoken agreement that I was continuing my apprenticeship.

I'm not going to lie. When I got home that night, I was a lot more aware of my surroundings. I was afraid - no, I was terrified - that I would sense something I hadn't before. It seemed cooler than usual in the lobby, but maybe someone had turned up the air conditioning. Or I was just imagining things. My apartment felt the same as ever, but it took me a long time to fall asleep.

I have an old but serviceable laptop, a hand-me-down from Jess who had upgraded for Shift_Dev, and I powered it up over breakfast the next morning and checked out the links Rosalind had emailed me. There were several ways to find out about a building's history, many of them online and several of those free. They geared many towards aspiring home owners, such as property and land entry records, deed and title searches, things that, along with a physical inspection, were typical of the house closing process. Census data could tell you who lived where and when, at least once every ten years, although the data was not accessible to the public until seventy-two years later for privacy reasons. There were websites which, for a fee, would tell you if anyone ever died at the property, if there were any fires, or even if meth labs operated there. Many of the sites, even the free ones, required you to register before you could find anything useful, and I held off on that for now. I soon became bewildered by the many sources of almost-information and decided that perhaps Rosalind's librarian could help point me in the right direction.

I discovered, in a PDF reproduction of an excerpt from a set of military memoirs that cropped up when I Googled my address, that my apartment building dated from the 1940s. It was a rebuild on the site of a previous home destroyed by fire. I couldn't find any information about the fire itself, and wondered: if people had died, suffered injuries or trauma by the fire, could such memories survive the building's destruction itself? Were they bound to the physical structure or the location? Regardless, the new construction was intended as multi-tenant housing, targeting GIs returning from World War II and entering white-collar professions. I found a couple of names, but further Googling just resulted in links to the same document and unrelated people sharing the same name; I wrote them down anyway.

My best sources of information were the building owners, residents, and neighbors, as well as any relevant real estate agents and/or property managers. There was a lot of unwritten, or at least uncirculated, tribal knowledge that could tell me everything I wanted to know - if only I knew how to ask. Rosalind appeared to have something of a network, and I figured I should ask her if I could speak to any of them. I didn't much care for my landlord, a retired software developer who was prompt with his rent demands, but lax on the maintenance. I had eleven neighbors, well actually ten, because there was an open unit on the third floor. But I seldom spoke to any of them except for Pierre, the flamboyant waiter who lived down the hall and, so he said, part-owner of Zero, a gay bar in The Grove. He was an avid runner and since his work hours were like mine, we sometimes left or returned at similar times, or saw each other in the park, where he often left me for dust. He was friendly enough, but was an incessant talker, and often strayed off topic.

"Well, I don't know about anything *newsworthy*, although you have to wonder about the couple in 1C, don't you? I've seen people running in and out of that place at all hours, could be friends or could be clients. Do you think they are selling drugs? I've been meaning to talk to Patrick for ages about them, but the man doesn't return my calls. Does he return yours?"

Retreating into the sanctuary of my apartment, I texted Rosalind and asked if she could send me the contact info of anyone in her network who might be able to help me. It was a school day, and I doubted she'd reply for a while, so in the meantime I steeled myself and took a bus to the Central Branch of the St. Louis Public Library. I didn't fight downtown parking on a weekday.

Nothing against libraries, but they're too "institutional" for me. The Central Branch occupied an entire city block, and for all its white stone and arched window grandeur, I still dragged my feet up the broad front steps. Given that it was late morning on a Monday, attendance was sparse, but I still had to fight the urge to always check my surroundings: too many doors, balconies, and of course book stacks.

I headed for the information desk and asked for Sophia. A stocky, pale-faced young woman standing by the elevator door to my right looked back at me. She had a shock of blue hair, wore a vivid orange blouse and gray slacks, and clutched at least a dozen hardback books in her arms.

"Are you D?" she asked, squinting at me. Eyeglasses attached to a cord dangled around her neck.

"I am. You're Rosalind's ex-student?"

"Mrs. Hill's, yes." She grinned as she walked over and set the books down on the counter. "Still can't call her by her first name, and she's even told me to."

"I guess you know why I'm here then?" I said, aware of the other librarian behind the desk, a white-haired black woman, watching us unabashedly. "Generally, I mean."

"Yes, but 'generally' doesn't help you, does it? Residential or commercial? Neighborhood? Approximate age?"

I told her and she gave me a curt nod before picking up the stack of books and heading back towards the elevator. "Come on then, you're heading in the same direction as me. Generally."

The elevator looked like they had designed it for hobbits, and not very many of them. Sophia stepped in and I had to stand with my arms pinned to my side to avoid touching either her or the walls. There was nothing uncanny about the panic that rose within me, just good old fashioned claustrophobia. At least it was only down one floor, so I didn't think she noticed anything "off" about me. I still needed her help, after all.

She guided me down a dim corridor to a low-ceilinged room a little larger than my apartment. Gray steel filing cabinets lined the side and back walls, but a double row of black laminate tables dominated the room, on which sat ranks of flat-screen monitors, keyboards, mice, and paperback-sized metal boxes that I assumed were computers. At the far end of each row sat a pair of huge standalone CRT monitors with what looked like large glass trays set under their screens.

A young black woman was the only other occupant of the room, sitting about halfway along the row to the right. She glanced up as we entered, frowned, then got back to whatever she was doing. Sophia sat me down at the farthest flat screen on the left.

"You can get to all of our digital archives from here, as well as certain public internet sites," she explained, clicking the mouse cursor in and out of a mercifully small number of screens. "You can pay for more access, but you don't need to if you have your own internet access at home."

I nodded. She showed me how to get to the city directory for the Tower Grove South zip code and lookup the history of those who had lived at my address. The History Museum possessed older hard copy city directories dating back to the Civil War, and Sophia knew an archivist there, but my apartment building wasn't ancient enough to send me down that rabbit hole. Swiftly moving along, she opened another screen where I could search an index of national, regional, and local newspaper articles that might be relevant. However, the articles themselves were not accessible from the terminal.

"It takes a lot of effort to scan them in," said Sophia. "And we don't have enough storage capacity for most of it, anyway."

"Can't you store it in the cloud?" I asked, attempting to sound somewhat knowledgeable. She just rewarded me with a withering look.

"So, once you know which articles you want to see, you make a note of the catalog number and then use this magnificent beast!" She gestured at the adjacent CRT with pride, and I remembered something that Rosalind had once told me.

"A microfiche terminal," I offered, trying to keep the question out of my voice.

"Reader, yes," she said with a smile that had only a hint of mockery. "Have you used one before?"

I admitted I hadn't, so she showed me how it worked. The machine itself seemed simple enough once you got the hang of the scrolling speed and direction. The devil was in deciphering the catalog number and finding the right drawer in the right filing cabinet.

"Don't try to put anything away!" Sophia warned me. "We've lost too many to misfiling already. Just stack them in this tray once you're done, and I'll take care of them later."

"Thanks," I said, suitably intimidated. She stood in silence while I typed a nervous first query and I looked up at her before I clicked the "Search" button.

"I was just wondering," she whispered, with a glance at the room's other occupant. "Has Mrs. Hill heard from Daniel lately?"

"Who's Daniel?"

"Oh, I guess not then. Okay, well, I've got to get on, but I'll come back and check on you in an hour or so, if you're still here."

She hurried out of the room with me staring after her. Who was Daniel?

If she came back, it must have been more than an hour later, because that was almost exactly how much time I spent slogging through the digital records. The city directory wasn't that hard to navigate, but all it offered were names. They were different names than those I had found earlier in the morning, but I still had to run follow-up searches of the newspaper indexes for each name as well as those of the current residents I knew, my landlord, and the building address itself. I worried I would be there all day, but there were only a handful of useful looking articles in the search results and I soon got the hang of the microfiche catalog system. Using the world's shortest pencil, I scribbled notes on a piece of scrap paper because I wrote more quickly, if less legibly, than I typed. By the time I had exhausted my search results, and my tolerance for squinting at the microfiche screen, I'd found a couple of interesting events, but nothing that I thought was going to keep me up at night.

All in all, I was quite proud of myself, the pride of the student who has completed a complex homework assignment well with due diligence. A part of me empathized with Sophia's inability to refer to Rosalind as anything other than Mrs. Hill. She was the consummate teacher, at least compared to the teachers I remembered. That sent me off on a wary excursion down memory lane as I took the bus home, my greatest achievements rubbing shoulders with my gravest errors. I was so self-absorbed that I almost missed my stop, and still focusing inward when I entered my apartment, I almost stepped on the envelope someone had slid underneath my door.

For a split-second, my foot skidded, and I grabbed the doorframe in panic to regain my balance. As the adrenaline surge subsided, I stooped over and picked up the envelope. It was plain and white, a single laser-printed "D" the only marking on front or back. I frowned; maybe this was from one of my neighbors, although only a handful knew my name and I couldn't imagine what was worth putting in a note that they couldn't say in person. Maybe it was some kind of invitation.

"One way to find out," I muttered and tore it open. Inside was a sheet of white paper on which was printed a single word in the same font as my initial on the envelope.

STOP.

CHAPTER ELEVEN

ALWAYS ROOM FOR IMPROVEMENT

I didn't know what to make of the note. Which of the very few things I was doing did the author want me to stop? Cooking at Hickory? Dating Jess? Running in the park? I had the distinct feeling none of those were the answer, and this might have something to do with my apprenticeship as a "memory eraser" to Rosalind, but who would know enough about it to want me to stop? And why?

My mind cooked up a series of unlikely theories as I prepared and left for work. Was Jess not okay with me spending time with another woman? She would tell me that herself, far more directly than with a note slipped under my door. Had Mike overheard any of my phone calls at work and wanted to prevent me from becoming distracted from my job in his kitchen? Again, Mike would tell me face-to-face, or at least over the phone. Was Martin lying when he said he wanted me to help his wife with her talent? Even if so, I could think of a dozen less roundabout ways for him to stop me working with her.

I wondered if Rosalind had received a note too.

I was donning my chef's apron at Hickory when this occurred to me. It would have to wait until after my shift, which meant I couldn't ask her about it until the next day. I sighed and tried to put it out of my mind, as I marshaled my forces and began our prep work for the evening. Some restaurants in the area closed on Mondays but not Hickory, and we were all the busier for it.

Another storm barreled through the area overnight, leaving cooler temperatures in its wake - by which I mean low-eighties instead of mid-nineties, the typical summer heat in St. Louis. I worked the lunchtime shift on Tuesdays, so Rosalind suggested we meet again at the Zoo afterwards, and she told me to bring my research notes.

We met at the same spot as before, a bench next to the sea lions exhibit. She wore much the same outfit as she had at the Botanical Garden, including the oversize sunglasses, except this time her sun dress had a safari theme. She rose as soon as she recognized me and there was an awkward moment when I wondered if we were going to hug. Instead, I said hello and began fumbling through my ratty backpack for the notes.

"Let's walk and talk," said Rosalind, waving off the notes. She smiled but seemed distracted, and for a while we walked in silence.

"I spoke to Sophia," she said at last. "She seemed rather scandalized by my choice of protégé."

"She was?"

"Indeed. But she said you soon got the hang of the microfiche reader, so that impressed her at least."

So, Sophia had been covertly checking in on me while I did my research, and being too caught up in what I was doing, I hadn't noticed. I wasn't sure I liked that.

"So, what did you find out?" Rosalind asked, pausing in front of the tiger enclosure. I pulled out my notes, a sheet and a half that I had typed up before going to bed the previous night, while it was all still fresh in my mind. She glanced at it while I talked her through the highlights, nodding at each point. She shrugged when I asked about whether the memory of the previous structure's fire could live on in the new building.

"I haven't seen anything like that before," she said, frowning. "But that doesn't mean it's not possible. We just don't know enough to be sure. What else did you find?"

"I couldn't find any murders. There was a shooting in 1998, after two roommates argued about their share of drug money, but no-one died, at least not that I could tell. Some guy electrocuted himself in 2004 trying to fix his stovetop, but that was the only death I saw. I couldn't find any other fires or any other records of traumatic property damage."

She continued reading for a minute or two. I had remembered to include citations for all my references, and they had bulked up the report, but there wasn't much detail besides what I had told her. I glanced down at the pair of tigers sunning themselves on the rocks below, heedless of the dozens of people gawking down at them, and I shifted, uncomfortable.

"Well, this is not a bad first effort," Rosalind said, handing my notes back to me. "It takes practice and more time than you may have had to spend yesterday to get a more complete picture."

Crestfallen, I felt like the kid in A Christmas Story who proudly handed in his report, thinking it was a masterpiece, only to get a C+. *You'll shoot your eye out!* I heard in my head.

"Did I miss something?" I asked, trying not to sound petulant.

"Sophia told me you were at the library for a little over an hour. I was there for three, and I've learned to look for patterns in otherwise insignificant pieces of information. For example, there was a man called Jim Berkowitz who lived there for at least five years in the eighties. In that time, three different women were recorded as living with him. After he moved to an apartment in Dogtown in 1991, the police convicted him of a felony assault against yet another woman. In my experience, domestic abuse can cause deep emotional scars and I have handled two such cases before. They were two of the worst."

I couldn't see her eyes through her sunglasses, but I guessed from her tone they would look haunted. What kind of emotional toll had these experiences taken on her? The physical toll was bad enough, but nothing a little rest and plenty of water couldn't help. But how many memories had she erased, of what kind? Was I really up to this?

Rosalind started walking again, and I followed. Ahead of us loomed the black skeleton of the Flight Cage, a remnant of the 1904 World's Fair from which the Zoo began. As a boy, I had loved birds and it had always been one of my favorite attractions, but now I found it menacing, just another cage, if larger than most. I turned off the path that led there, and Rosalind glanced at me but didn't object.

"I don't judge you for your past," she said. "And neither does Martin. We appreciate you confided in us, and that you're moving forward. Everyone has secrets, D, and yours is not the worst I've heard."

It was comforting, but I then remembered something. "Who's Daniel?"

Her step faltered for a moment, then she sighed and looked at me, her features grim. "I suppose Sophia asked you about him? She always had a soft spot for Daniel. He's my son."

"Oh." I guessed from her tone that this wasn't a subject she wanted to discuss. And it was none of my business anyway.

"There's something else I wanted to show you," I said before the silence became awkward. I rummaged in my backpack, retrieving the white envelope with its cryptic, threatening message inside. "Someone slid this under my door while I was at the library yesterday morning."

She read the note and frowned, stopping under a shady tree and examining both paper and envelope. "That's strange," she said at last. "Have you ever received anything like this before?"

"No. Have you?"

She shook her head. "No texts, or phone calls, or emails? You're not throwing wild parties in your apartment and pissing off your neighbors? No?"

I recounted my theories, except for the one about her husband, and she agreed they all sounded far fetched. She handed the note back to me, then stood staring into space and chewing her bottom lip until sighing again. "I don't know what to make of that, but you should keep it. I can't imagine how it could apply to what I'm teaching you, but it wouldn't be the first time something has surprised me during this journey. However, I feel further vindicated in one of my training recommendations for you - you should take up karate."

My skepticism must have been obvious, because she raised her eyebrows and cocked her head. "You disagree?"

"You really think I'm going to need to fight people doing this?"

She laughed, but there wasn't much humor in the sound. "I hope not. But there's much more to karate than fighting. It's a philosophy, even a way of life to some. Mental fortitude is as valuable as physical fortitude, more so in many ways. What happened to you at Stengel and Sons concerns me; you allowed your emotions to get the better of you. I worry what might have happened had I not been there."

I did too, but I was trying not to think about it. And I wasn't sure that karate was the answer. I didn't want to get better at fighting people. I didn't want to fight people at all. "What else?"

"What else?"

"You said that was one of your training recommendations for me. You have others?"

She pursed her lips, and once again, I felt like an unruly student. "Listening is an acquired skill. It took me months and, I now realize, many narrow escapes before I could clearly hear the source of the memory, that 'quietest voice' I told you about before. Hear it, join it, hold on to it as the memory dissipates. How musically inclined are you?"

My heart sank. This was going from bad to worse. "I mean, I enjoy listening to music, but I've never been able to play an instrument worth a damn. And Jess forbids me from singing along to the car radio."

"Then that is something else we must work on. Perhaps a visit to the St. Louis Symphony would be worthwhile."

"Okay," I said. Except for that morning in the Botanical Garden, she had always been very businesslike in her dealings with me, but with an undercurrent of good humor that put me at ease. Not today. It was almost as if she didn't want to be there, and it made me uncomfortable.

"Are you sure it will help?" I asked when she failed to elaborate. "I don't hear much of anything during these, well, while I'm experiencing these memories. Except for the screaming door."

She cocked her head again. "What do you experience?"

"Temperature swings mostly. It was freezing in Colton's apartment. I felt it as soon as we left the elevator. The stock room at Stengel and Sons, too. And the Crestwood house was burning hot. Well, it was on fire, I guess. In the memory, I mean."

She stared at me for a few moments, then grimaced before delving into her purse and handing me a business card. The characters GWK, which seemed to stand for Gateway to the West Karate, encircled a red sunburst. A phone number, an email, and a street address on Manchester Avenue, which I guessed was in Maplewood or thereabouts, filled out the card. I looked at it, then looked at her.

"Call them," she told me. "Tell them Martin and I referred you. Try an introductory class if you like. I wouldn't be recommending this if I didn't think it would help. But you would have to commit to it."

It sounded like a challenge, and probably was. Maybe it was her almost dismissive mood, or perhaps it was the unsettling and inexplicable turn my life had taken since I first met her in Colton's building just a few weeks before, but I had grown tired of being on the defensive.

"Alright then, I will." I put the card in my back pocket, didn't quite know what to do with my hands, and folded my arms instead.

Rosalind gave me a thin smile. "I'm glad to hear it. Let me know how your first session goes. Now, I do apologize, but something has come up to which I must attend. One of these days, we'll have to spend more than half an hour here. Take care, D."

Without waiting for my reply, she turned and strode towards the northern exit. As soon as she was out of earshot, she began an animated conversation into her phone and continued to do so until the late afternoon crowd swallowed her up.

"Karate?" Jess exclaimed when I told her that night at a Spanish restaurant in the Grove. In a rare planetary alignment, she also had the night off work, so we were celebrating with dinner and a movie. I grinned at her over a table crowded with tapas plates, and bit into the enormous shrimp I had just painstakingly peeled. "That I can't wait to see!"

I shrugged. "Rosalind seems to think it will improve my self-control."

"You don't sound convinced."

"I don't see how learning to fight better helps with my temper."

"It's not just about fighting, you know. Depending on the discipline, there's a lot of meditation and breathing exercises, so you can approach conflict with a clear head."

"When did you become an expert on karate?"

"I'm hardly an expert, but I took lessons for a while in high school." She paused and chewed, deep in thought. "My parents insisted. Self-defense. Being a young woman in a big city and all that."

I frowned, protective instincts aroused. I'd heard far too much "locker room talk" to dismiss the sense in that, but it irked me. "Maybe you should come too," I said. "It might be fun to share a hobby like that."

She raised her eyebrows. "Why? Are you looking for a sidekick in your ghostbusting career?"

"It's not ghostbusting," I protested. Jess enjoyed teasing me, but I was determined not to take the bait. Not yet anyway. "I signed up for a free lesson this Saturday at noon. Come with me."

Determined not to procrastinate, I had called before I even left the zoo. The guy I spoke to was friendly enough but sounded rushed and I didn't get the a chance to name-drop Rosalind and Martin.

"I'll think about it," she said. "Eat up, or we'll be late for the movie."

It was nonsense, but Jess was very particular about getting good seats in the theater, so I ate up.

It surprised me when she texted on Friday night and said she wanted to come to the lesson.

"I've been thinking about what you said," she told me after I picked her up the next morning. "It would be fun to do something new together. And I'll enjoy kicking your ass!"

Gateway to the West Karate occupied a nondescript storefront in an unremarkable strip mall dominated by a Target store. It was further down Manchester Road than I had estimated, just west of Interstate 270, so we didn't arrive as early as I had planned. Almost a hundred degrees of sun blazed down as we hurried across the black asphalt parking lot, hoping that the building's air conditioning would be up to the task.

A wall of cold, pine-scented air greeted us as we entered the dojo, a term repeated multiple times during my phone call. There had been plenty of photographs on their website, so I had a rough idea of what to expect. Slate gray matting, bordered by about four feet of pine laminate floor, dominated the almost perfectly square space. Motivational and instructional posters adorned the cream-colored walls, except for opposite the entrance, where there hung an enormous portrait of a white-haired but formidable-looking Japanese man. Blinds covered the windows, underneath which were cubbies for shoes and socks; everyone in the dojo was barefoot, so we followed suit. Jess grumbled about her family home under her breath - mostly.

"Welcome," said a well-tanned man, approaching us with a clipboard in hand. The white robe he wore was the one I recognized as the uniform for karate, belted in black. He stood a little shorter than me, his black hair close-cropped to disguise a receding hairline, and I doubted there was an ounce of fat on his stocky frame. He smiled at Jess, then at me, and ticked off our names as I gave them. "Excellent. We'll get started in just a moment. Please find a space on the mat."

There were about a dozen other students, so this wasn't hard to do. We were all dressed in loose athletic gear, a dozen variations of workout, or running shirts and shorts. More than half were women, including a couple of young girls accompanied by their parents, and a wiry, gray-haired woman who tilted her head defiantly when I caught her eye. Apart from a young black guy standing in the opposite corner, everyone else was Caucasian, including the three white-clad instructors who lined-up before us.

"Okay," said the man with the clipboard. "Thank you all for coming. I am Sensei Allen, and I'm the Chief Instructor here. To my right is Sempei Richard, to my left is Sempei Donovan, and they will both be your instructors if you choose to continue your journey with us. For make no mistake, karate is a journey and only you can tell how long it will be."

There was more of this, but I only half-listened. I thought I recognized Donovan, a lanky guy with tight blond hair and a stubbly goatee. For a moment, his gaze rested on mine, then drifted away. I shook my head and tried to focus, but I knew it was going to bother me until I could place him.

He seemed to avoid me as he and the third instructor - a silver-haired but no less physically intimidating man with piercing blue eyes - walked among us during the lesson, while Sensei Allen stood underneath the enormous portrait and directed. We bowed, we stretched, we learned some basic striking and kicking techniques, while he explained the importance of practice, of repetition and muscle memory, of breathing and meditation.

"In moments of crisis, there is no time to think," Allen explained. "Anger, fear, adrenalin. They are your enemies. If you follow this journey, you will be better aware of yourself and your surroundings, calm under pressure, focused on your adversary, whoever or whatever that may be."

To the disappointment of some, we didn't spar in our first lesson. Jess grinned at me as if she had been relishing the chance to take me on, a sentiment I didn't share. Instead, the Sensei asked his fellow instructors to demonstrate some common self-defense techniques, which involved Donovan throwing a series of punches at Richard and the older man effortlessly blocking them with his arms. The blocks all had Japanese names using words like "soto" and "uke", which I forgot more or less instantly, but I noted the moves and I began to realize karate was as much about defense as offense.

I figured this was all building up to a sales pitch, and when it came, the pressure was no higher or lower than I expected.

"Beginner or master, you will get out of karate as much as you put in," Allen said. "Three lessons a week, four if you can swing it, and daily practice is what I would recommend. You can sign up now if you wish, or call or go online later."

"What do you think?" Jess asked as the lesson wrapped up and we reclaimed our shoes. I took my time retying my laces before I answered, weighing my defiant acceptance of Rosalind's challenge with the time and financial commitment Allen was asking for. Jess's face gave nothing away as I looked up at her.

"I don't know," I admitted. "It sounds good, but I don't know how we'll both find the time. It's hard enough scheduling a dinner date."

"We can be flexible," said Allen, appearing at my elbow. I didn't jump, honest. "Beginners start by attending their own classes until they get the hang of the structure, but we teach all skill levels together. Jess and D, right?"

I nodded, fearing the hard sell. He smiled ruefully. "I have to give the sales spiel. That's the point of the free class. But at least you have a better idea what you're dealing with. How did you hear about us?"

"Friends of ours," I said after a momentary pause. "Rosalind and Martin Hill."

"Ah!" Allen said, and his eyes lit up. "What a great couple! And she's a force of nature, let me tell you. Looking at them, you'd think Martin would be the one to worry about, but *I* wouldn't make that mistake. I've known her a long time, trained and sparred with her often. We studied here under the same master." He shook his head and sighed. "I wish she'd stayed here and taught, but she wanted to experience other martial arts. Our throws didn't satisfy her. She still trains here from time to time though, and she always had an eye for talent."

I stared back at him, somewhat abashed. Out of the corner of my eye, I could see Jess grinning.

"Let us know," he said, and clapped me on the shoulder before hunting down another potential customer.

"You'd better watch your step now," said Jess with a mischievous smile. "You know two women who can kick your ass."

"No-one is kicking my ass," I grumbled, not sure of that at all, and reached for the door.

"Dex?"

I froze. No-one had called me by that name for a very long time. Slowly, I turned to find Donovan, the assistant instructor or whatever Allen had called him, standing a few feet away. And then I remembered who he was.

"Donovan Brooks."

"It *is* you! I wasn't sure. The ponytail threw me off, and it's been a long time. How are you?"

I clutched my leather bracelet, then forced myself to let it go. Calm under pressure, right?

"D?" Jess was there, and just reminding me of that fact.

"Jess, this is Donovan. We went to UMSL together. Back in the day."

"Back in the day is right!" He grinned, but his eyes searched mine, and I thought I knew what he was wondering. Sure enough: "What happened to you? After the expulsion, I mean. I never saw that coming, dude. There were tons of us doing Es and shit."

"Yeah, well, we didn't all pay the same dues," I said, unable to keep the bitterness from my voice.

He grimaced. "No, you're right about that. At least you landed on your feet, it looks like. Good-looking girl, you look good yourself, if you don't mind me saying."

"Always room for improvement."

"Absolutely, and you've come to the right place! I started here six years ago, made Nidan last December. It's life-changing."

I blinked. "Did what now?"

"Nidan. Second degree black belt. Sorry, I forget not everyone knows the terminology."

I couldn't help but be skeptical about that. Just as the pause grew awkward, his eyes narrowed. "Did I hear you say you know Rosalind Hill?"

"I do, and it seems everyone else here does too."

"By reputation, if nothing else." He nodded. "I've never sparred with her myself, but I've watched her in action. She could give Sensei a run for his money. A formidable opponent."

I hadn't spoken to Donovan in over fifteen years. He wasn't a friend, just a friend of a roommate, someone I'd swapped inappropriate jokes with over a keg once or twice. Locker room talk. I felt uneasy, without knowing why.

"D, we're going to be late," said Jess, placing a hand on my arm.

"Right." I forced a smile. "Why are we surprised when we run into old acquaintances? Good to see you again, Donovan. Maybe we'll be seeing more of each other."

He returned the smile and gestured toward the door. "Maybe we will. I won't keep you."

I had turned back towards the door when he added, "Stay on Rosalind's good side, Dex. She *is* a force of nature."

CHAPTER TWELVE

YOU WANT TO DO THIS?

I usually got Tuesday, Thursday and Sunday nights off during the week, as well as Saturday lunchtimes, but Jess's schedule was more variable. Money was a bigger issue. I could afford two lessons per week, but beyond that was a stretch. Jess said she would leach from her parents if she had to.

"Dad's always nagged me about taking up self-defense classes again," she said, as I drove her home from GWK. "Let's just sign up for a couple nights a week and I'll make as many classes as I can."

"You definitely want to do this then?"

"You don't? I thought Rosalind wanted you to."

"She recommended it. But..." I couldn't think what to say after the "but". I wasn't sure why I was so reluctant, and the only reasons I could come up with were, to be honest, lame excuses.

"Tell you what," Jess said after it was clear my sentence had died at birth. "Let's wait until after next weekend. You haven't forgotten about Chicago, right?"

Some idiot in a bright red Camaro chose that moment to weave in front of me as we approached a red light, and I screamed a few expletives as I stamped on the brakes. Chicago, right. My birthday trip, planned before our fight after Kenya Day. We were still doing that then.

"Course not. I wasn't supposed to book anything, was I?"

"No, D, I got it. You got the weekend off work, right?"

"I put the request in. I'll double-check tonight."

And I knew I had thought about requesting time off, but I wasn't sure I'd done so. Sure enough, when I mentioned it to Mike that night, he frowned.

"Not that I recall. Did you text or email?"

"I don't remember," I said with a sinking feeling. Jess was going to be furious.

"Did you have plans?" asked Mike.

"My girlfriend booked a weekend in Chicago for my birthday. I must've just forgotten to tell you."

Mike grimaced. "Well, I haven't set next week's schedule yet. I could put TJ on all the weekend shifts, but I'd want to talk to him first."

"Let me," I said, and Mike nodded.

TJ was cool about it. I texted him and he replied later than night that he'd take the weekend.

Still owe you for when I broke my arm, he texted.

We're quits now, I replied.

Disaster averted, I texted Rosalind to let her know we'd attended the introductory karate lesson and that we would "sort out our schedules" while in Chicago, which seemed suitably ambiguous. Oddly, she didn't reply until Tuesday evening. It wouldn't have bothered me, but I'd picked up a strange vibe from our meeting at the zoo and I was worried that I'd offended her, perhaps with my lack of boundless enthusiasm for her training suggestions. I wasn't checking my phone every hour, not really, but I was relieved when it finally buzzed as I prepared fettuccine carbonara for me and Jess.

Glad to hear it. Out of town. Be back later this week, maybe. Practice.

Practice what? I wanted to reply, but decided against it. Besides, Jess was stealing chunks of chicken from the pan, and I had to admonish her.

Other than the relentless heat, the rest of the week passed uneventfully, and I found myself getting excited about the weekend. Jess and I had only stayed in a hotel together once before, the previous New Year's Eve, after a raucous evening downtown. A full weekend away, in another city, was a step up in our relationship. I felt like it was a watershed: on one side was a guy clawing his way back into society, just trying to hold down a job and his own place to live, on the other was someone having a purpose in the world and someone to pursue it with. I was ready.

Or so I thought.

We took Amtrak rather than drive, because neither of our cars were that comfortable for a five-hour-plus journey, and because Jess got irritable when I yelled at other drivers. This meant catching a Lyft at 6am that Friday morning to the uninspiringly named St. Louis Gateway

Transportation Center. A little early for me, but since it was early July, the sun had already risen, and that, combined with a large Starbucks dark roast, kept me sufficiently awake as we found our seats in the train carriage. The journey to Chicago's Union Station was no shorter than driving, but at least we could both nap before Jess plugged in her phone and showed me maps and websites of attractions she wanted us to visit. I was happy to just be with her and do whatever she wanted to, but what *she* wanted was my input.

"We can't do *all* of this," she snapped after I said, "Yeah, that looks good" one too many times. "There's enough here to keep us occupied for a week, and we have two days."

"Oh. Where are we staying again?"

"The Great Lakes Hotel. It's just off Michigan Avenue, north of the river. A few minutes' walk from Navy Pier."

"Let's start with what's close to there then," I said. "I'd prefer walking to taking public transport, especially the subway. And don't tell me again that it's called the L."

"They have Lyft in Chicago too, you know," she sighed, before grinning. "That's cool. I can work with that. And are you sure you're cool with meeting my grandparents?"

"Of course."

Jess had visited family in Chicago almost every year growing up. Despite her ongoing irritation with her family in St. Louis, she loved her grandparents, and we would visit with both sets during the weekend. Her dad's mother had died of breast cancer a couple years before, but James Evans still lived in the family home in Evanston, insisting he'd continue to do so until they carried him out in a box. We'd planned that visit for tomorrow afternoon. First up, after we hurried through the bustling maze that was Union Station and emerged into the not-any-cooler scorching sun of downtown Chicago, we caught another Lyft to a Spanish restaurant near our hotel. There Jess's mom's parents, Gathii and Atieno Maina, joined us. The Kenyan expats were a diminutive but lively couple, clearly known and liked by the restaurant staff, who kept bringing us extra samples of the many tapas we hadn't ordered. I had been almost as nervous as when Jess first introduced me to her parents, but before I knew it I was laughing at Gathii's delightfully bad joke telling and his wife's gentle mockery. Atieno had heard from her daughter that I was a chef and wanted to hear about this passion we shared. Jess laughed, and we all dug into the enormous bowl of paella that was one of the best things I could remember eating at any restaurant ever.

"It is our favorite place to eat when we come into the city," Gathii explained, his accent sounding as rich as I imagined it had been when they walked off the plane from Nairobi in the 1970s. He had already dripped some sort of red sauce on his shirt, but the fabric's colors were so vivid you couldn't notice. "We came in here one day to shelter from a thunderstorm and ate one of the best meals we've ever had. That was, what, twelve years ago now?"

"Yes, you still had your practice," said Atieno, picking daintily at her food. Her sun dress would have put one of Rosalind's to shame. "Gathii was a dentist, and I was his hygienist," she explained with obvious pride. "Forty years we worked until Covid. If he could, he would work still."

"Eyes not what they were." Gathii tapped his thick, round glasses with a cheerful grin and forked another mound of paella into his mouth.

I found them delightful. They adored Jess, who seemed content to let them ply me with questions, jumping in only to guide the conversation away from any sensitive topics. The only blemish on the meal was the dark glances I caught emanating from a pair of young white couples at a nearby table. I thought I recognized the type, resentful that anyone with *that* skin color would have the temerity to sit in the same restaurant and spoil their lunch. I caught one guy's eye and gave him the barest shake of my head; he stared back for a moment, then looked away.

Gathii and I argued about the check, which he wanted to pay for in entirety. In the end, I persuaded him to leave the tip to me, while the women rolled their eyes. I slapped two twenty-dollar bills on the table and excused myself to use the restroom. Which was where the trouble started.

I was washing my hands, staring impassively at my reflection in the mirror above the sink, when I heard the toilet in the single stall flush. As awkward as any guy when confronted with anyone else using the Men's room, I tried to finish up only to see the door open behind me. Out stepped the same guy at whom I'd just shaken my head in the dining room.

He paused for a moment, registering who I was, then smirked as he stepped up to the sink I had just vacated. He wasn't as tall as me, but he was well built, his Cubs shirt stretched to impress over his chest and shoulders. His hair and eyes were as dark as mine, but his skin was paler, perhaps from Italian or Greek heritage, I guessed. I bit my lip as I dried my hands and reached for the door handle. Five more seconds. That was all I needed.

"Why do you even like this food?" he drawled. "There's not a fried thing on the menu."

Perhaps it was lingering resentment over how Jess had been harassed at work recently, or more likely the barely suppressed frustration of any non-fully white person in a white man's world, but my body reacted far more quickly than my brain did. I pivoted, grabbed him by his shoulders, and rammed him against the stall door. His head smacked the metal with a satisfactory thud and water splashed both our faces from his still-wet hands.

"I know more about food than you ever will, you racist fuck." I hissed the words, furiously blinking water out of one eye, my face mere inches from his. His lips drew back from his teeth and he snarled before shrugging me off and we stared at each other in mutual animosity. It could have ended there, but then he grabbed my shirt and threw a roundhouse punch.

He was fast and in less cramped quarters things may not have gone well for me, but as it was his elbow jammed against the stall door behind him and I had time to flinch before his fist more or less bounced off the side of my head. It still hurt. We both cursed, then he threw another punch with more or less the same result. I finally got my own hands up, my left pawing at his shirt while I drew my right back for a vicious counterstrike. Numbing pain flared from elbow to shoulder as my arm collided with the ancient air hand dryer, tearing it from the wall with an abrupt metallic screech. We both froze and gaped at the scratched and dented mechanism dangling abjectly from its electrical wires and then time, in that peculiar way it does when adrenaline floods your system, slowed down. If this guy landed a real punch it was going to hurt, and I thought back to the karate lesson and Sensei Allen talking about calm under pressure, of ways to defend yourself against an assailant, of the different blocks with Japanese names I'd already forgotten. But I remembered the demo and Donovan throwing a punch at the other instructor, who had blocked it with a sort of outside-in movement, and I was ready for the next punch, twisting my right arm up in the same way. Amazingly, it not only prevented the blow from landing but forced my opponent's arm down and gave me the opening I needed to finish this while he was off balance. I gave him a savage knee in the stomach.

He went down hard, with a surprisingly high-pitched grunt of pain, and curled into a foetal position with his hands over his groin. Well, I was aiming for his stomach - honest. I stepped over him and opened the door to the dining room, pausing to check how incapacitated he was, but all he did was shoot me a murderous glare through watering eyes.

Time to get the hell out of there.

I brushed myself down and fought to slow my breathing as I hurried back to the table. "Are we paid up?" I asked. "Because I could use some sunlight."

Jess narrowed her eyes, but her grandparents rose without complaint and bade cheerful farewells to the staff. The skin on the back of my neck prickled as I followed their ever so slow progress toward the entrance, looking resolutely forward even as I listened for any hint of my adversary.

We made it to the street, and I insisted on walking them back to their car, parked in a garage on the next block. Atieno thanked me with a smile, but Gathii gave me a curious look before taking her arm and turning down the sidewalk.

At the same moment, Jess grabbed mine, fingers clawing into my flesh. "What did you do?" she hissed.

"Taught someone a lesson," I muttered, but before I could elaborate, a shout rang out above the lunchtime traffic from behind us.

"You wanna fight me like a man, big guy? Come fight me like a man!"

We were almost at the crosswalk, but didn't have a walk signal. I disengaged Jess's hand from my arm and turned to see the guy from the men's room and his buddy following us. They stopped as soon as I turned, about ten paces away. Other pedestrians gave us a wide berth.

"You want to do this?" I said as calmly as I could, although I could feel my body shaking with adrenalin. "Because we can do this. You and your other racist friend."

That got people's attention. Two young black guys, defying the summer heat with black t-shirts and baseball caps, turned from where they were preparing to cross the street and looked first at me, then at the two white men who now both looked wary. The standoff dragged on for what seemed like hours, until Jess laid her hand on my arm again, gently this time.

"We have a walk signal," she whispered. "Let's go."

Letting out breath I didn't know I was holding, and with a slow and deliberate turn, I allowed Jess to guide me across the street, her grandparents several steps ahead and other pedestrians still giving us plenty of cushion. I heard some half-hearted insults from behind me, but it didn't sound like they were following. By the time we reached the other sidewalk, the tension began to dissipate and I could take a deep, shaky breath.

"I'm sorry," I said as we rejoined Gathii and Atieno. "I let my temper get the better of me. It just... well, there's no good excuse." My prison counselor would have been proud.

"There is no helping those people," Gathii said sadly, although I thought I caught a glint in his eye. "Hate rules them. It is best to ignore them if you can."

I disagreed, but I wasn't about to start that argument. I just nodded and turned to Jess, who looked like she was swallowing her own instinctive words.

"D's very protective of me," was all she said, taking my arm properly.

Gathii smiled. "I am glad to hear it."

"It was nice meeting you, D," said Atieno with apparent sincerity. "Our Jess is lucky to have found herself a good man."

"Oh, I think I'm the lucky one," I replied, and she beamed. Jess raised an eyebrow.

"Come see us again," Gathii said, holding my gaze as he shook my hand before turning to Jess. "Be patient with your mother, Jessie. She does what she thinks is best for you."

"She always has," Jess replied and hugged her grandparents in turn. "I miss you both. I'll visit as often as I can, I promise."

CHAPTER THIRTEEN

GET OUT!

"What the fuck?" Jess said as soon as the parking garage elevator door closed on her grandparents. She dropped my arm and rounded on me, any gratitude for my "protection" smothered by an angry glare. "I introduce you to my grandparents and you almost start a fight in their favorite restaurant? What were you thinking?"

"You had your back to those assholes," I protested, holding up my palms in placation. "They were giving us dirty looks and making snide comments to each other the whole time. I know your grandfather saw it."

"Yeah, but I didn't see him try to start anything." I thought that wasn't a reasonable observation, but let it pass.

"That one guy basically came after me in the bathroom. I couldn't let it go."

She opened her mouth, shut it again, then impaled me with her eyes for several long heartbeats before letting out a heavy sigh. "Oh, D, you need to do something about your impulse control. Seriously."

"I know, I know," I agreed. "I was less worried about taking on him and his buddy than I was about someone calling the cops. That sort of attention I don't need."

"No, you don't. And nor do I. Are you okay? Can we go back to enjoying our weekend now?"

Was I okay? I'd almost got into a fistfight in a restaurant in front of my girlfriend's family and was lucky that no-one had called the cops. My heart was still racing, but in a cooling down, post 100 yard dash kind of way. I needed to move on, wanted to move on, but a part of me was still rattled even as we went about our day. Maybe that's enough to explain what happened later.

It was still a little early for us to check into our room at the Great Lakes Hotel, but there was a speakeasy-themed bar next door, so we treated ourselves to a drink first. Jess studied the bartender in detail, and I thought made rather a show of examining her drink and the layout of the bar itself. I told her to stop. "I didn't check out the kitchen at the restaurant. You don't need to be giving them the third degree," I said quietly.

"Just picking up pointers," she protested.

"We're on vacation," I insisted. She stuck out her tongue, but at least stopped being obvious about it.

The single front desk clerk at the hotel was friendly enough, but she looked rather harassed. There were two couples ahead of us in line, one of which had some problem with their reservation. As we reached the desk, the clerk, a short black woman in her early twenties with dreads halfway down her back, took a long drink from a bottle of water and fixed her smile in place before asking how she could help us.

"I can't believe they're leaving her to handle a Friday afternoon all by herself," Jess grumbled as we rode up to the tenth floor in the elevator. Fortunately, our check-in process had gone off without complications. "We got a great rate too. I wonder how this place is doing."

The room was pleasant enough, if a little on the small side. There was just enough space to walk between the king bed and the TV stand-cum-minibar-cum-desk to get to the efficient bathroom, but it looked clean and the bed was comfortable. I was all for giving the bed a more rigorous test right then, but Jess insisted we should do some sightseeing first.

"If we start now, we'll never go anywhere," she said, and while I didn't disagree, I also didn't see a problem with that. But I allowed myself to be lured out of the room by the promise of Navy Pier.

Opened to the public in 1916, Navy Pier had charted an erratic course through the twentieth century. It had always included public spaces as well as supporting both commercial shipping and a World War II training center for the United States Navy. Waves of revitalization came and went with mixed success until a more ambitious re-imagining in the mid-1990s introduced the now iconic Ferris wheel, museums, theaters, shops and exhibition spaces. It was now Chicago's most visited attraction, which I heard as loud and crowded.

I wasn't wrong, but once we made it through the Ferris wheel line, we had a car all to ourselves, then followed that up by taking a speedboat trip out on Lake Michigan with only a couple dozen other people. Somehow, I knocked my sunglasses off my head and into the lake halfway through the tour and had to squint at the remaining handful of sites the guide described over the PA. Jess suggested we buy replacements at one of the gift shops back at the pier, but they were overpriced; I lose or break sunglasses with alarming frequency and hate spending more than a few dollars on them. We settled for poking around the small botanical garden for a while before sauntering back towards our hotel, stopping to eat a light meal in the rooftop beer garden of an Irish pub not because we were that hungry, but because we knew we wouldn't want to go out again once we got back to the room.

"Shall we watch a movie?" Jess asked with mock innocence when we closed the door.

"Very funny," I said, and pulled her down with me onto the bed.

It was a very pleasant end to what, despite my lunchtime altercation, had turned out to be a thoroughly enjoyable day. Had I not been determined to get some ice to melt overnight in my water glass, then that is how we would have remembered it. But no, D cannot drink tepid water, not after rediscovering the joy of abundant ice in polite society. So I threw my shorts and T-shirt back on, grabbed the bucket with its plastic liner bag off the minibar, and left the room in search of the ice machine.

Perhaps because it was a high-rise with only a handful of rooms per floor, the Great Lakes hotel had only setup ice and vending machines on odd-numbered floors. I had a choice between going down to the ninth or up to the eleventh, and since our room was next to the stairs and furthest from the elevator - and who takes a hotel elevator one floor anyway? - I decided to walk up empty-handed and then back down with the heavier burden of a full bucket of ice. My contented self-mockery lasted until I set my hand on the handle of the gunmetal gray door that had a big number '11' stenciled in black on it.

A wave of heat washed over me, not the already stale summer heat trapped inside the stairwell, but a dry, furious heat that promised flame and smoke and death. I recoiled, the hair on my arm standing on end. That familiar sense of otherness crowded out my recollection of the bedroom in Crestwood. Something was here that shouldn't be, and knowing more about how these things worked and how to deal with them brought me little comfort. I can't explain why I didn't just turn around and walk two flights down to the ninth floor, unless it was now knowing that the phenomenon existed, I couldn't ignore it, and my failure at the hardware store on South Grand rankled. I licked my lips and took a deep, shuddering breath. Then I pulled the door open.

For a few confusing seconds, the burning heat ebbed away almost entirely, although my perception of wrongness persisted as if I had entered a parallel dimension that almost looked the same but in which the angles were all tilted a fraction of a degree. I stepped through the doorway, but I couldn't see the ice machine and assumed it must be closer to the elevator. I started down the hallway and, in an instant, the heat was back, and with it a tightness in the air that made it difficult to breathe. Though I could see no smoke or evidence of fire, if I closed my eyes I could feel it, lapping up against the walls, writhing around my legs, surging ever higher. "Listen," Rosalind had told me before, and I both wanted to and desperately feared to, despite my suspicion that she and I didn't experience these things the same way. Maybe that was why I became so disoriented: I couldn't commit to embracing the memory, hoping to channel it away, yet the sensations persisted. I stopped moving, closed my eyes and tried to ignore everything, tried to push the heat and reek of smoke away. All sound, real or imagined, grew muffled and although my ears didn't pop, I staggered, eyelids flying open as my arms flailed towards the walls to brace myself. I could still hear screams of terror and pain, but it was as if I was underwater. As I drew level with a pair of doors facing each other across the hallway, my rapidly blinking eyes saw what I was sure were tendrils of smoke snaking through the air. Someone was trapped! No, someone *had been* trapped. This wasn't real, this was a recording, a memory, and if I just retreated, edged back down the hallway, the sensations that seemed so real would fade into the slate-gray walls. But I didn't move. I stared at one door then the other, certain I could see smoke and there were, or had been, people in those rooms, and why weren't they trying to get out? My eyes blinked furiously as my skin tingled, whether from heat or fear I didn't know, and panic uncoiled within me like an awakening dragon. I banged on one door, then the other with my fists, tried in vain to turn their handles, pull them open, but it was so hard to breathe. And it was so hot! What could I do? What could I do? Then I saw, six feet beyond the door on my right, gleaming halfway up the blistering paint on the wall, my salvation: a scarlet pull alarm! I lurched forward like a sailor aboard a storm-tossed ship, grabbed the handle, and yanked it downward.

There was a split-second when it seemed like the entire hallway was holding its breath, then emergency lights began strobing and the air was rent by a repeating klaxon that sounded like half a dozen seriously pissed off cats being swung around by their tails. I stood, frozen to the spot and panting, until one of the room doors opened and a short, middle-aged man with wiry gray hair and wearing a Kansas City Chiefs jersey peered out. He flinched when he saw me, as I was looming right outside his room.

"Is there a fire?" he asked. Part of me wanted to yell at him that the fire alarm was going off late on a Friday night and so that was a good working assumption, but I was also asking the same question of myself. My mind insisted there was a fire, that somewhere nearby, perhaps in this very room, terrified people were screaming, unable to flee from the flames; yet none of my physical senses could confirm any of it.

"Doug?" called a woman's voice from inside the room. The man looked questioningly at me for a couple more seconds, then took a step back and glanced over his shoulder.

"I don't see anything, but there's a guy outside our room. Maybe we ought to get out."

"Yes! Get out!" I cried, rousing myself into action. I wasn't sure if the fire was real, but the alarm was, and I could hear shouting and the slamming of doors from elsewhere in the hallway. Turning towards the elevator, I saw a pair of younger couples hurrying toward me, their eyes wide, not panicking yet but wondering if they ought to be. Right, no elevator in a fire, go back to stairs. Now.

I allowed myself to be swept up by the exodus. Guests from higher floors choked the stairwell, and I stopped dead on the threshold, hearing someone behind me curse. Between my disorientation and my rising panic, I couldn't make myself move either direction. Then I heard someone calling my name. Jess. I stumbled down two half-flights of stairs to see her waiting by the door to the tenth floor. As soon as she saw me, she grabbed my arm and hung on as we descended as fast as the congestion from ten floors of fleeing guests allowed us.

By the ninth floor, my panic was easing and remnants of whatever that was on the eleventh were fading. It had not been as vivid as either the Crestwood bedroom or the South Grand alleyway, but I was increasingly sure it had only been a memory, an Imprint as Rosalind called them. I was ashamed of myself for my poor reactions. Worse, I had that awful feeling that comes with realizing that your mistake may have scared, or at least inconvenienced, a lot of other people who were going to be mad at whoever was responsible. I had little hope I could avoid the blame, and I was not disappointed.

The stairwell exited into a well-lit alleyway, sliced between the hotel and its neighboring high-rise. Hotel guests spilled from the exterior door in both directions, standing in groups and giving the malodorous garbage skips as wide a berth as possible. The hectic red and blue lights of a Chicago Fire Department truck flashed from the nearer end of the alley, and a couple of helmeted figures stood at that end of the crowd, answering or deflecting questions. Closer to hand, the front desk clerk stood in animated discussion with a taller man, wearing thick-rimmed glasses beneath a huge Afro, and another firefighter. Afro guy wore the same standard-issue black hotel shirt and pants as the clerk and held a tablet, which he waved around until the fireman, who in his uniform with all the equipment hanging off of him looked about as broad as he was tall, put a restraining glove on his arm.

"Can I have everyone's attention please!" The firefighter's deep voice boomed down the alleyway, and everyone turned and quieted. "If you are staying in a room on the eleventh floor, please come talk to me."

Around a dozen people filtered through the crowd towards him, faces uncertain. I recognized the guy in the Chiefs shirt, accompanied by a wisp of a woman who must be his wife. He didn't look at me, but my shoulders had already slumped.

"Were you on the eleventh floor?" Jess asked, frowning at me. I nodded, not taking my eyes off the firefighter as he talked to each of the guests.

"That's where the ice machine was."

It was Chiefs fan's turn. He shook his head in response to a question, and then I saw the penny drop. He started searching the crowd with his eyes. Looking for me.

"I pulled the alarm, Jess," I whispered, just before he found me. I raised my hand at the same moment that he pointed toward me and realized I was still carrying the ice bucket.

"What?" Jess asked.

"I thought there was a fire. I felt it, or remembered it."

"Jesus, D!"

The firefighter began walking toward me. Some of the other guests backed away, others lingered in fascination.

"Good evening, sir," he said, taking off his helmet to reveal a wide, black face, sweat beading on an almost bald scalp. The badge on his chest read "Dupree". His eyes flickered to Jess, standing at my side, then back to me.

"Good evening, officer," I replied, as calmly as I could.

He flashed me a grim smile. "Am I correct in understanding you were on the eleventh floor of this hotel when the alarm went off?"

"I was. I pulled the alarm."

"Did you now?" His eyes narrowed. "And what was your reason? The hotel monitoring system has detected no evidence of a fire, and neither has my crew."

I sighed. "It's hard to explain."

"I'm sure it is," he said softly. He glanced at Jess again. "Are you aware that it is a Class 4 Felony to set off a false fire alarm? You've pulled two trucks and almost twenty men away from any potential real fires."

My heart sank. I couldn't get something else on my record, not now.

"I thought I saw smoke. I felt the heat and I heard people screaming. I just wanted to get ice." I shook the bucket as evidence and wondered if I sounded as crazy as I felt.

Officer Dupree gave me a long, shrewd look. "Stay here," he said and walked back to the hotel staff, who were both staring in my direction. I tried to ignore them, and the other guests who stood in groups whispering. I forced myself to look at Jess, who returned my gaze inscrutably before looking away. Her hand found mine and gave it a brief squeeze.

"Okay, everyone," called Officer Dupree. "The building is secure. We've confirmed it was a false alarm. You may return to your rooms. We apologize for any inconvenience, but I'm sure you agree that your safety is the hotel's top priority."

From the look of things, not everyone was in total agreement with this. Several guests gathered around the hotel staff, and I heard the word "compensation" several times. The Chiefs fan shot me a venomous look before slinking down the alleyway to join the line for the elevators.

"You okay?" Officer Dupree asked as he rejoined us.

"I don't know. Am I?"

"Well, in other circumstances, you probably wouldn't be. But you were on the eleventh floor of this hotel."

I frowned. "And so..."

"And so you're the fourth person in the last two years to pull that same fire alarm with no sign of fire in the building."

He let that sink in, his eyes never leaving mine.

"What does that mean?" I asked at last.

"Hell if I know. Something's going on up on that floor, but I don't know what it is, and neither does the hotel. False alarms happen all the time, in some hotels more than others. We let some go, but after a while we have to fine them. I hate fining this place. They're good people and their business has been hanging by a thread ever since the pandemic. I don't know if they'll pass that down to you, but I can't say I'd blame them."

I couldn't either. But an extra charge on my hotel bill was still better than a felony charge.

"Look," he said, putting his helmet back on. "I'll see what I can do about the fine. When all is said and done, I'd rather we had a hundred false alarms caused by people who weren't sure than one tragedy caused by no-one taking action. Talk to the hotel, apologize. But I'd stay away from the eleventh floor if I were you."

He rejoined his fellow firefighters, barking instructions, and within a couple minutes the trucks were pulling away. Being Chicago on a Friday night, a crowd had gathered on the street to watch the spectacle, but they dispersed soon afterward. Jess and I lurked in the alleyway's mouth until they were gone, and by the time we entered the lobby, there were only a handful of guests still waiting for the elevator. One or two glanced in our direction, but if they recognized us, they didn't show it.

The front desk clerk and her colleague did recognize us. I could see politeness and irritation doing battle as I walked up to the desk, hands spread in apology.

"Guys, I'm sorry. I really thought there was a fire. I was wrong, and if I've made things difficult for you tonight, I apologize."

They exchanged looks and then the man sighed, took off his glasses and rubbed his eyes.

"We try not to rent rooms on eleven," he muttered. "But we can't pass up the business, not now."

"What's wrong with the eleventh floor?" asked Jess.

"Don't know. Just seems to bother some folks. You're not the first person to set off that alarm."

"I still say it's haunted," said the desk clerk. "We had a housekeeper refuse to go up there, too. In the end, she quit."

"That wasn't the only reason she quit. But still. Most folks are fine, but it doesn't take many to get us a bad reputation. Didn't you look at TripAdvisor before you booked?"

"Yeah," said Jess. "Everywhere gets bad reviews, believe it."

His laugh was hollow. "Maybe. Look, the fire department said they'd try to cut us a break, but if we get a fine, I gotta pass it on to you. It's in the terms and conditions, and we can't afford to make any exceptions right now."

"I understand," I said, wondering how much a fine like that might be. My credit card limit was pretty low.

We rode up to our room in silence. I felt somewhat numb, as though the rush of adrenalin had scoured me clean of emotion. Once or twice I thought Jess was about to say something, but she kept her own counsel until we closed our room door behind us. Then she thumped me in the middle of my chest hard enough for me to stagger backwards.

"What the actual fuck?" she growled. "This was supposed to be a fun, relaxing getaway for your birthday tomorrow. Are you *trying* to spend the night in jail?"

"You know I'm not," I replied, my voice flat, weary. "I wasn't expecting it, an imprinted memory or whatever Rosalind calls them, not here. Maybe I should have run from the damn thing. I still can't handle them, and I don't know if I'll ever be able to."

She glared at me and set her hands on her hips, which was every bit as intimidating as the thump on my chest. "You need to let others help you, then. I don't know if karate lessons are the answer, but perhaps you should listen to someone who's supposed to have been 'handling them' just fine for a lot longer than you."

I hung my head. Jess never has minced words, and she was right. I couldn't do this alone.

"Sure. I'll give them a shot, if I can still afford it after whatever fine they give me here."

She continued searching my eyes for long seconds, then relaxed and reached for me. We stood, holding each other in silence for a while, her pliant warmth and sharp floral scent soothing me more than any words ever could.

Excerpt of email recovered from closed account, owner untraceable. Destination account also closed and untraceable.

From: (address withheld)
To: (address withheld)
Subject: St. Louis 2023-07 #2
Sent: 2023-07-25 23:06:14 UTC

…and it's possible, of course, that the idiotic note has actually had its intended effect. However, I'm intrigued by the coincidence and frankly find it implausible. I suspect our mentor knows exactly what she is doing, and it's entirely likely she awaits a challenge better suited to her protégé. I see no evidence that they know about the relapse at the hardware store.

I wonder… Our latest student locked her first Tether earlier today, guided solely by my other student. It was messy, but it was still a tremendous step for both of them, and even though I dislike her personally, I am pleased with her progress. We need all the assets we can get, if I understand Astbury's latest projections correctly…

Chapter Fourteen

SO MUCH SORROW

"It's always a risk, staying in large hotels," sighed Rosalind. "Especially the older they are. Too many people, and too many potential lingering memories. We always look for B&Bs ourselves. I hope you're not getting discouraged."

"I was just trying to enjoy a weekend away with Jess. It was more annoying than discouraging. Especially when they slapped the extra grand on my hotel bill. Although I guess it could have been worse."

I drummed my fingers on the passenger-side dash of the Clubman and tried my best not to scowl. We were parked outside a brick bungalow in Shrewsbury while we waited for Mark, the realtor associate of Rosalind's, who I had met in Crestwood. I was recapping the highlights of the previous weekend's Chicago trip to pass the time. Rosalind was sympathetic, and indeed seemed to be back to her normal convivial self instead of the distracted, rather abrupt person I had last seen at the Zoo. I hadn't yet asked where out of town she had gone, and wasn't sure I would.

"It could have been a lot worse. I've been worried about you after what happened at Stengel and Sons. I wish you had avoided the memory in that hotel. You need a lot more practice before you're ready to tackle one alone."

"I didn't intend to 'tackle it'," I grumbled. "I should've let it be, I know. But I seemed drawn to it somehow. It's hard to explain."

"I'm sure it is, even to me. You might have had a narrow escape, so let's just be grateful that you did. Did you at least enjoy the rest of your weekend?"

"Yeah, apart from that, it was perfect. It's amazing what you can see there within walking distance of that hotel. We were out and about all day on my birthday and then her grandfather insisted on buying us dinner at this upmarket steakhouse on Michigan Avenue. Nice enough guy, but I don't think he likes me much, or Jess either, for that matter. I prefer her mother's parents."

Rosalind grimaced. "Family can be difficult. Believe me, I know." Her phone buzzed, and she glanced at the notification. "Mark says he's five minutes out."

"And we can't wait in the front yard?"

"We don't want to spook the neighbors, D. We're supposed to be discreet. Besides, the car has air conditioning. Do you want to go over the research one more time?"

"Sure, what there is of it. I know I need the practice. And the preparation." I almost added "and the money", but restrained myself. She gave me a shrewd glance. "Have you given any more thought to karate lessons?"

It was my turn to sigh. "Yeah, I've come around to the idea. Jess and I want to do them together."

"Splendid! Martin and I joined GWK together, too."

"Cool. We were going to start with twice a week, beginner lessons on Saturday mornings and a general session on Tuesday evenings, and see how things went. I was going to call them on Monday."

"Were? Was?"

"Yeah, well…" I shifted in my seat, even more uncomfortable than usual despite the cool air blasting me. "My credit limit is pretty low, and the fine ate up a lot. I need to pay it down before I take on the cost of karate, too."

"Well, that's unfortunate," she said after a pause. "I think you need the karate to develop the self-control to better handle these phenomena. Perhaps I could share part of my fee with you, say 20%, provided you are able and willing to research the location in question. We could even make that a standing arrangement. It wouldn't be much, a few hundred dollars, but it may help."

"That would help a lot. Thank you!"

"It seems only fair," she said, smiling. "Besides, you already put some time in on this one."

I had. When Rosalind had called me midweek to tell me about another "job", she suggested I practice my research skills now that I had a better idea where to go and what to look for. I agreed and resolved to spend as much time as I could at the library, poring over microfiches of newspaper clippings and whatever else it would take. I had been so caught up in my research the previous day that I lost track of time and arrived a few minutes late for work, apologizing profusely to Mike. However, I felt more confident that I had turned over all the stones that were there to be turned over, and found out all that I could. It still wasn't much.

"They built the house in the late sixties, only one owner. They must have been a young couple when they moved in. The husband died twelve years ago, the wife continued living there until she passed last year. No records of any crime or illicit activity except for a burglary in 1983. Kids all moved out by the early nineties. No fires, no other natural disasters, nothing notably alarming."

Rosalind nodded. "I didn't find anything else either. It happens. Not every memory we encounter corresponds to an event that is public knowledge."

"So what do we do?"

"We take extra care. Even when we anticipate what the memory may be, we should always be prepared for it to be something else. When we don't know at all, we must be ready for anything."

I frowned. That didn't seem particularly useful to me. I was just about to say so when a black Lexus turned onto the street and parked on the opposite side of the road from Rosalind's Mini.

"Sorry I'm late," Mark said as he climbed out of the driver's seat. His ruddy face looked even darker than usual, and sweat beaded his brow. "Closing in Richmond Heights took longer than I expected."

"This is a pleasant neighborhood," said Rosalind, turning off the Mini's engine while I untangled my legs from the passenger side of the car. "Martin and I bought our first house together a couple of streets over."

"Really? I didn't know that. I've sold a few in this neck of the woods over the years. But not this one." He scowled at the bungalow, and at the "For Sale - Price Reduced" sign planted in the modest front yard. Someone had been cutting the grass, although weeds had infiltrated the wilting flower beds.

"Ten months on the market. Ten! A house like this normally sells within two in this market." He led us up the crooked front path, dabbled with his phone for a few seconds, and after a cascade of beeps extracted the key from the white lock box hanging on the front door handle.

He paused before unlocking the door and shot a thoughtful look at Rosalind.

"I don't see the things you do, or feel the things you feel. Not normally. But in here... well, you'll see."

I held my breath as he opened the door, flinched at the warning beep of the security system, and tried to calm my racing heartbeat. Then we followed him inside.

The house was empty.

I don't mean just empty of furniture, walls bare of pictures, carpet cleaned, leaving a vague, resinous scent. I sensed nothing unusual at all, no difference in temperature that the AC couldn't explain, no "presence", nothing that tried to fool my senses into thinking something was there that wasn't. We walked through the living room with caution, glancing to our right at a kitchen in serious need of updating and a meagerly lit open space where a dining table might have stood before passing through a doorway into a corridor. It was dark, and I guessed it led to bedrooms and bathrooms. Mark's hand hovered over a light switch.

"Do you feel anything yet?" he murmured.

I caught Rosalind's eye, and she frowned. "Do you, Mark?"

"Not yet. It's in the master bedroom. That's where I feel it. That seems to be where everyone feels it."

"Feels what?" I said, a little louder than I meant to. But the sepulchral whispering was creeping me out. Why couldn't I feel anything?

"So sad," he said before standing up a little straighter and flicking the switch. Yellow light illuminated a straight hallway about twenty feet long, with two closed, dark wooden doors on each side and another at the end. "Last door on the left. I'll wait for you outside."

We didn't move or speak until the front door closed behind him.

"Remember what I've told you before," Rosalind said as she led me down the hallway. "I'll take the lead on this one, but try to contribute if you can. Breathe. Try to stay grounded in the real world. Hold on to something if you need to."

She grasped the door handle, then smiled at me before turning it. "Think of it as grounding an electrical circuit if you like. There's a potential here that we need to drain away. Nothing can hurt you here. Remember that."

I didn't think that was how electricity worked, but before I could object, she opened the door and entered the master bedroom. In a physical sense, it was as empty as the rest of the house, although the wallpaper was more garishly floral than one of Rosalind's dresses. A bay window dominated the wall ahead of us, half-covered by heavy maroon drapes which left enough space between them for midsummer sunlight to stab through, illuminating the swirling motes of dust whose dance we had interrupted. Another doorway at the end of the wall through which we had entered led to a tiny en-suite bathroom accented in shocking pink tiles.

"Do you sense anything unusual?" Rosalind asked, eyes half-closed and head turned to one side.

"It's a little colder," I said, closing my own eyes for a moment to concentrate. "That's it."

She nodded. "I feel that too. The gentlest of cool breezes. And, oh, the faintest murmuring, no, singing I think." She looked back at me expectantly, and I shrugged. I didn't get it. If Mark said he and others picked up a strange vibe in this room, why was I not at least as overwhelmed as I had been in the Chicago hotel?

"Ah." Rosalind had taken a couple of steps toward the window, and I followed hesitantly. The temperature plunged with each step, as if this was a walk-in freezer, not a bedroom. My teeth were chattering by the time she stopped in the middle of the room, underneath an ornate, if dated, gold and crystal chandelier, and her eyes were wide as she turned to me.

"You feel something more now, I presume?"

"I'm f-freezing," I stammered. "It's like I'm outside in the middle of a blizzard, not inside on a hot summer day." Something more. "I swear I can taste fresh snow, like I'm catching flakes on my tongue."

"Very good," she murmured, nodding her head in approval. "I feel the cold too, if not the snow. But the song..." She faltered, and blinked rapidly. "So much sorrow."

"So what do w-we do?"

"I'm going to listen, listen carefully for the one voice among many. If you truly hear nothing, perhaps you can look for a pattern in what you're experiencing. Look for something out of place and concentrate on it."

I absorbed this, uneasy and still trying to reconcile the brutal cold I felt with the sunlight leaking through the drapes. As soon as I had said it, I couldn't dismiss the blizzard in my imagination, for all that I could not see it. Wind howled around me, tearing mercilessly through and under my t-shirt and shorts that were no protection at all. Snowflakes bombarded my skin with such fury that I closed my eyes and turned my head away. At that moment, I realized that the source of the wind, of the snow, was in the far corner of the room next to the window, and that was when my ears popped and the floor pitched sideways. I staggered towards Rosalind, hand out instinctively to brace myself and avoid knocking her over, and my hand met hers, similarly outstretched. We clutched each other as the light dimmed, the cold and wind and the snow fading away to reveal a darker, older room, furnished with tasteful elegance, bed, dresser and wardrobe of some deep-colored wood, photographs of a young and growing family adorning the walls. And through the gloom I saw her, a tiny wizened woman, staring out of the window, tears glistening on her cheeks. Then she turned to face us.

I had a dog growing up, a black Labrador called Seamus. He was my joy, an unfailing companion even as the gulf opened between me and the rest of my family. One day, when I was fourteen, he refused to get up from his bed in the corner of my room. I carried him to the car and my mother drove us to the vet, but there was nothing they could do. I cried for what seemed like days, but my grief for Seamus was nothing to what I felt pouring from the little old lady in that bedroom in Shrewsbury.

Breathe.

My heart pounded in my chest, not from terror but from the burden of this woman's sorrow. She gave no sign she could see us, while looking mournfully about the room. I remembered my research: this must be the woman who had just died, but her husband had died a decade earlier after forty years of marriage. A long life together, a happy life I hoped, now ended. Amidst the depths of her own sadness, I felt a pang of my own, imagining what it must be like to be so close to someone for so long and then have them taken away. She needed closure, I realized, and maybe I could help give her that.

I closed my eyes, or at least I thought I did, although the vision before me changed little at first. My hand was sweaty where it held Rosalind's, and I was panting. I sensed her shaking slightly, then I forced myself to take the first of several deep breaths. Immediately I sensed a shift, as if the entire room had blinked out of existence and reappeared a split second later, a few atoms to the right. What was that sound? A crooning, almost a lullaby, so soft at first I wasn't sure it was real, but building, enveloping and soothing, calming and reaffirming. The old lady now sat in a delicate wooden chair in front of the open window, drapes tied back. She nodded her head in time with the lullaby, eyes closed and lips trembling. I felt such compassion then that I had rarely known before. I felt sure that theirs had been a life full of love, that her only regret was living so long alone after he passed. *But you're not alone*, I thought. *Acknowledge your grief, yes, but treasure the memories of the life you shared. He is alive within you still, as are all those hopes and dreams and joys and troubles and the love, the love that yet beats in your heart. Don't let sorrow for his passing diminish any of that.*

Something gave. A dam burst, and I sank to my knees, then collapsed from there as all conscious thought drowned in a torrent of emotion. I lost track of time; it could have been seconds or minutes before I regained my sense of self, my head resting on the carpet with what felt like a nice bruise throbbing in the middle of my forehead. I looked up to see Rosalind gazing thoughtfully at the door to the bathroom.

"How do you do it?" I croaked, covering my mouth as I coughed.

"Not easily," she murmured, then sighed. "I think they were happy here, but she was so lonely after he passed. I hope Martin and I go together in an accident or something quick and painless.

"You helped, D. I don't know if you felt it, but I did." She smiled, as brightly as the sunlight piercing the drapes. I climbed slowly to my feet, lightheaded and my heart still racing a little, but otherwise just tired. And thirsty. Why was dehydration a side effect of the experience?

This time Rosalind had thought to bring a cooler full of ice-cold bottled water. We left the house, and I sat on the grass verge, huddled in the slight shadow of her car, slaking my thirst while she updated Mark on our success.

"Do you mind if I...?" he pointed at the house. Rosalind laughed and gestured for him to enter, then sat down next to me as he disappeared inside.

"This means a lot to me," she said quietly, not taking her eyes from the front door.

"What does?"

"You helping me. You have a long way to go, but... It's nice to finally share this with someone."

"I still don't really know what I'm doing."

"Was nothing different for you this time?"

"Well, the memory was different. No death or mortal peril. I mean, I guess the death had already happened, but she was so sad! No wonder others have sensed it."

"That's interesting, isn't it? It was just as strong and as demanding to deal with. Think about all the other people in and around your friend Colton's apartment, and the rest of that boy Xavier's family. They sensed nothing. Yet here, even Mark felt something and others besides. Fascinating."

"Why is that?"

"I have theories, but I don't know. I'm making this up as I go." She smiled, seeming rather tired I thought.

"You did something in there, in that bedroom. I remember thinking I could tell which direction the blizzard - what I thought of as a blizzard - was coming from, then suddenly it felt like I was falling from a height. What was that?"

Her brow furrowed as she glanced at me. "Interesting. I experienced it as the loudest explosion imaginable. My ears are still ringing."

"How could that be? I couldn't hear a thing." She shrugged, and we both took another drink of water.. "No, I was definitely falling, like an airplane out of control, or how I imagine that must feel. I was so disoriented until I remembered to breathe. And then I could think."

"Good," she said, and climbed to her feet as Mark emerged from the house, smiling with relief. I followed her lead and wondered what the two of us looked like.

"Thank you!" he cried. "That's the first time I've come out of that house without a cold sweat. You're a miracle worker, Mrs. Hill!"

"Oh please don't call me that," she shuddered theatrically.

"You are though! I know you say it's not an exorcism, but whatever it is you do, you do it well."

"Yeah, what do you say we do?" I asked before I could stop myself.

"We solve problems. People like Mark know what I do, and soon what you will do. We don't need business cards."

"Well, I feel like we need something. I'm tired of Jess cracking jokes about me being Ray the Ghostbuster."

"That would be cool," said Mark with a grin. "You could paint a logo on the side of the Mini and rent an old fire station with a pole and everything."

"Please don't encourage him," huffed Rosalind. "There are no such things as ghosts. But if you want to design a business card, D, be my guest."

"Maybe I'll do that," I said, grinning myself. Mark's obvious pleasure at what we had achieved in the bungalow was infectious.

"Say," he said, brow furrowing. He stared at us in silence, then scratched the side of his nose. "I may have another job for you, but... Well, do you think you could *pretend* to be exorcists?"

CHAPTER FIFTEEN

I DON'T DO EXORCISMS

"I don't know," said Rosalind slowly. "Why would we?"

"I have these friends, well, they're more my wife's friends than mine, to be honest. From church. Only they just bought a house in Kirkwood and, well, they think it's possessed by evil spirits."

Mark grinned rather shamefacedly. Rosalind arched her eyebrow, and I stifled an urge to laugh.

"I wasn't involved," he added hurriedly. "In the sale, I mean. But it sounds like it might be in your neck of the woods."

"I don't do exorcisms, Mark. I don't believe in evil spirits anymore than I believe in ghosts. Sorry if that offends your beliefs; I know your church is very orthodox."

"It is." Mark stood up straighter and lifted his chin. "We may be devout, but we're not medieval. I think you could help them, but they'll accept the help more easily if you acknowledged their beliefs. And I'm pretty sure they'll pay; heck, *I'll* pay to stop hearing them complain about it."

Rosalind looked at me and I shrugged. I was pretty intrigued; she taught at a Catholic school, but how Catholic was she? Not enough to go to Mark's church, from the sounds of it.

"I'm game," I said. "Just tell me where and when."

Mark said he'd get back to us with some times that would be acceptable to his friends. Then he handed a plain white envelope to Rosalind and drove off. She peered inside at what looked like a wad of cash, then extracted three hundred-dollar bills and passed them to me with a smile.

"Congratulations, D. You're on the payroll."

I accepted the money almost reverently. The occasion seemed momentous, but I could think of no momentous words to say.

"You always get paid in cash?"

"By Mark, yes. He doesn't have enough resources to cook his books. Others issue me checks if their bureaucracy is sufficiently labyrinthine, or they've got great accountants. Or tax lawyers." Her smile turned mischievous. "I do a lot of tutoring."

I nodded, thinking furiously. "When do you think we can do this next job? Next weekend, maybe?"

"You're anxious all of a sudden."

"Yeah, well, if I can get another payout like this by next weekend, I should be able to pay off my credit card before I get slapped with interest. And that means I can start karate lessons sooner."

"Good," she said, nodding. She opened her mouth and then closed it again before continuing a second or two later. "You need time to do the research and we'll have to see when, and if, these friends of Mark's will have us, but next weekend is workable. Although I'm really not sure I can keep a straight face while performing an 'exorcism'!"

She drove me back to my car, this time parked at the Shrewsbury MetroLink stop. Before I got out of the Mini, she handed me a manilla folder containing a set of stapled printouts.

"Breathing techniques, from a variety of sources, including some of the most-respected karate practitioners alive today. Study them, practice them. You will learn about them all in your lessons eventually, but I think it's a good idea for you to get ahead of the game. There are a couple of YouTube links in there as well, if you prefer watching to reading," she added with a grin.

"Thanks!" I said and meant it. I prided myself on keeping in shape by exercising and eating right, but with no other purpose than self-care. Now I had another purpose: mastering the phenomena that had disturbed me my entire adult life, and helping others in the process. If I had to put the work in - studying karate, poring over microfiches of newspaper catalogs, learning to breathe properly - I was willing to do it.

I called GWK as soon as I got home. Donovan's voice on the other end of the line did not deflect my determination, and I told him that Jess and I would like to start lessons the week after next.

"Good to have you on board, Dex! D, I mean. Sorry, man."

"No worries," I said, and texted Jess the details. *I'm still gonna kick your ass*, she texted back, and I chuckled as I got ready for work.

The week flew by. I read through the half-dozen or so articles on breathing and tried to practice, although I felt more than a little foolish huffing and puffing while checking my notes. Rosalind heard from Mark that his friends would be "thrilled" to have us perform our exorcism on Sunday afternoon, which I could do after my lunchtime shift at Hickory. Jess, upon hearing about it, insisted I kept my promise and allow her to come along and watch; I tentatively mentioned this to Rosalind, who didn't mind at all.

"She'll be increasingly curious until she does. Martin was the same way. He came to a few, got bored, and now just lets me get on with it."

I wasn't sure comparing Jess with Martin was fair, but then I had only met the man once. Regardless, I dug for details about the house in question, which were thin on the ground. It was barely a decade old, a tear down luxury rebuild in a hilly and wooded part of the suburb of Kirkwood, west of downtown and the park, east of Interstate 270. The original owners had moved to Dallas for the husband's new job just over a year ago, and there was no record of anything untoward happening in all that time. Was that suspicious? Hard to tell, but I kept looking until I was pretty sure there was nothing to be found - on public record anyway.

"Are you sure you're looking in the right places?" Jess asked on Thursday night. We'd had dinner and sex in roughly that order. Then she'd begun peppering me with questions about our upcoming job, undeterred that I really didn't know very much.

"I'm looking where Rosalind is looking," I replied, more defensively than I would have liked.

Jess gave me a brief frown. "I'm not questioning that she knows what she's doing," she said, trailing a fingertip absently over my chest. "You can find a lot of good information in old local newspapers and conventional web sites. But those aren't the only sources out there."

"Where else would you look?"

"I'd talk to people. Discretely. And not in person, of course, no-one does that anymore."

"We don't? I thought we were doing that right now." She thumped me in the side.

"You know what I mean. You don't have to go door to door like a Jehovah's Witness. There are all sorts of online chatrooms, everything from neighborhood and community groups on Facebook to paranormal channels on Discord. It's amazing what people talk about once you get them going. Most of it's crap, of course, but it's easier to focus on what you want to know than reading content targeted to the public."

I turned over to face her. "Have you been asking about this place in Kirkwood?"

"You never gave me the address, did you? Actually, if you want to know, I've been looking for other people who experience what you do, maybe even do what you do."

"What do I do?"

"Whatever you want to call what you do with Rosalind. Exorcise ghosts. Erase imprinted memories. I like the second description better, for what it's worth, but there's a lot more material out there related to the first. It's hard to know exactly what to look for, because you've been pretty evasive about the details."

I bit back an irritated retort. Her tone wasn't accusatory, and she smiled as her fingers resumed their idle caress of my bare skin. I responded in kind and sighed.

"It's not something I've been comfortable thinking about, let alone talking about," I admitted. "I don't know how it works. For the longest time I thought it was all in my head, some lingering after effects of the drugs I experimented with in college, or maybe me just going crazy. I'm not sure about that anymore. There's something out there, something real, and it's strange and scary and I don't know why I can sense it and almost everybody else can't."

"Maybe they can, just not nearly as strong."

"Maybe. I can tell you more if you like. I trust you, Jess, more than anyone."

She kissed me, and that ended her interrogation for that time.

I was a little concerned that Jess was asking around about hauntings and exorcisms and others like me, but she waved it off and said she was going to be too busy to do much more because the second half of her Shift_Dev course was about to start up. I decided to believe her and focus on the upcoming job.

Unfortunately, that preoccupation distracted me from my job at Hickory. Right before Friday night's service, I discovered I had, for the first time, burned the brisket, not entirely, but enough that little of it was usable. I cursed myself more vocally than I had ever barked at my line cooks; it was entirely my fault. I had been thinking of Sunday afternoon and forgot to set the timer. This wasn't an inexpensive mistake, and I feared how Mike would take it. As it was, he regarded me with a grim expression, sighed and rubbed at his eye patch before telling the servers that brisket was off the menu that night. I saw little more of him during the evening, but then I kept my head down, obsessing over the smallest detail of what I was doing, terrified of screwing up anything else. It wasn't until we had shut the doors and were cleaning up for the night that he invited me to join him in the dining room. I followed him meekly, trying hard to suppress the fear that I was about to lose my job.

"Is everything okay?" he asked, sitting across from me in a booth in the otherwise empty dining room.

"I'm really sorry," I said, aware that I was repeating myself but unable to think of anything else to say. "I fucked up. There's no excuse. All I can do is promise it won't ever happen again."

Mike grimaced. "Mistakes happen. I won't pretend it doesn't hurt, but it's not gonna close us down. Business is good, and you're part of the reason for that. But you've been acting distracted lately and I'm not the only one who's noticed. Is everything okay?"

He seemed sincere, and I had no reason to believe otherwise. Mike genuinely cared about his employees, which was why we all loved working for him. But I feared to push his tolerance and goodwill too far.

"I've taken up a new hobby," I said, choosing my words with care. "I'm excited about it, and it's been taking up more of my time. But I know my job is more important, Mike. I'll get my head back on straight. I don't want to let you down."

"Just don't let yourself down. You're a great cook, D, and a lot of restaurants would be lucky to have you. *I'm* lucky to have you. I don't expect perfection, not from you, not from anyone. But I do expect you to pick yourself up and dust yourself off after you fall down. You nailed the rest of your shift tonight, and that's what I want you to focus on. Forget the brisket; it'll be a treat for my dogs. I promise they'll eat it much too fast to notice or care that it's burned!"

I laughed, and he grinned. And, just like that, the tension that had built throughout the evening dissipated, like an erased memory.

"Thanks. I appreciate it."

"Of course," he said, rising from his seat. "Now get out of here. I wanna catch the end of the Cards game."

All things considered, it was better than I expected and maybe more than I deserved. I resolved to give my actual job the attention *it* deserved.

I brought a change of clothes with me for my Sunday shift, not quite my Sunday best, but better than the old T-shirt and jeans I cooked in. I didn't have time to go home before picking up Jess, so changed into a navy polo shirt and khakis in the employee bathroom. Charity, one of the line cooks, wolf-whistled as she saw me slink out of the kitchen and I grinned sheepishly; I thought I looked more like an appliance store salesman than anything else.

Jess - whose idea of Sunday best was a t-shirt without a lurid design and jean shorts that covered most of her thighs - and I met Rosalind at Kirkwood Park, so we could carpool to the client's house. We took my car, three adults being a bit of a challenge for the Mini Clubman. Rosalind had gone full skirt suit, in a shade of navy, just lighter than my shirt. She stared at Jess for a moment, who had got out to move to the back seat, then shook her head.

"I wish I could still wear shorts like you do," she told her, passing her a cooler.

"Oh, I bet you still could," said Jess, looking Rosalind up and down. "But you rock the suit."

I coughed, and they both laughed as they slid into their seats. I was already questioning this arrangement.

"So, Jess," Rosalind began in a business-like voice as I escaped the parking lot and headed north on Geyer Road. "D tells me you've been doing some research of your own."

"Has he now?" said Jess, and I squirmed in my seat.

"It's only natural to be curious. Martin was the same way, although he's mostly just concerned for my mental health these days. I'd be interested to hear what you have found, or answer any questions you have. However, I must ask you to allow us to do our job this afternoon. It requires focus and is not without danger."

"I understand," said Jess, after a pause. I glanced in the rear-view mirror to see her frown as she looked out the window. "Why is it dangerous? You erase memories that have imprinted themselves on a building somehow, from what D explained. How does that work? I assume you don't just whip out a wand and speak some Latin-sounding incantation."

Rosalind glanced at me, as if I had any idea how to answer that. Or maybe she was trying to gauge Jess's skepticism. All I had to offer was a shrug.

"No, there are no wands, nor are there usually bibles, rosaries, or holy water. Think of it as freeing something that is trapped. You just have to find the key to the trap and let it out."

"So this something is real. I mean, it's aware."

"No, I don't think so." Rosalind frowned. "I've never got that impression. Maybe that's not the best analogy."

"I don't want an analogy. I want to know what's actually happening," Jess said, a belligerent tone creeping into her voice. "What are the actual risks?"

"I can't tell you that," Rosalind replied, cool and unruffled. "I'm not a scientist. This isn't something you look up online. There is some mental state that allows me to connect with these phenomena, to let them flow through me and away."

"It's like unblocking a pipe," I blurted. "The memory, the Imprint, is trapped behind a blockage. Find where that blockage is, then you can loosen or dislodge it so the Imprint can drain away. Be Erased." And I thought of those moments when my ears had popped, as if in response to some significant pressure change: was this a side-effect of Rosalind "connecting with the phenomena" or "finding the blockage"? If so, why?

Jess clucked her tongue. "That's another analogy."

"It is, but it's not a bad one," said Rosalind. Her phone buzzed within her slim leather purse, but she ignored it. "The blockage can be hard to find, and once dislodged, it flows through you with whatever is behind it. You might make a good teacher, D."

"Well, let's not get ahead of ourselves," I said, but I was pleased. I had struggled to describe these experiences to Jess, and the plumbing analogy had just come to me. Maybe I was getting the hang of it.

Jess let out an exasperated sigh. "I still think we need to understand the mechanics of all this, how memories get imprinted, how you erase them. What actually happens, and what else might be affected? What effect does it have on you?"

"I don't disagree with you, Jess," said Rosalind, half-turning to look back at her. "And perhaps you can help. But for now, we have to, as you Americans say, get our game faces on."

So saying, she reached inside her blouse and extracted a gold cross suspended from a fine chain around her neck, and set it atop her clothing.

"I teach at a Catholic school. Gold Cross, as a matter of fact."

"Do you have a bible and holy water in your purse?" asked Jess. "Because I forgot mine."

"I do have my bible actually, but the only water we'll need is in the cooler. I won't make a big deal about it, and I hope they won't either."

Jess smiled. "Twenty-first century exorcists, how times have changed! It's about time they remade that movie anyway."

I had only seen The Exorcist once, one night in college before my expulsion, and someone had thought it would be fun to drop some acid before we watched it. I'm not sure how much of the weird shit I remembered was in the movie and how much in my overstimulated imagination, but I had no desire to watch it again to find out. What I didn't know, until Jess told me the previous night, was that the movie was said to be based on true events that occurred in St. Louis. In 1949, a fourteen-year-old boy from Washington DC started behaving strangely, and when this worsened and a series of unexplained physical marks appeared on his body, the family was advised to seek the help of a Catholic priest. These marks allegedly included the words "Go St Louis" and so the boy found himself at the Alexian Brothers Hospital on Broadway, attended by several Jesuit priests. Led by Rev. William Bowdern, they spent three months attempting to banish the possessing demons from the boy, their most significant case of possession and exorcism recorded in 300 years. The details are shrouded in secrecy, the source of the movie being a book written by someone who interviewed some of those involved, and, by all accounts, the movie was even more fanciful than the book. Nonetheless, I was glad that the wings of the hospital where this had all happened had been torn down in the 1970s and so we wouldn't ever be asked to do a job there. I hoped.

While I'm not a religious man, I couldn't help offering a quick prayer that we wouldn't face anything like that today. I bet God, if he or she was listening, had a good chuckle over that.

It started raining as we arrived at a house nestled in the dense, undulating woodland of western Kirkwood. I drove down a long, steep driveway and pulled up behind Mark Zellars' Lexus, then we hurried along the paved path to the covered porch that spanned the width of the two-story house, dodging several dozen plant pots arrayed like chess pieces mid-game. It was so quiet; I could almost believe we were in the rural heart of the state and not in the midst of St. Louis suburbia. I peered at the house's exterior while Rosalind rang the doorbell; the brick, hardie board siding and triple-glazed windows looked expensive, immaculate and unimaginative. "We have money," they said, "but we can't be bothered to think about it."

Mark opened the door, squinted at Jess, and invited us inside. I sensed nothing unusual as we stepped into a vast great room. It opened to a kitchen at the rear right that would make Jess's mother drool. Closer to our right, a grand staircase swept up to a second-floor balcony, and to our left, a doorway led toward the garage. A two-foot-tall wooden sculpture of Jesus on the cross hung over a stone-clad gas fireplace, and an assortment of other religious pictures decorated the walls. The scent of something herbal, maybe sage or juniper, was strong enough to make the inside of my nose itch, and as soon as I thought about it, I was fighting the urge to sneeze. Standing before the cream leather couch in the center of the area were our clients, a darkly tanned man of about my height and build with a trim black beard and receding hairline, and a short blonde woman who nonetheless looked taller as she was painfully thin. They held hands and looked at us nervously. Mark introduced them as Janice and Ricardo Gutierrez, and us as "Mrs. Rosalind Hill and her associates". I heard Jess struggle to suppress a snicker.

"Can you tell me about your spirits?" Rosalind asked the couple. They glanced at each other, and the woman blushed.

"It started soon after we moved in last Fall," said Ricardo in a husky baritone, and told us a halting tale of "spirits" and "manifestations" and "unnatural noises" plaguing them in the middle of the night. It irritated me at first - you'd think he'd have the story straight by now - but then I realized he was embarrassed. They both were. I felt a pang of sympathy: I had not done well in explaining the unbelievable either.

Rosalind extracted a pocket-sized bible from her purse as Ricardo stumbled to a halt. Janice's eyes flickered downward, and she offered a hesitant smile. "Can you help us?"

"I will most certainly try," Rosalind said, wringing every last microgram of Britishness from her accent. What a show-woman.

We left them with Mark while Rosalind led Jess and me up the staircase. About halfway up I felt it, the prickling of my skin and a rippling of heat, just before Jess whispered, "What is that smell?" I caught it too, a musky perfume that overpowered the herbal scent from downstairs. If unrelated to the phenomenon we were there to investigate,

Janice must go through a lot of whatever product that was. Before I could think more about it, we were at the top of the staircase and the heat almost knocked me over. Yet it wasn't the airless, crushing heat of the house in Crestwood, or of the hotel in Chicago. This was a sultry desert heat, a heat that writhed around me like an invisible serpent, seductive and deadly. I felt no fear, just a strong desire to find the source, and I followed Rosalind, in silence, down a short, wide corridor to the closed double doors of the master suite. She was blinking rapidly, brow creased in a puzzled frown, nostrils flaring as she laid her hand on the door handles. Oh yeah, breathe. I remembered the articles she had given me, and tried to focus on diaphragmatic breathing, slow and deep, deep and slow, which meant I wasn't paying attention to what she was doing when my ears suddenly popped. Then she opened the doors, and we walked in on an orgy.

I must have stumbled into the back of Rosalind, and I heard a muffled gasp as I regained my balance. I stared at the four poster king bed that dominated the room, or more accurately at the five naked bodies in and around it. One man sprawled on top of the sheets, straddled by two women who seemed at least as interested in each other as they were in him. A third woman was bent over one side of the bed, clutching the sheets as the other man took her from behind. They were all white, late teens or early twenties, attractive and very energetic. I'm no prude, and I'll confess to having seen my share of porn over the years, but this was different, the kind of virtual reality experience porn addicts dream of. I couldn't look away and felt my body respond with an instinct as primal as it was powerful. I wanted to join in, to tear off my clothes and leap onto the bed, to grab and be grabbed by other naked bodies, male or female it didn't matter, I just wanted pleasure, to abandon myself to lust, craving that sweetest of releases.

Breathe, dammit. Not pant. Deep, slow breaths. Listen? That isn't helping.

There was a shift, a flickering of the currents that swirled around me. For a disconcerting moment, I thought I saw another body on that bed, a body I dared not think about. *You can't do this here,* the embattled rational part of me protested. *This isn't your home, not anymore. Leave them alone.* The flickering returned, stronger now, violent like a nightclub strobe, and my lust was tempered with nausea. Hands grabbed my belt buckle, and I felt a moment of panic, before the vision steadied abruptly, all five - and only five, thank God - men and women suddenly turning towards me, startled and embarrassed, as a faint matronly voice crept into the edge of my hearing.

"...all well and good, but you've had your fun. It's time to get dressed and go home."

"Just a little while longer. It feels so good!"

"No. All good things must come to an end, and the end... is... now!"

The explosion of desire that followed was almost indescribable. It consumed me, rampaging through my body, stopping my heart and breath, as if those exquisite moments before orgasm had been distilled and amplified and drawn out over unbearable eons. And that doesn't do it justice. As reality crawled back into my consciousness, I felt spent, used up, struggling to stand. I found myself near the foot of the bed and grabbed the nearest post for support, drenched with sweat and panting desperately.

"What the fuck just happened?" said Jess, awe in her voice. She was at my side, her hand on my arm. I looked blankly at her concerned expression, then she glanced downward, and I was aware of a spreading warmth below my belt. Mortified, I realized I had actually orgasmed, standing fully clothed like a boy in the throes of puberty staring at the top shelf magazines at a newsstand. I tried to cover myself with my free hand, and Jess bit back a giggle.

"Well, that was interesting."

I looked over my shoulder at Rosalind, whose face was deeply flushed as she steadied herself with the other bedpost. Her wide eyes gazed back at me, her chest heaving as she drew in deep, calming breaths. I flinched when I realized I was staring at her chest, and she laughed shakily.

"I haven't had that much fun in years. Although personally, I would have preferred more men."

"What are you talking about?" demanded Jess. "If I wasn't here and know better, I would've been sure you two just got it on. What *was* that?"

"I think I'll let D tell you later," Rosalind replied, an amused curl to her lips. "We need to compose ourselves before we go back downstairs. That was more of a struggle than I expected."

"What was more of a struggle?"

"Well, to use D's plumbing analogy: it was a stubborn blockage with a lot of pent up water behind it, and I think we were draining it with a rather leaky pipe."

The words hung in the air for the space of a breath, then we all dissolved into uncontrollable laughter.

CHAPTER SIXTEEN

CARE FOR A LITTLE WAGER?

Embarrassed as we descended the staircase, I did my best to keep Jess between me and the Gutierrezes. Rosalind kept things professional, soberly informing them that the spirits should no longer trouble them. Janice closed her eyes and whispered what I assumed were prayers, while her husband thanked us profusely. They didn't offer us anything, nor did we ask. I think everyone was happier after we walked out the front door.

Mark caught up with us in the driveway and pressed an envelope into Rosalind's hand.

"Um, so what was it? Evil spirits or not?"

"Very naughty spirits, from the sound of it," muttered Jess. I elbowed her, and she swatted me away.

"You don't normally ask me, Mark," Rosalind said. "You're content to just hear the job is done."

"I am! But these are friends and, well, I don't think I've heard you laugh before. It didn't sound like any exorcism I ever imagined."

Rosalind glanced at me and Jess. "We did try to maintain that illusion. Suffice it to say, the experience was a little unusual. Or rather, more unusual than usual."

He boggled at her and I turned away and stuck my fist in my mouth, coughing as cover. My sides ached from our fit of giggling upstairs. I didn't need any more.

"There's something else," he said, as we raided the cooler in the backseat for bottled water. "I don't know if it's connected to you or not, but remember that family in Crestwood? Well, I heard from Dre Adams, the father, this week. He says they're thinking of putting their house back on the market."

"Oh no, why?"

"He wouldn't tell me at first, but then it sort of spilled out. Someone left an anonymous note in their mailbox."

Jess stirred next to me. I had told her about Xavier and his family, and I knew what she was thinking. I remembered the note that was slipped under my door a few weeks back.

"What did the note say?" I asked.

"'Leave, or it will return'. Laser-printed on plain white paper." I caught Rosalind's eye, and she shook her head almost imperceptibly.

"Did they go to the police?" asked Jess.

"They did. Weren't too helpful from the sounds of it."

"I can imagine. Dammit, racists suck!"

Mark stared at her for a moment, as if taken aback by her vehemence. There was a time, early in our relationship, where I might have tried to intervene on Jess's behalf, but I knew better now.

"Yeah, I agree with you," he said at last. "I see racism all too often in my line of work, but usually in more subtle ways. I didn't know whether to advise them to stay or go, or even if it was my place to say anything. It's tough for all of them, but especially on the children."

He blushed as he realized what he'd said, but Jess smiled grimly.

"It's every family's decision. We never received any notes like that, not that I know about anyway, but believe me, there are many other ways for racists to make you feel unwelcome."

The wild and playful mood gave way to a more brooding one as we drove away. I drummed my fingers on the steering wheel as I tried to process what had happened and what we had heard. Rosalind appeared lost in her own thoughts, while Jess fumed in the backseat. She stayed there even after we dropped off Rosalind, but when I made to turn towards her apartment, she leaned forward and gripped my arm.

"No, take me to your place. And tell me everything you saw in that bedroom."

I did as she asked, and she wrung every last detail out of me. She all but dragged me from the car and up to my apartment, then set upon me with a savagery that was as intoxicating as it was intimidating.

Afterwards, she propped herself up on my chest, her elbow digging into my ribs, and gazed at me. I basked in that gaze and reminded myself how fortunate I was.

"Do you think the Gutierrezes both saw what you guys saw?" she asked after a while. The rain had returned with a vengeance and was hammering against my bedroom window, and I listened a little longer before replying.

"Hard to know for sure, but I doubt it. I think they both sensed something, enough to bother them, but from what I've seen you have to intentionally tap into the full memory, otherwise you just get glimpses. How did it affect you?"

Her brow furrowed. "It got hot suddenly. I noticed that when we were climbing the stairs. And it was a weird heat, almost... almost like it was caressing me. It got stronger when we were in the bedroom, but I didn't see any visions like you guys did. I might have been too busy watching you and Rosalind, though."

She laughed and dug her fingernails into my chest.

"I'm glad you enjoyed yourself."

"Of course! I think it would be rather fun to have some erotic spirits around to spice things up in the bedroom."

"You think we need to spice things up?"

"Well, you know I'm always game to try something different."

"How can you be sure it would be erotic? Or pleasantly so? Clearly, these things don't affect us all in the same way. They don't affect most people at all. Maybe the husband and wife reacted very differently to what was happening."

"I guess so. I wonder why. What percentage of the population notices these - what did you call them? - imprinted memories at all, and why some more than others? I can't believe no-one has studied this. I can't believe Rosalind hasn't studied this."

"She may have, but she claims not to know more than she's told me."

Jess snorted. "I can guarantee that's not true. Why aren't you more interested in what's really going on?"

"Who says I'm not? But I'm mostly grappling with how to handle the effects it has on me. I can't let it reduce me to a cornered animal and pass out or pull fire alarms every time I go up against one of these things. I guess my interest is more practical, and yours theoretical."

"You need to understand both, I think," she mused. "And I can't believe Rosalind is the only one doing this kind of thing - erasing buildings' memories, if that's what we want to call it - in St. Louis, let alone the wider world. She knows more than she's telling you, and if she won't tell you more, I think you should find and talk to others."

"Yeah, maybe we could start a club: the St. Louis Erasure Society or something."

She narrowed her eyes, then grinned. "Catchy name! I always thought you were a bit weird, D. That's one of the reasons I like you. But this is turning into some Grade A weirdness. I think you need my help."

"I'll take anything you give me."

"Yes you will."

The rest of August passed with no more "erasures", and I wondered again why there weren't more of them. Were Jess's suspicions correct? Were there others out there doing what Rosalind did? If so, it seemed hard to believe she wouldn't know about some of them at least.

I got little chance to ask her, as she claimed she was busy preparing for the new school year. I dismissed the kernel of paranoia Jess had nurtured and focused on the path forward, despite my past popping up at unexpected and unwelcome moments.

For the first time in months, Fiona and I found mutual openings on our calendars and had lunch together at Angelo's on The Hill. It's a smaller and, in my opinion, underrated bistro with a basic menu where every dish is cooked to perfection. We sat in the tree-shaded patio out back next to a gurgling stone fountain and listened to one of the cooks singing through an open window in an off-key baritone.

"I'm glad you and Jess are back on good terms," Fiona said, sweeping her ponytail over one shoulder as she prepared to dig in to her lasagna. She'd dyed her hair purple since the last time I had seen her; maybe she was aiming for all the colors of the rainbow. "She sounds like she's the stability you need. I hope to meet her one day."

"Yeah, me too," I replied, twirling my fork amidst a plate of fettuccine carbonara. "As long as it's just you. Well, maybe Eric and the kids too, as long as he's up for it."

"Eric's fine. He's more tolerant than you give him credit for." I let that pass. I didn't rate Eric's tolerance for me highly at all.

She paused and stared at me over a mouthful of pasta, deep in thought. Her eyes were as dark as mine, although set in a paler, delicate face. The effect was vaguely unsettling.

"I talked to Mom last night," she said finally. "She asked about you."

I took a drink of lemonade. We were at the Rest of the Family part of the conversation. "Oh yeah? Checking to see if I'm in or out of jail?"

"D."

"It's what she cares about, isn't it? And how else would she know?"

"She... well, she cares about you more than that, even if she won't admit that to anyone, including herself." Fiona tore into a breadstick, but only nibbled on a tiny piece of it. "Anyway, she asked if you'd been in touch with Cousin Steven lately."

I set my fork down. Fiona watched me with a wary look on her face.

"That's as good as asking the same question," I said, trying to keep all emotion from my voice. "Why would I be in touch with that piece of shit?"

"I'm sure not willingly. She seemed to think you had gotten involved in something shady, and that he was involved. I think she's worried about you."

I snorted, but it genuinely puzzled me. How would Mom know anything about what I was doing, outside of the excerpts of my life fed back to her via Fiona? What was I "involved in" that she would consider shady? Maybe hanging around with a married woman, but I hadn't said a word to my half-sister about Rosalind - that was a part of my life that she didn't need to know about, not yet anyway.

"I don't know what she's heard or how," I said after a while, staring at my plate as I stirred the remaining pasta with my fork, appetite fading. "I promise you I haven't spoken or otherwise had contact with him since my sentence came down, and nor do I intend to. You know I take full responsibility for what I did, but he put me in that position. And didn't lift a finger to help me once I was there."

I lifted my chin in defiance and met her gaze. She didn't flinch, but she didn't blink either. Before the silence became uncomfortable, she reached across the table and covered my hand with hers. She didn't say anything; she didn't have to.

We wrapped up our lunch with small talk that was amiable enough, but not for the first time our family's dysfunction left a bitter taste in my mouth. I was broody and irritable when I got to work that evening, snapping twice at Greg within minutes of my arrival. Mike, whose spider-senses were finely tuned, was there for the second one and took me aside under the pretext of discussing that night's specials.

"You okay, D?" he asked, pinning me with his oddly disconcerting one-eyed gaze. "Greg's been doing a lot better the last couple of weeks, you've said so yourself. Don't want to tear that down, do we?"

I sighed, then took a deep breath. "No, you're right. I just... Well, I had lunch with my sister today and you know how the rest of my family is."

He grimaced. "You've told me. I understand, but don't bring that in here. We're your family too, in a way."

I hadn't thought of it that way, but I got the point and nodded my acknowledgment. Mike returned the nod and turned to go, then paused. "By the way, there was someone here at the lunch service who asked to see you. Left a message." He dug into his pants pocket and pulled out an antique money clip, stuffed with cash and other papers of presumable importance. He slid out a yellow post-it note and handed it to me, then headed back to the dining room.

Hi D! Been a while. Came to see you, but you're not here. Call me. Colton.

And a telephone number. I frowned and fended off those twinges of guilt that I'd made no effort to check back in with Colton since that night in his apartment. I didn't think he'd have stopped by just to call me out on that, but what else could he want? Was he looking for help? Or friendship?

I didn't have time to think about it right then. They needed me in the kitchen. So I shoved the note inside the back pocket of my jeans and resolved to deal with it later.

"Later" turned out not to mean the next day, or even the rest of that week. In my defense, I was more tired than usual. Jess and I had started our karate lessons a couple weeks earlier. I had imagined that the Beginner lessons would be more or less a continuation of the free one, a gentle introduction to the art. I was spectacularly wrong.

"The only difference between Beginner classes and General classes is that only new students attend the former," Sempei Richard told us at the end of our first Tuesday night. I stood sweating and panting with my hands on my hips, while Jess walked in tight circles with her hands on top of her head. There were ten other students, all adults and only a couple of whom I recognized from our free lesson, including the defiant gray-haired woman: she was the oldest of us, yet she appeared only a little out of breath.

"You must practice and you must study every day," added Donovan. Sempei Donovan, I reminded myself. He had treated me the same as every other student that night, not acknowledging our past acquaintance, and that was fine by me.

At the end of that first lesson, we received our white *Gi* and *Obi*, the heavy cotton canvas uniform and belt. We should have received them when we arrived, but there had been some sort of mixup, which infuriated Sempei Richard. Halfway through the lesson, a young woman with a blonde pixie cut walked through the front door of the dojo carrying two white cardboard boxes. She set them down and scuttled over to the side of the mat nearest Donovan, with whom she exchanged a few quiet but heated words. She stood there in sullen silence for the rest of the lesson, and I got the weird idea that she was watching me in particular. Judging by the scowl on her face, Jess might have thought the same; there was certainly an edge to her sparring that gave the rest of us pause.

"Don't we look dapper?" Jess said, admiring her reflection in the dark front window.

"Ready to take on the world, even as lowly white belts!" I grinned, but I meant it. Wearing the uniform felt like a statement of intent or commitment.

"Do they fit okay?" asked the blonde, glancing at Jess but focusing on me. She was tanned and well-toned, the build of a woman who was no stranger to a gym or, more likely, a dojo. "I'm Lana, by the way. I just moved up to the General class a few weeks ago."

"They're fine," I said. She looked at me with expectation until I introduced Jess and myself in that order.

"Good. See you around, D. Jess."

I feared an explosion, but Jess just raised an eyebrow, then laughed about it when we were driving home.

"That chick just gave me a whole lot of motivation," she said grimly.

I wouldn't have thought more about it, but I had the nagging sensation I had seen the blonde before. She kept popping up, usually towards the end of our lessons. And just in time for sparring, I thought sourly, as Jess's sparring partner. The penny dropped when we caught her kissing Donovan in the parking lot one night; they grinned as they recognized us. He gave us a cheery wave, and they slid into the Mustang parked right next to my Elantra. Good for them, I thought, walking around my car after they drove off out of sheer paranoia, while Jess watched hands on hips.

Things escalated when we saw both Donovan and Lana at the Run Into Fall 5K in Forest Park.

Jess and I had met during the previous year's race, my first ever 5K. My neighbor Pierre had persuaded me to run, then somewhere between the bus stop and the starting line had acquired a rainbow-colored Afro wig, a ridiculously overlarge pair of sunglasses, and a couple dozen like-minded and dressed companions. Among them were Jess and her girlfriend Nina, a petite and alarmingly thin Thai student, who announced that they were the "B" contingent. I lost track of all the new names but Jess's, dazzled by those emerald eyes and her dark complexion, which I've always found an alluring combination. I joined the group as they ran together for most of the race, to cheers from the occasional spectators, then with one kilometer left, the serious runners put on a finishing burst, Jess among them. Surprised, I had tried to catch her, but fell a few meters short, much to her obvious glee. We had all gone to Zero afterwards, my first and only ever visit to a gay bar, much to Pierre's delight. Far too much alcohol and innuendo later, I was leaving to walk home when Jess barred my way and demanded my phone number. Three weeks later, we were dating, something I hadn't done in almost fifteen years. So, although the race was not technically our anniversary, we treated it as such and had vowed we would run it for as long as we were together. I was happy beyond words we had made it to this second run.

Adding some spice to this year's race were Rosalind and Martin, who had run it every year since its inception twelve years before. Rosalind had been delighted to hear we were running too, adding "I do hope you can keep up!" Her husband had looked like a runner, and didn't disappoint, but I couldn't picture her that way until we met outside the registration tent before the race. She wore a white running shirt and shorts, neon orange shoes, and had pulled her hair into a ponytail through the hole in a silver Cardinals baseball cap. She waved to Jess and me as we approached, and I couldn't help notice the muscle tone in her tanned arms and legs. I remembered what both the Sensei and Donovan had said about her at GWK: she was "a force of nature." It looked like I might be about to find that out for myself.

"What do you think, D?" she asked as we joined the masses heading towards the starting line. "Think you have a shot against the British contingent?"

"Oh, definitely," I said, ignoring the grin on Martin's face, then grunted as Jess planted her elbow in my ribs.

"Sabotage!" I cried in mock outrage. "You're supposed to be on my team!"

"Look!" she hissed, and as I turned to see who or what she was looking at, I recognized them, Donovan and Lana strolling our way, accompanied by a compact older black man with short gray hair and black wraparound sunglasses. Before I could move, Lana spotted us and tugged Donovan's navy T-shirt.

"Dex! Mrs. H!" he cried and plunged forward to seize me by the hand. Lana followed in his wake with a tight smile while their companion hung back.

"What are we, chopped liver?" Jess asked Martin in a stage whisper, which Donovan likely chose not to hear.

"Hey Donovan," I said with as little enthusiasm as I thought I could get away with.

"Dude, it's great to see so many GWK students out here. You're the third group we've run into."

"Always happy to see our new Sempei out here, too," said Rosalind. I detected the frostiness in her tone, but he seemed oblivious.

"Gotta lead from the front! And that's what I plan to do, anyway. Care for a little wager, Dex? Me and Lana against you and Jess?"

"Sure," snapped Jess before I could even open my mouth. "Shall we say fifty bucks, combined times?"

Donovan looked taken aback for a moment, then grinned. "You got it! Fifty bucks each, that is."

I nodded mutely. Unless the high tech shoes and form-fitting apparel were just for show, I wasn't sure I fancied my chances against Donovan, and hoped that Jess could pick up the slack.

"Mind if we get in on that?" Rosalind asked. "Even if we're in a different age bracket than the rest of you." She looked pointedly at the couple's older companion, who made a show of not paying much attention, although I was sure he was.

"Sure, Mrs. H," Donovan said with a cheerful smile, although he bit his lip before saying so. "Let's compare official times after the race. I'll wait for you guys at the main desk."

Jess snorted, and Lana laughed. Donovan grinned, then nodded to each of us, including Martin, who he finally appeared to have noticed. He and Lana rejoined their companion, who whispered something in Lana's ear; she shrugged. I glanced at Rosalind who frowned, before sighing and stretching one last time.

The gun sounded soon afterwards. It took a few moments for the runners ahead of us to clear the way, and then we were off. I was determined to follow Jess's pace, but now I had to worry about Donovan and Lana, too. I didn't care about Rosalind and Martin: if the older

British couple beat us I would be suitably humble, but I discovered I really didn't want to lose to my cocky, half-remembered college buddy who had disappeared as quickly as all the others when shit went down.

Martin and I had the longest strides, but I carried more weight and it wasn't all muscle. Donovan, Rosalind and Jess purred alongside us, each hinting at more than met the eye. Only Lana soon appeared uncomfortable, drifting away from the rest of us before clawing her way back; her and Donovan's un-introduced companion was nowhere to be seen. The weather was perfect, not too warm and overcast, with a breeze that promised rain long after we'd run the race. The course undulated through Forest Park's east end, starting near the Zoo's south entrance and looping anti-clockwise past Barnes Jewish Hospital and Chase Park Plaza to the Art Museum on the northern side, then skirting the edge of the Zoo to complete the circuit. As we approached the halfway point, I found myself alongside Donovan, who ran with an erect, almost lazy posture that suggested he was holding back.

"The trick," he said conspiratorially, "is to listen to the pace of the pack. Then, pick your moment, and..."

I swear it was as if he doubled his pace, leaning forward now and opening up a significant lead. Martin appeared from just over my right shoulder and hung with him, but I struggled to close the gap. I ran to stay in shape, but I wasn't a *runner*. Jess went with them too and then stayed back, and I knew she was holding that reserve, ready to best me in the final sprint. "Go!" I grunted, waving her on, and she grinned and set out in pursuit.

"Just us now then." I looked to my right to see Rosalind's grim smile, her cheeks pink as she matched me stride for stride.

"Did we lose Lana?" I puffed, and she laughed, jerking her head backwards before gesturing ahead.

"We can still see them. Let's not give up so easily, eh?"

Something about the way she said it goaded me on. Who said anything about giving up? That said, I realized I had already accepted that Jess, Martin and, yes, Donovan were going to beat me, and was falling back into my familiar Tower Grove Park jogging pace.

"Fuck this," I spat, gave myself a quick mental dressing down, and upped my pace. We passed the 4K marker and Rosalind started falling away, but I was hunting now. I was determined to pass at least one of the other three, not because of the bet, but to prove to myself and, yes, to Rosalind that I could. My chest began burning, and for a moment I wavered, but as we turned into the final stretch with the zoo walls across the road to our right, I could see them. Two hundred meters left, and

Donovan and Martin were neck and neck, ten meters ahead of an already furiously sprinting Jess, who was twenty meters ahead of me. Knowing I couldn't overhaul Donovan grated on me. I tapped what reserves I still had, determined to sprint to the finish. I dipped my head, dragging my body forward and charged those last few dozen strides, stumbling as I crossed the line and having to push myself up off the ground with one hand so as not to wipe out. The light applause I heard must have been for someone else.

When I had recovered both balance and dignity, I slowed to a walk and looked first for Jess. She sauntered a few paces away, hands over her head, taking great shuddering breaths and scowling. Martin was nearby, looking back and searching for Rosalind; he nodded as his eyes skated off mine. Donovan was nowhere to be seen.

"I couldn't catch up with the bastard," Jess growled, then grinned. "But you almost caught up with me! You might have a chance next year!"

"That he might," said Rosalind, arriving at our side on Martin's arm. She smiled, but there was something calculating about the way she looked at me I wasn't sure I liked.

"I think you might be ready, D."

CHAPTER SEVENTEEN

THERE'S ALWAYS HOPE

"Ready for what?" I asked, but I thought I knew.

"To take the lead on our next memory erasure. I'm warming to that term, by the way. You've been training hard and are showing me the necessary determination. In teacher's terms, I think you're ready to retake the test."

She smiled, with just the barest hint of mockery. I was both pleased and alarmed, but it wasn't the time or place to debate the issue. Friends and family of those who had completed the race mingled in a loud, sweaty and occasionally boisterous crowd, and that still wasn't an environment I was comfortable in.

"Dex!"

I turned to see Donovan striding towards me, phone in one hand and waving to me with the other.

"Lana pulled her calf muscle halfway through," he said, frowning. I suppressed my irritation at his use of my old nickname and adopted what I hoped passed as a sympathetic expression. "I'm gonna go find her. We parked closer to the Art Museum, anyway. I'm not sure how you four finished, but I figure we lost the wager for sure. I'll bring the money to your next lesson."

"Don't worry about it," I said. "If she's hurt, I think that lets you off the hook."

He stared at me. "Oh no. We'll honor the bet. Make your decisions and accept the consequences, that's what I say. Jess. Mr. & Mrs. H."

Nodding to each of us in turn, he stalked off. I glanced at Rosalind and she raised an eyebrow.

"Just let me know," I told her as we headed for our own vehicles, and she nodded in satisfaction. I wondered how long I would have to prepare myself.

Not long as it turned out. Rosalind called me on Thursday evening, just as I was settling down to watch the Cardinals in the NLDS decider.

"Nicole Kelly called me this afternoon. I don't know if you remember her..."

"The blonde in Colton's apartment. The property manager." That day was seared into my memory, and I could still visualize the taller and not unattractive woman who had been waiting with Rosalind outside Colton Lynn's door.

"Very good." Rosalind sounded half-impressed, half-amused. "Apparently, the building has another issue that she'd like us to look into."

"The same building?"

"1500 Locust, yes. Martin, love, can you turn that down for a minute?"

I heard a crowd roar in the background and, glancing at my muted TV, I realized they must be watching the game too. Lead off homer in the first inning, that's the way to start!

"D? You still there?"

"Yes, sorry. That's strange, isn't it? We've only had a handful of jobs since that day, unless there were others you didn't tell me about, and two of them are in the same building?"

"It's unusual, certainly. But not unprecedented. I once worked three jobs in a month at a motel on Watson Road. That was a couple of years ago. I think it's closed now, torn down to make way for a new car dealership."

"That's a pretty big coincidence."

"Oh, I agree. It's possible that one imprinted memory in a building somehow makes it easier for others to occur. That might be what's happened in the building on Locust, probably before we dealt with the one in your friend's apartment. We simply don't know enough."

I knew Jess wouldn't let it go, but it probably wasn't worth worrying about. I asked what we knew about the new Imprint.

"Not much, other than I believe it's the apartment directly above your friend's. I suspect Nicole believes I didn't properly take care of things last time, and it's possible she's right. She's still prepared to pay the full fee, though, as long as we can get this done soon, preferably next week.

I'll bring over the research I gathered last time, although you should probably check for any recent events of interest just to be on the safe side. And for practice."

"Okay, will do."

"Oh, and D? Have you talked to your friend lately?"

"Colton? No, I haven't." I felt a stab of guilt, remembering the message he had left for me at Hickory. It had been over two weeks now and I had forgotten all about it. The note was probably still in the back pocket of my work pants, which had gone through at least one laundry cycle. We hadn't quite been friends, but we had shared a traumatic experience and I owed him at least a callback.

"I see," Rosalind said after a pause. "I asked after him, but he's no longer living there."

"What? What happened?"

"Nicole just said he terminated his lease. She thinks he moved elsewhere in the city, but didn't know where."

That didn't sound good to me. Colton had been proud of living in his own place again, and despite the disturbing events leading up to his apartment's Erasure, I couldn't imagine he'd had any better options, even if the place had still made him uncomfortable.

After confirming my Hickory schedule, Rosalind said she'd get back to me on a time for the Erasure. I thanked her, but was a little distracted. The Cardinals had just given up a home run of their own and I was itching to hunt down Colton's note. I found it during the next commercial break: sure enough, the somewhat matted post-it was wedged in the back pocket of a pair of pants in my dirty laundry hamper. His writing had smudged and faded but was still legible, although it may not have survived another wash. For a moment, I entertained waiting until after the baseball was over to call him, then berated myself. I'd been tardy enough.

"Oh, hey D," Colton said after picking up on the second ring, his surprise unmistakable. "I was beginning to wonder if you'd ever call. Not that I could blame you, I guess."

"Sorry man. Things were crazy for a while, then I couldn't find your note. Just did." I hesitated. "Hope you didn't need anything too badly at the time. I was pretty useless for that."

He chuckled, and something about it reassured me. That didn't sound like paranoid Colton, or wasted Colton. That sounded a lot like the guy I knew in high school.

"Oh no, it was nothing like that. Just wanted to catch up. Still feel guilty about that night in the diner and, well, afterward."

I laughed with little humor. "Lot of guilt going around. Hey, you wanna try getting dinner again? Maybe somewhere other than that diner - I'm not sure I could face another slinger."

His laugh was genuine, at least. We agreed to meet at JJ's Deli in Soulard early Sunday evening, which gave me a clue to where he had moved.

It was a simple walk from Hickory west down Cherokee to Broadway, then north past the Anheuser-Busch Brewery into Soulard proper. Half residential, half industrial, Soulard was an eclectic neighborhood. Home to a Farmer's Market and the hub of St. Louis's annual Mardi Gras celebrations, it had resisted most attempts at gentrification, and as I was in no particular hurry, I allowed myself to drift down side streets, peering at red-brick homes and apartment buildings in various states of repair and decor. The morning's cold front had passed, taking its rain showers but leaving a breeze to counter the building warmth from the sun beaming down from an almost clear sky. Even the unmistakable scent of brewer's yeast as I got closer to the brewery couldn't dispel the pleasure of a stroll on a late summer's day, and I suddenly wished Jess was with me.

JJ's was a hole-in-the-wall on Sidney Street, dwarfed by more renowned bars and eateries. It had miraculously survived the COVID-19 pandemic largely on the back of its incredible potato salad, and it was all I could do not to order before Colton arrived. His arrival mere minutes later saved me from social impropriety.

"D! Good to see you, man!"

"You too, Colton," I replied, and I meant it. He looked better than I remembered, eyes clear and clean-shaven. A lanyard with a photo ID hung around his neck as he wore a bright red polo shirt and khaki pants. He grinned when he saw me looking at it.

"I work the scheduling desk now. At the courier service. Previous girl quit, and turns out I have a knack for it."

"Good for you," I said, smiling. The steps forward were so important. "Shall we order and grab that last free table?"

We did so, potato salad and some sort of sandwiches each, then lapsed into an awkward silence while we waited for the food to arrive at our table in the back corner. I think we both had things to say, but neither one of us knew where to start.

"Look, I want to apologize for not checking up," I said at last. "I was pretty freaked out after that thing in your apartment, and well, it's a poor excuse, but my life got a bit complicated."

He barked out a laugh. "Dunno about you, D, but my life was already complicated."

A young girl with pale skin, pink hair, and about twenty piercings emerged from behind the counter with two plates which she set down, correctly, in front of us. I thanked her, and she smiled her acknowledgement, which Colton appeared to find amusing.

"That was some wild thing though," he continued, after savoring his first mouthful of potato salad. The early evening sun slanted down into my eyes, but at least my seat faced the door. "You remember that British chick? I don't know what she did that night, but I never had more temperature problems."

"We've kept in touch," I said. "So what happened? I thought you liked that place. Apart from the weird shit, of course."

He grimaced and took a long drink of water. "I did like it. But I wasn't really comfortable after that, you know? And then the landlord announced he was hiking the rent. I mean *really* hiking it, and that was the final straw. I'd been seeing this other guy from down the hall, Derrick, whose lease was about up anyway, and he told me he'd found a two-bedroom apartment a couple of blocks from here, on 12th, and needed a roommate. So I moved in with him. Counselor was cool with it."

His expression grew wary, and I smiled. "Probably for the best. I'd have done the same thing."

"Right? Who needs that shit?! Derrick's a good guy, works maintenance at some condos over on Chouteau. They love him there, although I guess they might be going bankrupt. I don't know why. But he'll land on his feet. He went through juvie and took a hard road to get back, just like us, and we're both clean and he'll find another good job. We'll be fine." His face fell for a moment. "I mean, good jobs are relative, right? It's not like before. It'll never be like before."

"But you're coming back," I said quietly. "Even if it's to a different place from where you were going. Finding the path is as important as following it."

"Yeah. You know. And I have found my path, I think, and someone to follow it with. When I say clean, I mean it. Not so much as a sip of beer since we last met. Maybe that was the wake up call I needed."

And maybe it was mine too.

I stayed and chatted for a while, longer than I expected. He seemed genuinely happy with where he was, with his apartment and his job, with his partner and his lifestyle. He was interested in my life too, and while I kept Rosalind and Imprints and Erasures out of the tale, I found I had plenty to say about myself, and that hadn't been true in a long while. We even felt comfortable enough to talk about the darker times, back when we had first met at the New Hope shelter. When I finally got up to leave, we shook hands and then shared an awkward embrace, promising to keep in touch. Maybe we would, and maybe we wouldn't, but I felt like Colton had the makings of a good friend after all.

We scheduled the other 1500 Locust apartment's Erasure for the following Wednesday morning. I was taking a chance that I'd feel well enough to work my evening shift at Hickory, but according to Nicole Kelly evenings were "difficult". Jess was happy though, as she had neither Shift_Dev nor bartending conflicts and could come along. As expected, she was intrigued by a second Imprint in the same building.

"Don't you think there's a connection?" she asked as we drove to our next karate lesson at GWK. "Wouldn't that mean something?"

"It's hard to tell," I said. "I'm focused on how I'm going to deal with this one."

She shook her head in exasperation. "You don't have a scientific bone in your body, do you?"

"I told you, we're the practical ones and you're the theorist," I grumbled.

"And I told you they're both important. What if there's more than one Imprint to deal with? What if they're multiplying somehow? How would you handle that?"

"I don't think Rosalind's ever seen anything like that."

"Oh, well, that's conclusive. Honestly, you're like kids blazing your way through a box of matches, thinking everything's okay because nothing's caught on fire yet."

I frowned. I didn't much care for the analogy, and not just because Jess was younger than me.

On Monday, I did my due diligence, checking at the library and online for anything interesting that wasn't in the research notes Rosalind had dropped off over the weekend. I found nothing, but there were still a lot of potential sources of memories we might face. Not everyone who made it out of a reentry facility stayed on an upward trajectory, and there were at least two documented robberies when the building had been a bank, although I couldn't imagine how that would impact a room on the top floor.

I grew increasingly nervous throughout the day Tuesday, trying, without success, to avoid thinking about Stengel and Sons, worrying that we were overlooking something in the research that could lead to the same disastrous result, or worse. I wanted to be well-rested for the morning, so after whipping up a salad and some pasta for dinner, I practiced some *kata* and went to bed early. Which was probably a mistake, I realized an hour or so later: I wasn't tired enough to fall asleep straight away and couldn't stop thinking about the Erasure and whether or not I was ready, and did I really know that much more than when I had failed before. Around 11pm, I threw off my covers in disgust and spent thirty minutes working on my breathing exercises, striving for the calm, centered sense of self they promised. It was almost midnight before I finally lost consciousness.

"I feel like I'm taking an exam," I told Jess while we waited for Rosalind inside 1500 Locust's lobby. I would have preferred waiting outside, but the early morning sunlight had given way to a persistent drizzle that was still battling the stench of burning plastic from a now-quenched car fire down the block.

"Is that why you keep fidgeting with your bracelet?"

"Probably." I stuck my hands in my pockets. I had dressed in my best shirt and pants, while Jess had opted for her "I'm Speaking" T-shirt and calf-length ripped jeans, which were very distracting.

"And you've done all your revision, I hope?"

"Not helping."

She laughed, and I grinned despite myself. The security guard, a stocky black woman with blonde highlighted dreads and resting bored face, glanced at us from behind her desk. I shot her a respectful nod, and she turned back to her dual monitors with no change of expression.

Rosalind hurried through the lobby doors, immaculate in her navy skirt suit as usual. She raised her palm as she approached, then shook out and furled her black umbrella.

"Sorry," she said, panting and pink-cheeked. "My substitute teacher was sick, and I had to enlist and brief one of my colleagues. It's just *Hamlet*, for crying out loud."

"You need a minute?" I asked, and her eyes narrowed.

"I'll be fine. How are you, D? Ready?"

Was I? I had been considering the trajectory my life had taken since the last time I stood in this lobby, almost half a year before. Different? Certainly. Better? I thought so, although I still had a lot to figure out. And some answers were here. I took a deep, diaphragmatic breath.

"As I'll ever be."

"Good. Nice to see you, Jess. Please don't dress up on our account."

Jess batted her eyelashes.

"I think she's here for her own entertainment," I said.

"Of course I am. I want to figure out what it is you two actually do."

"When you work that out, please let us know," laughed Rosalind. "Is Nicole here yet?"

"Haven't seen her."

Right on cue, the lobby doors opened again and in walked Nicole Kelly, brushing beads of rain from her charcoal suit and shaking her ice-blonde hair disdainfully. I sensed Jess stir beside me.

"My apologies," Nicole said to Rosalind, waving an identification badge at the security guard before walking over and casting doubtful looks at both me and Jess.

"You remember D, Nicole?" Rosalind said, the ghost of a smile on her lips.

Nicole nodded. "You were here last time. Mr. Lynn's friend."

"Pleased to meet you again, Nicole," I said, extending my hand. After a moment's hesitation, she shook it.

"D is now my apprentice," Rosalind continued. "He will handle the situation today."

"I see." Nicole's gaze lingered on me for a moment, then switched to Jess. "And who is this?"

"Jess Evans," Jess said, shaking Nicole's hand and brandishing a replica Sonic Screwdriver. "I'm capturing data for subsequent scientific analysis."

Rosalind coughed discreetly.

Nicole blinked, then turned to me and lowered her voice. "As I've told Rosalind, I'm concerned about the recurrence of this... issue. Your friend Colton Lynn isn't the only tenant who's moved out recently, and I'm under pressure to raise rents to cover the shortfall. There's even talk of abandoning use of this property for those coming from reentrance facilities and targeting young professionals instead."

"That's not fair! Where would all the current tenants go?" This wasn't quite the same story I had heard from Colton, but the effect would be the same: push out those who needed it in favor of those who wanted it.

"I don't think that's seen as a primary concern," Nicole said. "The facilities I work with to place people here are worried at the prospect and the exodus. They're holding candidates back for now, and that isn't helping. I really need whatever this is to be fixed. For good."

So no pressure then. I glanced at Rosalind, but she just watched me with a neutral expression.

"Colton's a friend of mine," I said. "And I know others like him. Heck, there was a time when I could have used this chance of a new start that you're giving people. So I won't rest until we've cleared this up for you."

Jess's hand found mine, and Nicole nodded.

"Good. Let's go up. It's a corner unit on the top floor."

The guard buzzed us into the elevator and we rode up in silence. I held my breath, waiting for the telltale signs of the Imprint to manifest, and sure enough the skin on the back of my neck began prickling as we passed "3". By the time the doors opened, I perceived the otherness, the presence beyond normal human perception, and I shivered at the sudden cold. The guard frowned at me as she stepped out of the elevator, then turned left towards the short end of the corridor. I followed, and we stopped almost immediately outside a door, plain and dark green, just like all the others. But no, this door was different. It was like Colton's old apartment door, and I was both intrigued and wary of what lay beyond.

Breathe. Stay calm. Focus. Embrace the sensations, but don't let them overwhelm you.

"The tenant isn't home," said the guard, unlocking the door and pushing it open a few inches. "She gave her permission. Just don't break anything, I guess. I have to get back downstairs."

Whatever she thought was going on, she didn't want any part of it, and I wondered what, if anything, she sensed from the room. Then I forced my attention back on the door, slowly pushed it all the way open, and crossed the threshold.

The apartment was identical in layout to Colton's, just furnished differently. Two Scandinavian-looking armchairs huddled around a glass top coffee table in the main living area, facing a TV stand from which a jumble of DVD cases had spilled. A cracked door to our right led to the bedroom and bathroom, and a small but functional kitchen lined the far wall. The temperature dipped as I moved further in the room, and I could swear I felt a wintry breeze tug at me, a far different sensation from the reassuring waft of the air conditioning. I paused next to a battered wooden dining table, strewn with piles of envelopes and advertising fliers with just enough room carved out for a bowl of half-finished cereal. Out of the corner of my eye I could see Rosalind, there if I needed her, and Jess, no doubt bristling with curiosity.

Breathe. Focus.

I closed my eyes. I knew something was there, something that some, perhaps most, people could not perceive. It didn't frighten me as it once had, but I still gave it due respect as I cautiously opened my mind and probed for what would release it, erase it. I still didn't have a clear idea about how this was done. Rosalind and I were both frustrated by her inability to define her approach, so I had simply decided to immerse myself in what I could feel, real or otherwise, and try to detect anything that stood out, something I could latch onto. I was looking to trigger the pressure change that seemed to signify the unblocking of the Imprinted memory, and if my plumbing analogy was naïve, it at least gave me a point of focus.

I lost track of time, seeing nothing, just surrounded by the pulsing cold and a potential of something behind it, implacable and powerful. Doubt and frustration prowled the perimeter of my concentration, but I hadn't expected it to be easy. I tried to ignore them and redoubled my focus. All I could think of was to chase each stab of colder air, try to follow each one back to its source. And that's when I found it.

I can describe this no better than as an almost imperceptible "catch" in the universe. Or as a subliminal message buried within a video clip. Or, well, I could rattle off many other analogies of questionable relevance or accuracy, likely annoying you as well as Jess, and frankly, none of us would be any the wiser. Suffice it to say that once found, it took everything I had to maintain my focus, as if staring at the faintest of stars obscured behind billowing clouds. I narrowed in on it, an almost infinitesimal point, and what do you do with a blockage? You push.

Nothing happened at first, but I soon grew sure that I was doing the right thing. I gathered my will and visualized it as a needle, tapering down to a point I could use to hook that catch, and apply all my force against it. And I pushed.

My ears popped, and the universe took a sickening lurch. I was on a flat rooftop, this rooftop, under a leaden sky. Tiny snowflakes swirled around me in the desultory breeze, but now I couldn't feel the cold.

Ahead of me, a young woman stood shivering near the edge, looking down at the streets below. She wore only a long-sleeved white blouse and dark ankle-length skirts, her long red hair loose and unkempt, and her hands rested on a swollen belly that could only mean one thing. Despair radiated from her, drawing me unwillingly to the edge of the roof beside her. I'm not crazy about heights at the best of times, and maybe that was a good thing because after getting close enough to peer down at a sprinkling of early twentieth century cars trundling along the dirt roads, I jerked myself back from the edge. I knew I wasn't there, but I had no idea what would happen if I tried to *do* anything in this memory, and I didn't want to find out. This close, I could see the woman's eyes - the girl's eyes, she couldn't have been out of her teens - were red-rimmed and bloodshot, her mouth set in a determined line. I didn't want to watch this. I wanted to reach out and pull her away, to comfort and reassure her, to find whatever help I could for her. But I wasn't really there. I was powerless.

"Don't do it," I said anyway, in my mind if nowhere else. "Come away from the edge. Please."

She started and looked over her shoulder. Disoriented, I followed her gaze to see another woman standing in the middle of the roof by an open door in a small hut that provided access from the building below. She was older, but her face was similar enough that I guessed she was family, maybe a sister.

"Come away, Mary." Oddly, the words didn't match the movement of her mouth, but I was sure the meaning was the same.

"No hope," said the girl at my side. Mary. My half-sister's name.

"There's always hope," I urged her. "There are always those who can help you, if you only know where to find them."

"Hope?"

"Hope. Come away. Mary."

Mary turned back to the rooftop edge and, for a horrified instant, I thought that was it. Then she took one slow, deliberate step backwards and then the entire scene dissolved and poured through me, all the despair, fear, and relief, filling me to bursting, threatening to wash me away with it into oblivion. I flailed for something to hold on to. I couldn't do this by myself, and then there was someone else there, someone I couldn't see, propping me up, and it was just enough. In an instant, the torrent became a trickle and the untidy, modern-day apartment swam blearily back into view.

I stood, but only because Jess and Rosalind supported my sagging body on either side. Sweat drenched me and my mouth was so dry I couldn't separate my tongue from its roof. Jess hung on, staring at me with concern as I straightened, and Rosalind let go.

"I'm okay," I croaked, and fought back a cough. The room was still blurry, although the cold and the wind and the otherness had all dissipated. The Imprint was gone. I had Erased it.

"Well done, D!" said Rosalind. "That was not easy. I am *very* proud of you."

I nodded, and that was all the movement it took. I fell to my knees and vomited.

Excerpt of email recovered from closed account, owner untraceable. Destination account also closed and untraceable.

From: (address withheld)
To: (address withheld)
Subject: St. Louis 2023-09
Sent: 2023-09-16 14:23:38 UTC

…but despite his irritation I confess I am intrigued by the protege's progress and curious about the mentor's methods of instruction. She's a teacher by profession, which might explain it, although I doubt these techniques lie in any curriculum she's ever seen before.

It's funny: neither were what I expected when I finally saw them in real life last week. No, I did not speak with or otherwise interact with them - I will respect your wishes even though I don't agree with or understand them. The mentor would be easy to underestimate. She reminds me of a protagonist in one of those cozy mystery series. Her protege looks all brawn, not brain, someone I wouldn't want to cross in a bar fight. Clearly, there is more here than meets the eye. There was a third person with them too, a younger woman, and my intelligence is that she's making insightful inquiries in corners of the internet about which she should have no knowledge.

Are you certain we shouldn't make an overture? Allies are surely better than adversaries…

Chapter Eighteen

WHEN CAN YOU GET HERE?

I still made it to work on time, and that was another victory.

Jess had cleaned up my mess while Rosalind brought me water, overriding my objections that I couldn't keep it down.

"The nausea should pass soon, if it hasn't already. Dehydration is far more serious. Drink."

I did as I was told, taking small sips at first, just to rid myself of the acrid taste of bile. Swallowing was painful, but by the time she brought a third glass I was able to drain it eagerly. I wiped my mouth with the back of my hand and hauled myself to my feet, albeit with the help of a kitchen chair, which continued to support me.

"I'll be okay," I said in a hoarse whisper, coughed and regretted it. My head was still pounding, but I remembered to breathe, slow and deep, and strength flowed back into my limbs. "Does anyone have any ibuprofen?"

Rosalind shook her head. "I wouldn't. It'll do more harm than good. Let your body heal naturally."

"Easy for you to say," I muttered, and Jess smacked me on the arm. She knows I'm a terrible patient.

Someone cleared their throat, and I turned to see Nicole standing in the doorway. I didn't know if she had stayed outside the whole time or had just retreated while Jess and Rosalind cleaned me up. Her expression was hard to read, perhaps curiosity and wariness, maybe a sprig of revulsion.

"So, did you fix it?"

Back to business, fair enough. Had I fixed it? It certainly seemed that way to judge from the flood of emotion that had all but overwhelmed me. If there was more to it than that, I wasn't sure I was up for this line of work.

"Yeah, I fixed it," is what I said, unable to keep a note of challenge out of my voice. Nicole raised an eyebrow and glanced at Rosalind.

"Yes," said Rosalind, with every ounce of classroom authority. "I observed the entire thing. D took care of the issue for you."

And she made sure I received the full $1500 fee too, refusing to accept a cut for providing me with all her prior research. Which, as she pointed out, hadn't been all that useful in the end.

"Sometimes it helps and sometimes it doesn't, but I always operate on the principle that the more you know, the better prepared you are. I got lucky the last time we were here - that murder was on the public record. I doubt anyone other than the two sisters ever knew anything about this."

"How do you know they were sisters, then?" asked Jess, who had forced the tale out of me as we walked Rosalind back to her car.

"I don't *know*, but it seems a reasonable guess. Anyway, the older and bigger the building, the more research you have to do and the greater the odds you'll miss the source of an Imprint. Which is why you should always be prepared for the unexpected."

"I need that on a T-shirt."

"Maybe I'll get you one for Christmas." Rosalind opened her car door, then turned back to me with a big smile on her face. "I really am proud of you, D. You've taken a considerable weight off my shoulders. Talk to you soon. Bye Jess."

"I'm proud of you too," said Jess, crushing me in a fierce hug as Rosalind drove away. "You're not afraid to face up to your fears, especially if it could help someone."

"With you by my side, I don't have any fear," I murmured and kissed her. We stood wrapped in each other's arms for some time, heedless of passers-by and the inevitable wolf whistle from a passing car.

By the time I got home, my headache had faded to a background throb, my thirst had abated, and my strength had returned. On top of that, I was on a natural high, the implications of what I had just done fully sinking in. I had accomplished something that few others had, that as far as I knew, most people didn't even know needed doing. I shared the love of the woman I loved, and had earned the respect of another woman I respected. And I had even reached out to an old acquaintance and perhaps begun a genuine friendship. I whistled - whistled! - as I showered and changed for work, and swaggered as I walked into the kitchen at Hickory. Life was good.

Which was when the wheels came off.

We were about halfway through the dinner service, a little busier with the NLCS game on TV. TJ, who had worked the lunchtime shift earlier, walked into the kitchen just after 8pm as I was furiously plating food for a table of six.

"Lost my phone," he explained, sidling past me. "Gonna check the break room."

"Okay," I said, dolloping pulled pork over the hoagies on two adjacent plates. I had just passed that order off for sides and was calling out the next one when TJ appeared at my side, phone in hand.

"Got it?" I asked, as I reached for the brisket.

"Yeah, it was under the table. Must've dropped it. Hey man, your phone is going apeshit in there."

"My phone?" Why was he still there and bothering me? He knew how busy this place got at this hour.

"Yeah, yours is the one with all the rave tones, right? All we need is a light show, dude. We can charge the customers extra."

What the hell was going on?

"Huh. Can you cover this order for me while I check? Since you're here?"

"Sure", he said as I squeezed past him and ducked inside the break room. Mike didn't like the staff having their phones on them while they worked, and I agreed with him. I opened my locker just in time for another Skrillex moment and saw notifications for three missed calls and at least a dozen messages. All from Jess.

I scanned the messages, which were all variations on "call me" with increasing capitalization and profanity. No voice mails - Jess hated them, and flat out told me once she would never listen to any I left for her - but her first call was twenty minutes ago. I called back immediately.

"Hey babe, what's—"

"Dad had a heart attack," she interrupted me. "He's in surgery. We're with Mom at the hospital, waiting. I know you're working, but I really need you. When can you get here?"

There was a lot of background noise, and her voice was somewhat muffled, but I could hear the panic running through it. I panicked myself for a moment, unsure what to do, but that wouldn't help anyone.

"As soon as I can," I promised, as calmly as I could. "Let me talk to Mike, and I'll text you when I'm on my way. Which hospital?"

"BJC downtown. Hurry, please."

"I will."

Mike wasn't in his office, so I tracked him down behind the bar where he was talking to customers and impeding Alison, the bartender. He raised his eyebrows when he saw me hovering on the threshold of the kitchen and excused himself.

"Problem in the kitchen, D?"

"Jess's dad's in the hospital, heart attack," I told him, my voice low and urgent. "I was wondering if I could leave a little early, after service, but before cleanup, maybe."

"Hell no! You're leaving now." He grabbed my arm and dragged me back into the kitchen. "I can help finish service tonight. Be there for your girl. What are you doing here, TJ? Your phone? Since you're here, can you finish up service tonight? D's got a family emergency to attend to."

"Sure, dude, I got your back," TJ said, looking at me with concern before turning back to the ticket he was working. I could've hugged him.

"Hey, take some of this with you," said Mike, and filled a half-dozen to-go boxes with pulled pork and potato salad. "In case anyone missed their dinner."

I thanked him and could've hugged him too, but there was no room and I needed to get going. I ran to my car, dumped the bag of food on the passenger seat, texted Jess, hoped Officer Kennedy wasn't prowling the neighborhood, and floored the gas pedal as much as I dared.

Twenty minutes later, I hurried into the ER at Barnes Jewish Medical Center. The place was packed, and I balked in the doorway, then forced myself inside, scanning the room for Jess and her family. She saw me first and almost bowled people over on her way to throwing herself into a fierce hug. I wrapped my arms around her and tried not to whack her with the takeout.

"What's the latest?" I asked. Over her shoulder I could see her oldest brother Jonathan standing next to a row of black faux-leather seats, murmuring to his mother who sat at the end. Zawida wore the absent expression of someone in shock and didn't seem to acknowledge whatever her son was saying.

"Still waiting to hear," Jess murmured into my neck. "Jonathan says that's probably a good thing."

"What happened? I mean—"

"Mom said he'd complained about being tired when he got home from work. Then the chest pains started when they sat down to dinner and he told her to call 911. Benefit of being a doctor, I guess. Mom called when she was in the ambulance with him. She was pretty freaked out. He was still conscious because I heard him telling her to calm down." She sobbed, and I gave her a gentle squeeze.

We walked over to join the rest of the family - Kioko was en route - and Jonathan shook my hand, surprising both of us. Zawida tried a brave smile but made no move and I didn't feel comfortable bending over to give her a hug.

I noticed Jonathan was wearing scrubs and frowned. He caught my eye and shook his head.

"Can't operate on family, D. Ethics and all that. Can't say I disagree. I'd be useless in there right now. But Dad's in good hands with Dr. Malik. He's one of the best there is."

"What's in the bag?" demanded Jess, as if noticing it for the first time.

"My boss gave me some takeout, in case anyone was hungry and... well, in case we're here for a while."

"Oh I'm in. Who else?" Jess dug into the bag and pulled out a couple of boxes, wafting the unmistakable scent of smoked meat around us, turning more than a couple of heads. "Come on, it'll take our minds off it for a while."

"You cooked this, D?" asked Zawida, her voice soft and frail.

"I did," I said, "well most of it, anyway." She smiled and accepted a box and a spork, but only ate a bite or two. Jonathan declined, professing lack of hunger as an afterthought. And I can't eat Hickory unless I'm starving; I'm just around it too much.

"Suit yourself," shrugged Jess, who had no such compunction.

We settled in to wait. Kioko arrived forty-five minutes later, flustered and apologetic, and Jonathan took his brother aside to bring him up to speed. A few minutes later, the seat next to Zawida opened up and Jess slumped onto it. I gave it another ten minutes, then volunteered to fetch drinks from a vending machine I could see in the far corner. I left the family sitting and standing in morose silence.

As I threaded my way towards the vending machine, it occurred to me to wonder about where I was. This was a hospital, and a large one at that.

How many memories were imprinted here? There was enough emotion just between the Evans family to create such a memory, and people must make hundreds or even thousands of such memories every year in this ER alone. Fear, worry, relieved joy, such a palette of powerful emotions to choose from. I could sense them from the real live people in that room with me, stifling and unnerving. But that's all I could sense. There were no unusual temperature swings, no pressure changes, no unease that something, if not someone, invisible was watching me. Why? Were any such phenomena drowned out by the genuine emotions of the weight of humanity in this room? If I were to venture deeper into the hospital, to the wards if not the operating room waiting areas, would that be true? I knew I didn't want to find out: I may have been still fresh from my success at 1500 Locust earlier that day - the same day! - but I had no illusions about my ability to handle more than one Imprint at a time.

"You gonna buy something?"

I started and realized I had been standing motionless in front of the vending machine for a lot longer than was reasonable to make my selections. With a muttered apology to the young black guy watching me stonily, I punched in the codes for two waters, a Mountain Dew and a Diet Coke, then almost dropped all of them as I struggled to wrangle the bottles into a mass suitable for carrying across the room. Flustered, I was halfway back to Jess and her family before I saw the surgeon was talking to them.

I stopped, not wanting to intrude. All four faces stared in sober attention at the balding, dark-skinned man wearing the same scrubs as Jonathan, no less imposing, even if the top of his head barely came up to his colleague's shoulder. His voice was earnest as he spoke to all of them, but especially to Zawida. When he finished speaking, Jess embraced her mother, who leaned into her daughter with closed eyes. The relieved smile on Jess's face told me what I most wanted to know. Jonathan asked a couple of questions and nodded at the answers. Kioko half-collapsed against the wall, eyes closed and lips moving in silence.

Calvin Evans had suffered a mild myocardial infarction, which was what surgeons like Jonathan called heart attacks. His colleagues had elected for angioplasty over bypass surgery, running two stents from his groin through his arteries to open blocked blood vessels and improve the flow of blood to his heart. It sounded excruciatingly painful, and my jaw dropped when I heard he was only under local anesthesia during the procedure. Once he moved from recovery to an overnight bed for observation, the family could visit him.

"I'll stay here," I told Jess, wrapping her in a long hug. "He needs to see his wife and children, and there's only so much room."

"You'll wait for me, though, right?"

"I will. Text me if you need anything."

She kissed me, then set off with Zawida and her brothers into the labyrinth of the hospital interior. After a minute, I walked as far as the entrance to the corridor down which they had disappeared, closed my eyes and concentrated. It was quieter here, and I fancied I could detect a faint background signal, like the tingling in the air before a thunderstorm. But maybe that was all it was, fancy. I could have gone further in, maybe, but after all, this had been another reason not to accompany the family to visit Calvin.

The ER was still crowded, so I waited outside, far enough removed from the doors to not block the occasional ambulance or other vehicle dropping people off. It was much quieter there, only an occasional pedestrian and the hum of the ceaseless Kingshighway traffic to interrupt my thoughts. It was a cool evening, a welcome harbinger of Fall to come, and the last ruddy vestiges of daylight lurked above the western horizon, beyond the silhouetted trees of Forest Park. I texted Mike to let him know Jess's father was in recovery, and started to text Rosalind, then thought better of it. Some troubles were best kept close.

I stared into the gathering darkness and thought about family. The last time Jess had seen all of hers together, she had stormed from her parents' home, and it was likely she hadn't spoken with either brother since then. Now faced with the unimaginable, they had come back together, and maybe Calvin's heart wouldn't be the only thing to heal. I wondered how my mother was doing, the first time I had thought about her outside of a conversation with Fiona for a long time. I may not be able to adequately explain my accomplishment that morning, but I'm sure Mom would have liked to hear something positive about me for a change. Heaven knew I'd disappointed her enough over the years.

"I thought I'd find you out here," Jess said, appearing at my side an hour later. "Brooding, are we?"

"We are. I am. It's been a day, but more so for you than me. How is he?"

"Groggy, quiet. Makes a pleasant change, actually." She tried to smile, but it came out as more of a grimace. I put my arm around her and she rested her head on my shoulder before speaking again.

"I think I'm going to stay with Mom and Dad for a bit. At their house, I mean. She's still in a bit of a daze, and I think she could use the company and the help, at least until he's well enough to go back to work."

"Makes sense. How long will that be?"

"Too early to say. At least a couple of weeks, I think. He's a doctor, and they're the worst patients, or so the saying goes."

I turned to face her, taking her hands in mine. "It'll be okay, Jess. This has been a terrible scare, but I know how much his family loves him, how much you love him. You don't have to put on a brave face, not with me. I already know how brave you are."

She tilted her head quizzically, then took a deep, shuddering breath. Tears welled in the corners of her eyes, and she wiped them away with the back of her hand before leaning in close.

"I love you, Jess." I whispered, stroking her hair. She nuzzled against me but didn't reply. She didn't need to.

CHAPTER NINETEEN

LEAVE WELL ENOUGH ALONE

I offered to call in sick on Thursday to help out, but Jess waved me off.

"Dad's coming home today, and Jon and Kioko are both taking time to get him settled in. That's more than enough fuss for Mom. I'm gonna go pack up some things and head over there after class."

I kissed her again before she left, and she smiled, but her emotional rollercoaster ride of the previous evening had ended in relief, gratitude, and a renewed commitment to her family.

"Call me later?" she said as she walked out my apartment door, and I promised I would.

Mike clapped me on the back when I arrived at Hickory later that morning.

"I'm glad to hear Jess's dad is doing better," he said, as I tossed my keys, phone, and leather jacket into my locker; it had turned unseasonably chilly overnight. "Please just ask if you need anything - rescheduling your shifts, whatever. Family's important, and you're my family D, you and everyone else here."

"Thanks, Mike," I said, touched and grateful to him all over again for giving me this chance, this job two years before. "Working will help, and especially working here will help. I appreciate what you did last night, and Jess's family appreciated the food."

"Good!" Mike smiled. "Don't forget, we've got a new line cook starting today. Davinia. I want you to take her under your wing. I know she's got the skills, but she's lacking in confidence, especially in herself. And I know you can help her with that."

"I will," I promised.

After my shift, I called Jess, but she was irritable, trying to track down a T-shirt she wanted to pack, so I left her to it and called Rosalind instead. Jess had told me that morning she was okay with it. She and Rosalind had struck up something of a rapport since the Hills had hosted us for dinner and we were all becoming friends. I gave Rosalind a quick summary of the situation and assured her that Jess's dad was on the mend and well cared for.

"Thanks for telling me, D," she said. "I'm sure Jess is worried sick, though. I imagine that's why she's moving back home for a while."

"She wants to help her mother, too." There was a pause.

"Yes, that too. You will take good care of Jess, won't you?"

"Of course!"

"Good. I think I'll give her a call in a bit."

"Yeah, you might want to wait a while. She's a cranky packer."

Of course, I couldn't blame Jess for worrying. Despite her frustration with her family, she still loved them and especially her father, who indulged her unwillingness to follow in her brothers' footsteps more than her mother had. I envied her. I wondered what I would do if something traumatic happened to my mother, or if I would even hear about it in time to do anything, and if I would. I shut down that line of thinking. The past was the past, and some things were best left buried.

But not all of them would stay there.

I surprised an odd look on Mike's face midway through Saturday night's dinner service. He wandered into the kitchen as I was coaching Davinia, a diminutive black woman with hair spiky enough for a goth club, through the peak of our busiest night of the week. I had put her on veggies, and it was clear she knew what she was doing, but the mechanics of dealing with the sheer volume of orders in an unfamiliar kitchen were stressing her out. I made sure she got her part of the order first and kept up a constant stream of what I hope was encouragement. So, I almost didn't notice Mike standing by the service counter, but I glanced up as I slid a plate of ribs onto it and saw him watching me. For a fleeting moment he looked scared, but then he smiled and told us to keep up the good work, before heading back to the front of house. I frowned, but couldn't spare the time to think more of it. The reason for his visit didn't emerge until the very end of the night.

"Hey, D," he said, taking me aside after I had just begun cleaning up. "There are some guests out in the restaurant who are asking after you, and if you could spare them a minute."

"Really?" I said, wiping my brow and wondering who on earth he could be talking about.

"Does the name Steven Rourke mean anything to you?"

I froze. Not just physically, but I was incapable of thought for several seconds. When my brain shuddered back into action, it dislodged memories of that name, flinging them about like shrapnel. It was a name I had hoped never to hear again, but that was just wishful thinking in a city as small as St. Louis.

"I can see it does," Mike murmured. "You know I won't ask, D. But I don't want any trouble."

"Me neither." I felt nauseous, and couldn't look at any of the food cleanup going on around me. I wanted to grab my phone and keys and leave, but I knew that might not work out well for Mike, and I owed him - whether he saw it that way or not.

"Shit," I breathed at last. "I'll go talk to him. Can you keep an eye on things back here?"

"You got it. Be careful."

"Oh, I know."

I washed my hands, as much to calm myself as anything else, then left the sanctuary of my kitchen and entered the dining room, which was still half full. The ALCS game in Oakland was still in the third inning, and there were two tables of green-capped fans riveted to one or the other of the wall-mounted flat screens showing the action. The table I was interested in was, of course, in the back corner. I walked toward it, slow and steady, fighting twin urges to flee and to throw myself howling at the two men and a woman sitting there.

"Declan!" said one man, grinning as he rose to his feet and offering me his hand to shake. He stood a couple of inches shorter than me, his twinkling blue eyes and pale, clean chiseled face still talk-show handsome, although his hair was more silver than red now. The black polo shirt and designer-faded jeans could not disguise a lot more girth around the middle than I remembered, but the big, blocky rings on every finger spoke of power and the willingness to use it, and they did not lie. I hesitated as long as I dared, then shook his hand. His lips twitched, then he gestured to the empty chair opposite his.

"Sit down, please. It's been far too long since we caught up with each other."

I sat and glanced at his companions. The other man appeared about the same age, which was to say late forties, black and almost bald, with a rim of very short gray hair. Circular rimless eyeglasses perched on a wide flat nose, but he had a solid build, his biceps bulging beneath a pastel blue and pink golf shirt. It took me a moment to place him, but then I remembered Donovan and Lana's silent companion at the 5K in Forest Park. I was sure I hadn't seen the woman before: she was younger and Asian, Japanese I think, short but lithe, and her every movement was careful and controlled, reminding me of a coiling snake. Both watched me in silence, and neither smiled.

Intimidated? You betcha.

"How long *has* it been?" Steven Rourke asked, brow furrowed in thought, although I suspected he knew exactly how long it had been, probably to the day.

"Sixteen years, give or take," I said, looking him in the eye.

He nodded. "Yes, that sounds about right. How time flies, although probably not as fast for you. Given that you spent most of it as a guest of Missouri Eastern Correctional."

"And more time after that, getting my life back together. But I expect you know that, too."

"I do. Information is the real currency, Declan. Although I hear you go by 'D' now."

"It's shorter." He grinned. "Aren't you going to introduce me to your associates?"

"It would be rude of me not to, wouldn't it?"

We sat there staring at each other for what seemed like an age. He had retained his affectation of an upper class British accent which I inevitably compared to Rosalind's, but while hers was natural and used to engender respect, his was intended to boast of superiority and instill fear. I had once got it into my head that he reminded me of Shere Khan, the tiger in the Jungle Book movie, one of my favorites as a kid. Steven Rourke had all the self-possession, menace and authority of Shere Khan and I couldn't shake the image of the poor snake gripped by one paw with a claw up its nostril.

I took a deep breath. "Why are you here, Steven? What do you want from me?"

"I want you to stop," he said.

The hackles went up on the back of my neck, and I forced myself to remain expressionless, or so I hoped. Three pairs of eyes bored into me, but I was damned if I was going to give them the satisfaction.

"I was wondering who sent that note," I said, mouth dry. I needed some water, but there was none left on the table. "A bit indirect for you, isn't it?"

"I prefer to keep things safely anonymous and civilized when I can," he said, baring his teeth in the beginnings of a smile that was betrayed by narrowed eyes. "If I start throwing bodies around, some might get hurt. Or get sent down for a decade or more."

"Can't have that."

"Well, quite."

"What do you think I'm doing that you want me to stop? Cooking barbecue?" From the corner of my eye, I saw the other man shift in his seat.

"Good God, no! On the contrary, I want you to dedicate yourself to this job. That was some very passable brisket. I think you may have a future as a cook, Declan, and we all deserve a future. Mike Szemis deserves a future, don't you think? Very big on giving people second chances is our Mikhail. Very admirable. I think Hickory deserves a second chance, too."

If his voice had gotten any colder, he'd be exhaling ice chips. I didn't need to pick apart his words to understand the not-so-veiled threat. I had heard and seen this before, and I wanted no part of it. Yet, this one thread to my old life would not be cut by wishing it so. And not without risk by any means.

"Come on, Declan, you're a bright boy. I've always thought so." Warmer now, almost convivial, the big cat toying with its prey. "Leave well enough alone and enjoy all the good things in your life."

He stood, and this time his companions stood with him, flanking him as he turned to leave. Before he did, he looked back over his shoulder. "Just a few minutes longer on that brisket next time."

Too shaken to get up for a while, I just sat there gawping at the nearest TV. Finally, the baseball fans across the dining room erupted in cheers and I came back to myself. Mike caught me on my way out and raised his eyebrows in silent inquiry.

"I don't know," I muttered. "I'll figure it out and keep you out of it."

Damn, I sure hoped I could keep that promise.

Sleep didn't come easy that night, haunted by ghosts that did exist, if only metaphorically. I went through the motions during Sunday's lunch service, and the kitchen was subdued and uneasy with the rest of the staff catching my mood. I didn't want to go to Clayton - I wanted Jess to come to me - but I had promised to join the family for Sunday dinner. Both Calvin's father and Zawida's parents had traveled from Chicago to be with their children and Jess was now sleeping in the basement, not because she had to give up her bedroom, but because she needed the space.

"Why did I do this?" she hissed after dragging me inside the front door. "I must be mad!"

"Don't be mad for loving your family," I said, and she stopped short.

"What the fuck is wrong with you?"

So I told her, and afterwards she sat with me in the backyard and held my hand while Jonathan grilled every edible vegetable known to mankind on the Evans charcoal grill. Calvin grumbled that he'd never eat meat again if his wife had her way, while Kioko tried to avoid answering one question after another from Zawida's parents, and Gathii turned to me at one point and winked slyly, and it was just such wonderfully normal family dysfunction that I almost cried.

"What are you going to do?" Jess asked me later, arms crossed over her chest as she stood on the front porch while I put my shoes back on.

"The best I can."

"Are you going to tell Rosalind?"

"I don't know."

"You should. She deserves to know."

"We all have secrets," I said, then sighed. "I'll figure something out. I have to."

To be honest, I didn't know what to tell Rosalind, and I dodged the issue by begging off the next Erasure when she called me a few days later.

"My head's not on right," I told her, cutting her off before she could even explain where and what it was. "This thing with Jess's dad, and stress at work, I don't want a setback so soon after my first success."

It sounded lame, even to me, and judging by the length of the ensuing pause, Rosalind thought so too.

"I see. Well, I wish Jess's dad well. Let me know when you're ready for another go."

I felt bad, and the fact I had disappointed her just added to my malaise. I tried to focus on Hickory, what I now thought of as my "real job", and for a while, heartened by Davinia's progress, I put aside my fear and uncertainty and took pleasure in helping her come out of her shell. Mike wasn't exactly solicitous, but he took every opportunity to praise what I was doing. I was grateful. In some ways, this was the dysfunctional family I had craved in the Evans' backyard. I couldn't, in good conscience, bring them trouble, and I didn't need Officer Kennedy lurking outside the restaurant most nights after my shift to know how real that threat of trouble had been.

Jess, of course, didn't see it that way.

"What's this I hear about you turning down a job with Rosalind because of some bullshit about my father?"

I had returned her call the following Thursday night as I huddled in the break room waiting for a torrential downpour to pass. Now I wished I had waited until I got home to call her.

"We're having dinner at the Hills on Sunday," she said after enduring a minute of my rambling excuses. "You can grow a spine and tell her the truth. Then you and your *friends* can figure out what to do next."

She wasn't wrong, but that didn't improve my temper. I had been neglecting my karate practice of late, earning some pointed criticism from my old buddy Donovan during our last lesson. I had twice lost my composure during sparring and almost hurt myself and my partner.

"You've got to remember that karate is more mental than physical," he said, taking me aside at the end of the lesson. "All the technical skill in the world is useless if you can't keep a cool head."

I was going backwards, it seemed, and that needed to stop. Ha ha. So maybe Jess was right, and it was time to open the door to another skeleton-filled closet. But I felt it was potentially dangerous knowledge, and I wasn't sure how much to say, how wide to open that door. I made my decision when I received another mysterious note just before going to dinner.

I was wrapping up the Sunday lunch shift at Hickory, cleaning and tidying and chuckling over Davinia's exasperated story about her young son's obstinate refusal to eat anything green, when Mike passed me a sealed white envelope. Turning it over, both sides were blank, and I looked back at him quizzically.

"Someone left this for you last night," he said. "In the middle of service. Didn't even ask if you were here, just that I give it to you. We were so busy that I forgot about it until just now. Sorry."

I shrugged, but now regarded the envelope warily. "Do you know who it was?"

"No, although he looked vaguely familiar, might have been a recent customer. Black guy, my age, bald. Ring any bells?"

"Not sure," I said, although I remembered Steven Rourke's silent companion. I hesitated, and Mike took that as his cue to turn his attention to his other employees while I opened the envelope. Inside was a plain white sheet of notepaper with a simple message.

"We need to talk. Please call." And a phone number, 314 area code. That was it.

I didn't know what to do or what to think. I assumed the guy was one of Rourke's goons, but then why would he reach out? And why this way, unless it was to somehow reinforce the threat to Hickory? It didn't feel right. I stuffed the note in the back pocket of my jeans and resolved not to call, at least not without discussing it with Rosalind, Martin, and Jess too. That's when I knew I had to tell them everything.

Rosalind and Martin lived in Webster Groves, on a quiet street off of Elm, lined with tall trees and expensive real estate. They said it reminded them of the streets on which they had each grown up back in England. Their house wasn't one of the biggest, but their front yard was - studded with immaculate flower beds arranged around a pair of enormous oak trees. The leaves were turning and the entire neighborhood was a riot of red, orange, yellow, and islands of coniferous green. It was a glorious early Fall day - or Autumn as Rosalind insisted on calling it - sunny and warm with a soft northerly breeze, and we sat around a patio table in their much smaller, but private, back yard. Rosalind served us salad and shepherd's pie (with minced lamb, not beef, thank you very much), while Martin poured glasses of Cabernet and I told them about Steven Rourke's visit to Hickory.

"And who is Steven Rourke?" asked Martin with a frown, but Rosalind answered before I could.

"He's a property developer, one of the biggest and richest in St. Louis. Made a name for himself gentrifying Benton Park, but I think he's expanded from there. I read an article on him on one of the news channel websites a few months ago, one of those rags to riches stories."

I snorted. "He was a fucking drug dealer. Resourceful and ruthless. For all I know, he's doing it still, and more besides, whatever respectable face he presents to the world. I guarantee more people know the real Steven Rourke than they let on."

"And you know that how?" asked Rosalind.

"Because I bought drugs from him when I was at college. Ecstasy, mostly, then some LSD. The rave culture fascinated me, more so than the music, just like my friends at UMSL. I became the guy who bought the drugs for the parties, and Steven had recently made UMSL his territory. I didn't know how, and back then I probably wouldn't have cared much.

He made sure I got what we needed, and that it was a good product for a good price. And after I got expelled, after campus police found drugs in my room, he took me in when the rest of my family disowned me, gave me a place to stay and a job as a courier until I could work out what to do next."

I paused and took a drink of water, not wine. Martin and Rosalind waited for me to continue, him stony-faced and her sad and pensive. Jess sat next to me in silence, but she had heard this all before.

"Before I could do that, I got jumped one night while out on a courier run. For Steven. And you've heard how that ended up. He made it clear to me that on no account could his name get dragged into it, although honestly, I don't think it would have helped me much. But I never heard from him again, not in prison, not when I got out of prison, not when I was living at New Hope, certainly not when I finally got my shit together, got a real job, got an apartment and met Jess. Met you. Not until the other night at Hickory.

"But I heard things, heard that he'd moved up in the world, heard that you didn't fuck with Steven Rourke. And so now I don't know what to do. I don't want to let you down, but I don't want to bring any trouble to Hickory, to Mike. He's been really good to me. And Steven is more than capable of bringing trouble."

"And this is who you've brought into our lives," said Martin icily. "I'm not sure how I feel about that."

I felt Jess bristle beside me and grabbed her wrist under the table, but I couldn't blame him.

"That's a little unfair, Martin," said Rosalind, not quite looking at anyone. "What bad choices D has made lie mostly far back in his past. Who are we to criticize him for that?"

Martin grimaced and shook his head. "Perhaps. But I'm not happy about it."

"It doesn't have to be an issue," I said. "If I stop."

Rosalind stared at me morosely. I felt bad saying it, but it was one option.

"Would that even help, though?" asked Jess. "I mean, it might help Hickory, but if he wants you to stop what you're doing with Rosalind, to stop Erasing memories, might that mean that he wants her to stop too? What does he know, and why does he care?"

I stared at her. The thought hadn't even occurred to me. I had been distracted all week just because Steven had reappeared in my life, threatening my livelihood, my place of work. I hadn't even stopped to consider how he knew about Imprints and Erasures, or how much he knew. Of course, he'd said nothing quite so direct - I had replayed the conversation so many times in my mind, like someone worrying a toothache - but I was sure that was what he'd been talking about.

"I don't know what he knows," I said at last, following an uncomfortable silence. The cool breeze had turned cold and gusty all of a sudden, and Rosalind slid closer to Martin, who put his arm around her. "It's possible it's just about me."

Martin and Jess both frowned, but Rosalind sighed and twirled the remnants of her wine in its glass. "It doesn't really change anything," she said. "I can't do this Chouteau Village job alone. I visited the place yesterday, and I sensed at least three Imprints, maybe more. You remember, D, what I said about old, large buildings?"

"Yeah. Chouteau Village? That's the job?"

"That's the job. It's been on the table since early summer, but I've been holding off until you grew strong and, frankly, good enough to help me. If you can't, I'm afraid I'll have to turn it down."

"Is that the condo complex built on the site of the old St. Mary's Infirmary?" Jess asked. "The one that's been in the news for financial troubles and so on?"

"It is," said Rosalind, her tone grave. "I suspect they're close to the brink, and I'm a long shot chance to stop more tenants from leaving. Probably closer now than earlier in the summer, but I can't do this without you, D."

"And what about Rourke? What about Hickory?"

She shrugged. "I can't give you a simple answer to either of those questions. I'm tired of putting off this decision. There's a hell of a lot of research we need to do to give us any chance of being prepared, and I don't want to start on it if you're not with me."

I looked away, into the shadows between the trees as the sun set behind the houses to the west. This was one of those moments where life offers you a choice between two paths, each leading to two very different futures. Neither of those paths gave me a clear view ahead, and both put either livelihood or friendship at risk. I knew I could, and likely would, agonize all night, sleepless, and still struggle with the decision. So I might as well decide now, and I went with friendship.

"I'm with you," I said.

CHAPTER TWENTY

BUT THE NOTES

"I'll help with the research," Jess promised, as we helped clean up the dinner plates and prepared for Martin's famous English trifle. "I can probably find things you guys can't."

Rosalind raised an eyebrow. "You sound like my students. Telling me Facebook is for old people."

"It so totally is," grinned Jess. "I'll hook you up with Snapchat."

"I thought it was all TikTok now. You're behind the times, Jess," I said and winked at Martin, who rolled his eyes.

We laughed and by unspoken agreement we left the subjects of Chouteau Village and Steven Rourke behind, and just enjoyed the rest of our evening together. I was grateful: I had made my decision, and I would stick with it, but I was well aware of the potential consequences.

Rosalind talked to her contact at Chouteau Village the next day and agreed that we would come out the afternoon of the Thursday after next to deal with their "unexplained issues". I didn't want to try an Erasure right before working the dinner service. Neither Jess nor Rosalind had any commitments that night either, and this would give us time to do what research we could. Or, rather, give Rosalind and Jess time to do research: they had both forbidden me from participating.

"If Rourke is watching you, it will appear that you're being a good boy and dedicating yourself to Hickory," Rosalind said.

I didn't voice my thought that Steven was perfectly capable of having Jess followed and putting two and two together, and reminded myself to tell her to restrict herself to online research. Which was probably unnecessary.

"How effective will our research be?" I asked, remembering my experience at BJC on the night of Calvin Evans' heart attack. "There have to be dozens of condos, old hospital wards, surgeries and so on, with who knows how many memories strong enough to be Imprints. Even if we could compile a list of the possibilities, there's no way we could memorize them all. And most of them are likely experiences that were never documented."

"All true. I won't pretend this won't be difficult, but we're not after specifics this time. As you rightly observe, that would be next to impossible. What we can do, however, is identify broad statistics and trends, help ourselves understand the likelihood of facing certain types of memories over others. And if there are standout incidents on the record, I suspect those will have a higher probability of Imprinting."

"That's a lot of likelihoods and probabilities."

"It's better than nothing," she said irritably. "It doesn't change the fact that we - that you - need to be prepared for anything. Practice your breathing, practice your focus, remember what worked for you last time, and practice that."

What had worked for me last time was instinct, but I didn't say that. Truth to tell, I was getting nervous. Not only was the specter of Steven Rourke looming over the whole endeavor, but I wasn't thrilled about the idea of walking into a building that used to be an old hospital, especially since it was clear Rosalind herself seemed intimidated by it. Not taking part in the research, while sensible, meant I felt excluded, that I wasn't privy to essential information, that I wasn't useful. So I did what Rosalind suggested, focused on practicing my *kata* and my breathing, and tried to remember just what the hell I had done in that top-floor apartment at 1500 Locust.

At Hickory, I did my best to conceal how unsettled I remained and to project the necessary professional calm in the kitchen. It helped that Davinia was exceeding mine and Mike's expectations and was the model of efficiency. If I had any criticism at all, it was that she was so serious about everything and rarely cracked a smile, let alone laughed, but we can't all be the life of the party.

"I really need this job," she told me when I asked if everything was alright after a grueling shift. "Two babies and my mom are depending on me." I masked my discomfort and wondered for the hundredth time just what Rourke might do if he found out I was defying him. When he found out.

Jess was busy finishing up a tricky Shift_Dev assignment that week. She missed Tuesday's karate - and thankfully, Lana's unnerving if flattering extra attention to me that night - and I didn't see her until Saturday. She was quiet and yawned all the way to GWK, but the lesson seemed to reinvigorate her and she was as chatty as ever as we grabbed a buffet lunch at a nearby Indian restaurant.

"Dad's going back to work on Monday," she said, ripping off chunks of Naan to scoop up her palak paneer.

"That's good," I said, trying not to let it sound like a question.

She shrugged. "Jonathan thinks he should give it another week, but doesn't want to argue with him. No-one wants to argue with Dad. He's getting away with murder."

"Are you going to move back to your apartment, then?"

"I don't know." She speared some tandoori chicken with her fork, then gave me a curious look while brandishing it in the air before her. "My lease is up at the end of the month, you know?"

"Oh. No, I didn't know." Real smooth, D. I took a bite of butter chicken, hoping to disguise my awkwardness, and we sat there for a few seconds chewing and watching each other. We hadn't talked about the future, especially not our future, both having quite enough on our plates dealing with the present. We both enjoyed living in the moment, sharing each other's company, with no particular pressure or obligations to each other. Or maybe that was just my perception. We had been dating for a year now. Was it time to think about the next step? Were we ready? Was I ready?

"I think we should talk about that," I said, trying to hide the caution in my voice. "I think there are other options."

"Yeah, I agree," she said, with a hint of a smile. "But perhaps I should give you some time to consider those options. I don't want to blow your mind right before you go to work. Besides, there's something else I wanted to talk to you about."

"Oh?"

"I've been doing this research for Chouteau Village. Yes, yes, I'm keeping my voice down. It's fascinating what you can find if you know where to look. And I don't mean in the microfiche room of the library, even if that's adorably old school. Anyway, I'm still working on that, but something started nagging me. Have you and Rosalind talked about the connections between all these Imprints?"

"Connections?"

"That would be a 'no' then. Honestly, have you no curiosity at all?"

"Sure, I'm curious about what I need to do so that I can walk into any old building without panicking and either passing out or doing something stupid. You know, like pulling a fire alarm."

She froze, then reached out and laid a hand on my arm. "Sorry, love. I sometimes forget what this does to you. I'm—"

"It's okay," I said, covering her hand with mine. "I'm curious now. What have you found?"

"Maybe nothing. But as I was reading about Chouteau Village and its financial difficulties, I thought of 1500 Locust. You've been there twice, once for your friend, Colton, and then again last month. They're having trouble with tenants leaving too. And then I thought of the hotel in Chicago, and I started wondering if there was a pattern."

I considered this. I hadn't given further thought to any of the places where I'd been part of Erasures, wittingly or otherwise. For a moment, I even struggled to remember them all. "So, what about the house in Crestwood? They were just a regular family with a scared little boy."

"They're not a 'regular' family, and you know it. Don't you remember what that real estate agent told us about the note they received?"

"Uh, I remember a note..."

"'Leave, or it will return'. Remember that?"

"Now I do."

"Someone wanted that family out of that house. What if someone wants people out of Chouteau Village, and 1500 Locust? There are plans to redevelop that block on South Grand where the hardware store is. Did you know that?"

"No, I didn't know that. But Jess..."

"What?"

"You're implying this is intentional. We don't know that. We don't know if it's even possible."

"No, we don't," she said grimly, then sighed and rubbed her eyes. "I stayed up until three-thirty this morning thinking about all this. Believe me, it isn't the wildest theory I came up with. But there has to be a reason these phenomena exist. Or an explanation, if not a reason." Her voice tailed off and her eyes lost focus.

I set my fork down, appetite gone. The idea sounded a little far-fetched to me based on the evidence, but that didn't make it any less disturbing.

"The bungalow in Shrewsbury was already empty," I said, breaking the pensive silence. "And the house in Kirkwood, well..."

"I know. That sounds like a practical joke more than anything else. Maybe I'm reaching. Maybe these are just old buildings with a bunch of other problems and that's why people are leaving. Or maybe I just need to cut down on the energy drinks after midnight."

"But the notes."

"But the notes."

I sat back in my chair, head spinning. As recently as a couple of weeks ago, I had had a single goal, an odd goal admittedly, but one I could almost literally wrap my head around. Now I was jumping at shadows, but perhaps that was because the shadows were only now visible. "Jess?"

"Mmm?"

"If there is intent to some of this, if someone or several someones are, uh, directing this... well, that would imply that they have something to gain."

"Yes," she agreed. "It does, doesn't it?"

"We know Rourke sent me the 'Stop' note. His main hustle these days is real estate. I wouldn't put it past him to use any means necessary to acquire property at a bargain price. He would absolutely take advantage of people getting spooked by unexplained phenomena. But as notorious as he is in St. Louis, and as alarmed as I am that he's even aware of any of this, I can't imagine in my darkest dreams that he could influence or control such phenomena."

Jess stirred the remnants of her meal. "You haven't exactly kept tabs on him, by your own account. Who knows what he's capable of?"

"Not this. He wouldn't still be living in St. Louis if he had, well, paranormal powers."

"Just because we don't understand it doesn't mean it's 'paranormal'," she snapped. "And maybe it's not him. Maybe he's an opportunist, taking advantage of coincidences."

"There's something else," I blurted, my hand reaching into my back pocket even though I knew these weren't the jeans I had worn to the Hills. I sure hoped I had forgotten to wash them. "Another note, dropped off for me at Hickory. I'm pretty sure it was the same guy who was with Rourke when he came to see me."

"What did it say?"

"Nothing much. A phone number and 'we need to talk'."

"Have you called?"

"Hell no. I meant to say something to Rosalind and you guys the other night, but I forgot about it."

She held my eyes for long seconds, and I swear I could see the cogs turning behind her dazzling gaze. Not for the first time, I thought I could lose myself in her eyes and right then, it was a comforting thought.

"Hmm," she murmured at last, breaking the spell. "I can't say I blame you. We should talk about this. There has to be a pattern here. I'm just not seeing it yet. All I know for sure is this is bigger than we thought. I don't know how much Rosalind really knows, but we need to tread carefully, D."

"I'll drink to that," I muttered, and we clinked water glasses.

CHAPTER TWENTY-ONE

LET'S DO THIS

In 1889, the St. Mary's Infirmary moved from its original location in a mansion at 1536 Papin, one block northeast of what is now the intersection of Chouteau Avenue and Truman Boulevard, to the first of a series of brand new buildings on the same site. The infirmary was run by an order of nuns known as the Sisters of St. Mary, whose original members had left Germany almost twenty years earlier and arrived in St. Louis at the same time as a major outbreak of smallpox. Bringing some experience in treating the disease, they became known as the "Smallpox Sisters," and most of their patients were charity cases, the poor, working class, and unemployed. As was common at the time, architect Aloysius Gillick designed the new six-story red brick main building in accordance with the Miasma Theory - that disease was caused by foul air from pollution or overcrowding - including high ceilings and wide corridors, many tall windows and excellent ventilation. The hospital included one of the first Catholic nursing schools in 1907, was one of the first to treat African-American patients from 1933 onwards, and boasted the city's first racially integrated nursing staff. Throughout the next two decades, it was the premier hospital for the African-American population of St. Louis, but as other hospitals became integrated in the 1950s, allowing black patients closer access to care and black nurses better pay, St. Mary's pre-eminence declined. By 1966, the last patients were discharged, and the building wound down its life in healthcare in a series of roles as a drug rehab clinic, a residential care facility, and a halfway house, before finally closing its doors in 1994. Attempts to renovate the buildings as lofts, condos, or apartments came and went, and all but the 1889 building fell into ruin and were demolished by 2016.

By this time, however, a new developer finally managed what others had not, and the Chouteau Village Condominiums opened amidst much fanfare three years later. Initially a success, the development had recently been in the news for all the wrong reasons, including a spate of burglaries and financial irregularities. Units that once had been snapped up were languishing on the market, and prices were tumbling. And, if you listened to the right people swallowing their embarrassment, you might hear whispers of "sightings", of "phenomena", of "ghosts".

"This looks like a nightmare," I said, tossing Jess's three-page research summary onto my Hyundai's back seat. "Hospital, drug rehab, halfway house, why not throw in a medieval torture chamber for good measure?"

"There's a reason Rosalind wants your help," said Jess. "I think she's been grooming you the whole time for this."

"Great," I muttered and rubbed my eyes. I had not slept well the previous night, and there's only so much coffee can do. Jess clucked her tongue, but held back whatever she was going to say.

"Look, I think you can do this, whatever it is," she said at last, resting her hand on mine. "Rosalind believes in you, and I do too. I know you'll try your best, and that's all anyone can ask of you."

I bit back a glib response, sighed and tried to turn it into a breathing exercise, although I doubt it fooled her.

Rosalind arrived a few minutes later and parked her Mini in the adjacent visitor-designated space in the Chouteau Village parking lot. We had arrived in two vehicles this time to impress upon our client how seriously we were treating their situation. I had dressed in my smartest clothes again, and even Jess had forsworn her standard T-shirt and shorts with a smart black dress she described as her "interview uniform".

"We look like a team of attorneys," she grumbled, smoothing her dress as we got out of the car.

"We look professional, as we should," said Rosalind. "D, are you up to speed?"

"As much as I can be, I guess."

She looked up at me, her expression thoughtful. "I think we should split up," she said. "Once we get inside, you take the fourth floor and above, and I'll take the lower floors."

"Wouldn't it be easier to do this together?"

"I don't think so. You seem just as affected when you help in one of my Erasures as when you do one on your own, and we only need one of us to trigger the Erasure itself. I think we'll both need all our strength to handle this. If there are more Imprints on the upper floors than you think you can handle, text me. I'll do the same thing."

It made sense, but I didn't like it. I glanced at Jess, who was grinning.

"This is awesome," she said. "I just got to hear someone say 'I think we should split up' in real life!"

"Glad you're having fun," I grumbled, then took one more slow, lung-filling breath. "Okay, let's do this."

A nervous-looking middle-aged woman met us in the entrance foyer, clutching a leather portfolio in one hand and a phone in her other. It looked like she shopped at the same clothing store as Rosalind, but on her the skirt suit failed to convey as much authority.

"Joanne Simmons," she said, fumbling her phone into the purse hanging from one shoulder and offering us her hand, which we all shook as we introduced ourselves. "Thank you for coming. Is there anything I can get you or..."

"Do you have the master keys?" Rosalind asked.

"Oh! Yes, they're in here somewhere."

As she searched for the keys, I turned away and closed my eyes. Memories riddled this building, far more present and menacing than what I had sensed at Barnes Jewish Hospital. The very air seemed to vibrate with warring temperatures, and my ears rang with a background hum of white noise. For a moment, the weight of six floors and over a hundred years of memory crushed me, and I recoiled before forcing myself back upright. *Breathe, focus, find your calm.*

I nodded to Rosalind, and she nodded back. She knew.

By unspoken agreement, Jess came with me. I took the master keycard from Joanne and we called up an elevator.

"I'll start down here," Rosalind said. "Stay in touch."

Jess waved her phone at her and pointed at it as the elevator doors closed.

"Where to first?"

"Let's go to six," I decided. "If she's working her way up, we'll work our way down and meet her somewhere halfway. I hope."

We rode up in silence. My nerves battled my fears, and my determination took them both on. I couldn't spare time for talk. I could sense multiple Imprints, distinct aberrations in how I normally perceived the world, all cohabiting uneasily in this relic of a building. How many were there? I knew I couldn't worry about that. I needed to focus on one at a time.

The door opened on six and I emerged with caution into the wide, well-lit corridor, aware of Jess at my side, but not seeing her. My mind was only partly aware of "reality", most of my attention reaching toward the source of the heat and what I can best describe as pulses of raw emotion, a slow strobe of adrenaline that battered me relentlessly as I walked down the hall. Without warning, it surged, along with an almost asphyxiating whiff of bleach. I balled my fists and closed my eyes, digging in as if I were standing on a beach, knee-deep in crashing waves and fighting the undertow. When I opened my eyes again, I was looking straight at a cream-colored apartment door on which a wrought-iron "608" hung.

"This is it," I told Jess. My voice sounded hoarse and I coughed, which was a mistake as it set off a hacking fit. My mouth was already parched. She passed me the water bottle we had brought and I took a swig. Okay. Here we go.

As a precaution, I knocked on the door. Joanne had assured us they had advised residents to vacate the premises for some kind of hygiene inspection that morning, but we couldn't rely on everyone listening to it, and I didn't want to barge in on anyone. No-one answered, so I swiped the key card and entered the apartment.

The heat alone almost knocked me over, and the waves of emotion threatened to overwhelm me. The longer I waited, the worse it would be, so I had little time to register the bright and airy spartanly furnished loft before closing my eyes and searching for the source of what I felt. Waves of anything have to come from somewhere, I reasoned. So follow them back, use whatever trigonometry lay buried in my brain from high school, and triangulate. I could hear patterns in the ambient hum now, the merest suggestions of voices, and I focused on where those were loudest and clearest. Whether it was because I half-knew what I was looking for or otherwise, I soon found the "catch", the knot that shouldn't be there. As soon as I concentrated on it, my forehead burned as if someone had turned a laser on me. Give up or go on? No, there was only going forward for me. Push.

Pop! Reality yawed sickeningly, and then I was elsewhere, or elsewhen. The same tall windows looked out onto blackest night, but the room was well lit with numerous lamps, either gas or electric. I couldn't tell, and that wasn't important, anyway. There were two beds in the room, one empty and the other surrounded by nuns, on which lay a young black woman in the throes of labor. It wasn't going well. The face of the woman, little more than a girl, was sweating and screwed up in pain, eyes wide and mouth open in a constant scream. One nun, gray-haired and grim-faced, bent over and worked furiously between the girl's legs, mercifully obscuring the details from my line of sight with her body. Another woman of about my age, from what I could see under her habit, sat on the bed and held the girl's hand, exuding compassion as she rode every anguished contraction with her, and I rode it too. Two younger nuns stood near the bed and prayed, eyes closed and lips moving fervently. The pregnant girl convulsed, her back arching and eyes rolling up into her head. The midwife barked commands to the others, and one of the younger nuns rushed from the room. I couldn't make the words out over a prevalent buzzing, like a chainsaw someone had left running and was now spinning around by itself in the dirt.

What could I do? I was just an observer, someone watching in pity from the future, no more able to influence events than if I watched the same thing happen in a movie. Yet, I had acted without expectation on the rooftop at 1500 Locust, and who could say if that was what had made the difference or not? What was there to lose?

"You'll be okay," I said to myself, to the universe at large, to whatever this was. She screamed, mouth open wider than I thought possible.

"You'll be okay."

"IT HURTS!" Deafening, distorted, primal, the sound of a mother fighting with every shred of her being to bring new life into the world.

"I know," I lied, but I told myself I had gotten a response and needed to keep talking, however inane I sounded. "These women, the nuns, know what they're doing. You'll see your baby soon."

"Soon?"

This time the voice was clear and full of hope, and then three things happened at once. The girl convulsed again just as the young nun returned with a bowl of steaming water, and then the midwife lifted something in her arms. The buzzing, which had dwindled during my unreal conversation, rose to almost deafening volume and morphed into a baby's cry, this baby's cry, as the nuns cut the placental cord and laid her in the exhausted and terrified young mother's arms. With that, the universe paused and then everything that was fraught, ragged, and twisted coalesced into a pure, ringing tone, the perfect mirror to the profound joy and love that mother gave daughter. My heart, so close to breaking, now sang with her.

The vision dissolved, and I was on my knees with my head resting on the wood laminate floor, gasping for air. I closed my eyes again and waited, one breath in and out, another, and slowly the sensations ebbed, the throbbing in my head subsided, and I pushed myself upright. Jess was right there, face full of concern and something else that I couldn't place, and I gave her as brave a smile as I could muster.

"Bad?" she asked, offering me the water bottle. I nodded, too weak to explain.

"Rosalind's on the second floor. She's done two Erasures already," she said.

"Not keeping score," I mumbled and heaved myself to my feet.

"I didn't mean—"

"Doesn't matter. Let's go."

I hadn't made a mess this time, although my stomach suggested it was still a possibility in the future. So we shut the apartment door behind us and continued down the hall. I was shaky and would have liked nothing more than to skulk back home to my apartment, or even to my car, to sleep, but I had a job to do. I was committed now, whatever the cost.

Sensing nothing else on the sixth floor, even after doubling back past the elevators to the other wing, we descended the gray concrete emergency stairs at that end of the building. I opened the door to the fifth floor, remembering the hotel in Chicago, but nothing happened. We walked the length of the wide corridor without me picking up anything more than the background sensations I had experienced in the lobby. Were there no Imprints on this floor at all, or had that first Erasure desensitized me?

That question was answered when the elevator door opened on four. If anything, my perception might have sharpened, because I could clearly distinguish two Imprints, one in either direction. I stood in the center of the corridor undecided, and glanced at Jess, who was frowning at her phone. She wiped her face clear of expression when she noticed me looking. And hid her phone behind her hip.

"Well?"

"There are two up here," I whispered. "One in either direction."

"So, which one first?"

Which one, indeed? The one to my left felt stronger, its tendrils of midwinter cold pushing back the fitful gusts of smoky warmth emanating from my right. I had recovered some of my strength, but would it make more sense to tackle what seemed to be the weaker imprint first, and then somehow summon the energy to deal with the stronger one? Rosalind might even arrive to help me with that one. But somehow I knew that was wrong, that I should pit my strength against the greater opponent first, while I still had it. And I shouldn't rely on Rosalind. This was my floor.

"This way," I said, and turned left.

The Imprint in Apartment 404 was of an old man with a dirty white beard and poor, threadbare clothes sitting at the bedside of a sleeping woman who, I was sure, was his wife. Or had been. She had just died, whether from some illness or natural causes, I didn't know. The man's grief and sorrow were almost overwhelming, but the part of me still rooted in the present recalled a bungalow in Shrewsbury, and I reminded him of all the good times, the trying times, the highs and the lows, but most of all the love that he still carried, and that was enough. I still wondered if I was communicating with the individuals in these memories, or somehow with the memories themselves, despite what Rosalind said, or if this was just a metaphor for the Erasure process. It would be a great conversation for another time, I decided, as I wiped my mouth and helped Jess clean the floor.

She had to support me as I stumbled from the apartment, but I shook her off by the time we reached 415. I was weak, far more tired than I had been after finishing the 5K a month before, but if this last Imprint was as weak as it felt, I thought I could deal with it. And I did, but only just. It *was* weaker, the catch easier to find, the memory of what I guessed was a young boy suffering from smallpox, vague and translucent. Despite this, I had trouble dislodging the catch, as if I couldn't aim properly. I struggled to assuage the boy's pain and confusion as they poured through me, somehow finding an extra reserve of strength at the last and sending him, I hoped, to recovery.

Afterwards, I sat with my back against the wall in the fourth floor corridor, nursing the water bottle and staring at the faraway ceiling, feeling utterly drained. Jess sat next to me, put her arm around my shoulders, and kissed my cheek. She was uncharacteristically quiet, but perhaps she was just giving me the time and mental space to heal.

After a minute, or an hour, or a year, her phone vibrated, and she peered at it, with the screen tilted away from me. She sighed in relief and gave me a gentle nudge in my ribs.

"Rosalind is done too. She wants us to meet her down on three."

"Do we teleport or are you going to drag me?"

"Walk or crawl if you must," she laughed. "I think she's tired, too. She's done five."

Five Erasures. Eight total, including mine. I didn't know what to think about that.

"Okay," I said, and forced myself to my feet, although I had to steady myself against the wall for a minute to allow the corridor to stop spinning before I could move.

I was shocked when I saw Rosalind. The elevators on each floor opened onto an almost perfect cube, flanked by enormous windows facing the street and the back lot. She was slumped on a chaise longue nestled under the front window, cheeks flushed red, sweat-matted hair plastered to her skull, her feeble left arm dangling almost to the floor, on which her phone rested. Her chest rose and fell as she took deep, shuddering breaths, and she smiled weakly as I tottered out of the elevator. I suspected I didn't look much better.

"Well done, D," she croaked, fumbling for her water bottle and shaking the last drops into her mouth. Jess hurried over and gave Rosalind her almost full bottle.

"Thanks, Jess," Rosalind said after several greedy gulps, then turned back to me. "I couldn't have done this without you. I almost couldn't do half of it. That was far worse than anything I had feared. I may have to take a sick day tomorrow."

She gave a soft laugh and closed her eyes, and for a moment I thought she had fallen asleep. When she opened them again, they contained a hint of her usual vigor.

"I'm sorry to have put you through this. It took me years before I dared to tackle two Erasures at once. You've just done three. You're a remarkable man. I think he's a keeper, Jess."

"Yes, he is," Jess said, smiling at me with obvious pride, and that might have been the best moment of my life.

"I can't believe you did five," I said, trying to convey all my awe of her in my voice. "I only managed the third because it was so much weaker than the other two."

"Yes, I had one of those as well. One of the three on this floor alone."

Our eyes met and something passed between us. I wasn't sure what it was then, but I think I know now.

We rested in silence for a few more minutes. Jess suggested I sit on an armchair by the back window, but I was afraid that if I sat down again, it would be hours before I would want to move. I could feel my strength returning, slow and almost reluctant, as if wary of how I would use it. By the time Rosalind struggled to her feet and attempted to smooth down her ruffled clothes, I could at least stand and walk unsupported. But I was going to sleep well that night.

"I told Joanne we'd be down in a few minutes," she said. "As much to motivate myself to get up as anything else." She paused, then scowled toward the eastern corridor. "I hope this was bloody well worth it."

She walked back and forth from one window to the other a few times, gingerly at first, then with increasing assurance. I joined her, to keep her company and to test my own wheels. Finally, we punched the elevator button and rode down to the entrance foyer, sweaty, exhausted, but heads held high.

And that was when the fun really started. Because Joanne wasn't in the foyer, but Donovan Brooks and Lana were. And they were in the middle of an Erasure.

At least that's what I thought at first. The elevator was still coming to a halt when that familiar prickling sensation began on the back of my neck. Rosalind shot me a look.

"You feel it too?"

"Yeah."

"I dealt with the first floor," she said, tired and confused, even a little defensive. Then the doors opened, and we saw them, Lana leaning against the wall opposite, eyes closed and silent lips moving, Donovan standing side on with his back to a tall window to my left where he could watch both her and the elevators. Both wore nondescript, loose-fitting blue shirts and pants, as if they were masquerading as some sort of maintenance staff. Donovan's eyes opened wide as he turned his head to look at us and his smile was grim. We stared back, and no-one else moved until the elevator doors started to close again, and by reflex, I stuck an arm out to block it.

"Hi, Donovan," I said, stepping out of the elevator first and trying to process what I was sensing. It was like and unlike what I was used to, almost a *backwards* view. Instead of something peering at us from somewhere else, we were the ones doing the peering.

"Dex." Donovan nodded and squared his body to face me, positioning himself between me and Lana. I was dimly aware of Rosalind hovering just behind my right shoulder, and the frustrated ping of the elevator meant Jess was keeping our options open. Donovan's arms hung loose at his sides, poised. It was as if we were preparing to spar at GWK. For a crazy moment, I half-expected him to lead us through the *kata*. His gaze flickered to Jess, lingered an instant longer on where Rosalind was lurking, then returned to me.

"Fancy meeting you here. What are the odds?"

His voice was measured, strained. Behind him, Lana grunted with effort, and a vision flashed before me, a vision of a crowd of people, of voices raised in anger, fear or alarm. Then it was as if something took that vision, that slice of memory, and *folded* it somehow, so that it lost its definition, but not its potency.

That's when I understood.

"You're not Erasing a memory. You're Imprinting one."

He opened his mouth, but didn't get to answer because several things happened at once. Lana let out a loud gasp and buckled against the far wall. I shifted my weight to my right, knowing I had to stop her from doing whatever she was doing, and that I couldn't go through a second degree black belt. Donovan shot the briefest of alarmed glances over his shoulder, and that's when Rosalind darted out from behind me and grabbed at him, one hand clutching his left elbow and the other gaining a fistful of shirt below his right shoulder. Surprise, a hint of fear, and an unmistakable stab of excitement rushed across his face, and his right fist punched her straight between the eyes. Her head rocked back, but she was already pulling him backwards. Before I could yell or do anything productive, she levered her downward momentum into a throw, planting her right foot in his groin and propelled him over her as she collapsed to the ground. His back thudded into the angle of the wall between elevator and window, followed an instant later by the double crunch of his skull bouncing off the walls before he landed in a tangled heap of limbs next to Rosalind, out cold. She raised her head for a moment, as if evaluating whether she had dealt with the threat, then dropped it down again, closed her eyes, and lay still.

I was paralyzed, I'd like to claim from exhaustion, but, to be honest, it was shock. All the scrappy, sloppy fights I had got myself into over the years were a joke compared to what I had just seen, brutal and clinical. Jess finally abandoned the elevator to kneel next to Rosalind, and I tried to rouse myself to action, but then I heard Lana moan and the full weight of the Imprint bore down upon me.

It says something about my progression as an Eraser that I instinctively opened my mind to it, to the heat, to the pulsing emotion, the stuff that our pattern-seeking brains naturally personify. It was fresh and raw, like a new-made sword cooling away from the forge. And it was too much, too powerful. I tried to make sense of the pulses, to find the catch in the Imprint, but I couldn't focus. Dazed, worried about Rosalind, beaten anew by forces I still knew so little about, I realized I just didn't have the strength. And, with rising panic, I didn't know how to pull myself away. I floundered, grasping at things that weren't there, feeling my consciousness ebb away.

There.

There's something.

Not a catch, not the Imprint, but something else fixed. Solid. Powerful.

Reach for it.

Reach, and...

Whatever it was, it wanted to grab me as much as I wanted to grab it. I didn't care, I felt its strength, its potential, and thought I could imagine a will directing it, a will that wanted the same thing I did. Could this be Rosalind, still conscious after all? I didn't have time to speculate. I needed to use this somehow to find the catch and erase this fresh memory Imprint.

It allowed itself to be used, allowed me to guide it, and was the strength to complement my will. I soon found the catch, where the pulses were coming from, and I wielded this strength, directed it against the catch, and pushed.

The catch gave, but instead of the now-familiar nauseating plunge into the imprinted memory, it was as if the heat and pulses pivoted somehow. Confused and disoriented, I felt panic rise within me again and fought it back, clutching my newfound strength for dear life. Had I cleared the catch? I couldn't sense it.

There must be another one, at least one more. The heat wasn't quite as hot, the pulses of emotion were somewhat weaker, and to the extent I could distinguish direction within whatever state of consciousness this was, they originated from somewhere else. Even with my unexpected ally, I found it increasingly difficult to concentrate. I had one more effort left in me, I decided. It was time to give everything I had and hope it was enough. I laid myself bare, naked to whoever or whatever was there to see, and *listened*. And there it was, faint but unmistakable, the memory of an echo of a whisper. I was being picked apart, knives of emotion slashing through my thoughts, but I hung on, desperate in my focus on what was, without doubt, a second catch. I was starting to lose grasp of the energy, the source of power I needed to destroy that catch, and the more I wrestled with it, the more I lost focus on the catch itself.

You have to risk it, an inner voice told me. *Harness what you have now, and throw it all towards the catch. And hope it's good enough.*

So I did. The universe exploded with light and a cacophony of sound, leaving me blind, deaf, and reeling. There was a tangle of bodies in front of me, a Brownian motion of humanity, and as if from far away the distant sound of voices yelling, screaming, crying in pain, anger and fear. I wanted so much to let it wash over me, but I couldn't. I had a responsibility, not just to Rosalind or Jess - I had a responsibility to myself. This was making a difference. This was one way that I could make amends for the mistakes I had made in my life, part of my path back to being a contributing member of society. I was saving myself by saving others.

A young black man lay bloody, broken and bruised on a stretcher before me, surrounded by a handful of animated men and women of the same age and color, two earnest young nuns and a pair of wary older white men, who I guessed were hospital orderlies. From their clothes, I guessed this was a memory from the 1950s or 1960s, not long before the hospital closed for good. Two of the women were yelling at the nuns, fingers stabbing at their injured friend, the orderlies and the nuns themselves, but their voices were too distorted for me to hear most of what they were saying. "Attacked" I heard, then "mob". An orderly tried to step in front of the nuns, and one of the other men rounded on him. This looked ugly, and was getting uglier.

"What about your friend?" I asked. "He's still alive. I can feel it. You have to help him."

Why had they all forgotten him? I could see his chest rise and fall, shaky, but unmistakable through his bloodstained, pink button-down shirt. Breath bubbled through his cracked lips, both eyes swollen shut. "Who the hell did this to you? And why?"

"... girl..."

"What? What girl? Is that one of you? Slow down, help him!"

"My girl..."

One of the screaming women sank to her knees, tears welling in her eyes as she rested her palm on the injured man's face.

"I love you," she said. "Don't leave me!"

"Never."

The injured man's right hand twitched where it lay on his stomach. Almost imperceptibly at first, it dragged itself up, over his ribs, across his twisted left shoulder, coming to rest atop the woman's hand. Her body shook with distress, and maybe relief, and she bent down to kiss the back of his hand where it covered hers.

The scene dissolved. I had a fleeting glimpse of Jess's wide-eyed face inches above mine, before that faded too, and the darkness took me.

Excerpt of email recovered from closed account, owner untraceable. Destination account also closed and untraceable.

From: (address withheld)
To: (address withheld)
Subject: St. Louis 2023-10 #3
Sent: 2023-10-20 03:04:11 UTC

...What have they done?...

CHAPTER TWENTY-TWO

A TOKEN
OF OUR
ADMIRATION

We stood as Martin Hill entered the waiting area outside the general admission wards at Barnes Jewish Hospital. I had only seen him in passing the previous evening, and he'd spared only a few choice words before focusing on his wife. I couldn't blame him, although I wasn't sure what else I could have done.

"She's finally awake, but still very weak," he said, pouring himself water from a dispenser. He looked exhausted himself and I guessed he hadn't slept much. "They're thinking about keeping her another night. Worried about the effects of the dehydration."

I wasn't quite sure what to say, so I asked the obvious question. "How's her nose?"

Martin snorted. "It's fine. They reset it, although the bruises are lovely. She thinks it's funny."

Jess smiled, but I had very mixed emotions. Rosalind had already been in one ambulance by the time I regained consciousness, as the paramedics were loading me into another. I had been more worried for her than about myself. I knew how bad I felt, but had no idea what had happened between her and Donovan, who was now being questioned by the police. The doctors had released me after an hour of testing and IV fluids, but all anyone would tell me about Rosalind was she was staying overnight for observation. Except Martin, who had poked his head in to provide a terse and expletive-laden update of her condition.

"She wants to see you both," he said now, sinking into a chair with a sigh. "Please don't tire her. I'm sorry if I snapped at you last night, D."

I shrugged. "You were upset. I understand."

"Yes. Well I'm sure we'll be having another conversation soon, but why don't you go back before she falls asleep again?"

The duty nurse directed us to a room about halfway down the ward. I held my breath as we walked toward it. So far, I had sensed nothing more intense than a low-level background "hum" of memory. I was certain there were Imprints in the hospital, but it didn't look like any of them were close. I still wasn't happy to be here, but I was happy to see Rosalind.

"Hello D. Hello Jess."

She lifted a hand for a moment in greeting, then let it drop back on top of the covers. She was propped up on a mound of pillows and still hooked up to an IV drip, as well as a rack of diagnostic equipment. Thick white gauze covered the bridge of her nose and most of the discoloration under her eyes. Wearing the standard issue navy hospital gown, she looked frail, a shadow of her usual self. She read my expression and flashed me a grim smile.

"You should see the other guy."

I chuckled and busied myself arranging chairs so Jess and I could sit close to Rosalind. The other bed in the room was unoccupied, which was convenient, but I didn't want our conversation overheard.

"I've been worried about you," I told her. "I'm glad to see you're awake and on the mend."

"Everyone's worried about me," she said, with unmistakable irritation. "They want to keep me another night, but I just want to go home. Martin makes an excellent nurse, and he can give me undivided attention."

"I'm sure the doctors are just doing what they think is best. I don't know what you told them, but it puzzled them why I was so dehydrated."

"What did you tell them?"

"That I had a fear of elevators and had been walking up and down stairs all afternoon. That's what I told the police, too. Joanne at least corroborated we had a valid reason to be in the building. I think she called it a 'safety inspection'."

Rosalind smiled and closed her eyes for a moment. I glanced at Jess, who continued to look thoughtful. She seemed like she wanted to say something, but when I raised my eyebrows in question, she shook her head.

"What happened to the other guy?" Rosalind asked, eyes open again.

I shrugged, but Jess answered. "Donovan? He woke up before D did, but after the police and ambulance arrived. He asked if you were okay, but he was probably just worried about what would happen to him if you weren't. Sulky little bitch."

Rosalind grinned. "You've no idea how long I've wanted to do that. He's always been a bit of a pompous git. And I actually had a reason to do it," she added, grin fading.

I shifted uneasily. This was a topic I had been dreading. "So we now know it's possible to imprint memories intentionally as well as to erase them," I said.

"Apparently."

"Do you think that explains why only a few memories ever get imprinted, because someone has to consciously do it?"

"I don't know. I suspect most are naturally occurring, but I'm too tired to really think about it right now."

"It explains the connections I found between Erasures," said Jess, glancing at me as she recalled our recent debate. "If they've been imprinting memories to scare people out of their homes, that's pretty effective and damn near impossible to prove."

"Perhaps," said Rosalind, with a frown. "I don't understand how Donovan and Lana benefit from that. Where did she get to, by the way?"

"She stayed with him until he woke up. She looked almost as bad as you guys did, but she was conscious. I was too worried about you to strike up a useful conversation, though."

"Yes, well, I daresay your next karate lesson will be interesting. I told the police I didn't want to press charges, and I guess Donovan doesn't either. It was all just a misunderstanding."

I was looking forward to a "useful conversation" with Donovan, although I had to remember he was a black belt.

Rosalind closed her eyes for a few seconds, then gave me a solemn look. "D, there's something I want to tell you."

"Mrs. Hill?" I turned to see a young redheaded woman dressed in a doctor's white scrubs standing in the doorway, flanked by a couple of nurses. "I'm sorry, but we need a few minutes to examine you. Could your visitors please wait outside?"

"Perfect timing," Rosalind muttered. "Hold that thought."

I only had another half an hour to spare before I needed to get ready for work, but I couldn't leave on that note. We returned to the waiting area, and Jess said she needed the restroom. Martin had gone, so I sat by myself for a few minutes, casting a vacant stare down the well-lit corridor leading to the elevator bank. So I saw Steven Rourke as soon as he emerged from one.

It took me a few seconds to recognize him, in part because of the Cardinals baseball cap but also because of the enormous bouquet he carried, crooked in his left arm. When he caught my eye, he grinned and stuck out his hand as I rose from my seat. I shook it reluctantly, and glanced behind him.

"No minders today, Steven?"

"I don't know what you mean, Declan," he said, releasing my hand. The warmth faded from his smile, but then it was only there for show. "I hardly think I need my *associates* in a hospital, do you? Although perhaps they could have used me."

His eyes glinted, and for a moment I glimpsed just how angry he was. Then his veneer of civility returned with a passable smile.

"Besides, Jamal is waiting for me downstairs. I'm just stopping to drop these off for the remarkable Mrs. Rosalind Hill, as a token of our admiration. Be a sport and take them to her, will you? I doubt you want me to give them to her personally." He offered me the bouquet and laughed at my suspicious expression. "They're just flowers. I bought them not five minutes ago from the gift shop here. But if you wish to examine them first, be my guest."

"Fine." I took the bouquet and noticed that the attached gift card envelope was sealed. "How do you know Rosalind? And who is Jamal?"

"You met him. He was the gentleman who accompanied me to Hickory that night not so long ago." He paused, allowing me to reflect on that. "As for Rosalind Hill, I know of her only by name, I'm afraid. And reputation. Jamal holds her in very high regard."

Then it clicked. Rourke didn't know any details about memories, how they were imprinted and erased, but he knew someone who did. So who was Jamal?

"You've got there, I see," Steven said, his voice quieter and hard-edged. "I warned you. I told you to stop. You should have listened. I want that building and I'm going to get it. You've simply delayed me for a while. What makes you think we can't add more tethers whenever we want?"

Tethers? "What makes you think we can't remove them if you do?"

"Indeed." He narrowed his eyes, and I thought I surprised a hint of respect from them as he nodded to himself. "Jamal tells me you picked a Two-Point Lock."

"I have no idea what that means."

"Neither do I, but Jamal was terribly impressed. I'll be in touch, D."

He clapped me on the upper arm, then turned and sauntered back to the elevators. He didn't look back.

"Who was that and why did he give you flowers?" demanded Jess, appearing at my side and making me jump half out of my skin.

"That was him. Steven Rourke."

"I thought so. That's why I didn't interrupt. What are the flowers for?"

"They're for Rosalind," I said and recounted our conversation.

"So I was right!" she said fiercely.

"Looks that way," I agreed. "Once Rosalind feels better, we probably need to have a bigger conversation about this."

"Is the doctor still in with her?"

We asked at the nurse's station, and were told that the doctor had moved on but no-one had got around to telling us. We hurried back to Rosalind's room, worried that she might have fallen back asleep, but she was too annoyed for that.

"She won't let me leave today," Rosalind grumbled. "She doesn't like this, and is concerned about that." There was a hint of a blush on her cheeks as she noticed the flowers and her eyes widened.

"D! You shouldn't have!"

"Um, well, actually I didn't," I said, embarrassed. Maybe I should have. "They're from Steven Rourke: a token of his admiration, he said." And I recounted all I had just told Jess.

"I see," said Rosalind, gazing at the flowers. "Well, there's a vase over there by the window, toss 'em in there. Can I see the card?"

I detached the envelope from a rose stem and passed it to her. The bouquet was a little large for the plain white vase she had indicated, but I tried to force it in anyway before Jess slapped my hand.

"For heaven's sake, give them to me," she said, snatching both flowers and vase from my hands. "I'll be back in a minute."

Jess left the room in search of water and maybe pruning shears, and I turned back to Rosalind. She was staring at the inside of a simple floral "Get Well Soon" card that she held in one hand, while the envelope dangled forgotten in the other. Her expression was unreadable. She replaced the card in the envelope, but didn't set it down.

"I have two things to tell you," she said, her voice weary. "But can I ask you a question first?"

"Anything."

"It's about something you said when you were telling Martin and I about Steven Rourke. You said he took you in when the rest of your family deserted you. What did you mean by that?"

Ah. Yes, I had said that.

"Don't worry," I sighed, rubbing one eye. "It's not a Darth-Vader-I-am-your-father-Luke thing. He's my mother's cousin, and decidedly the black sheep of the family. They don't get on. He's one of the reasons I haven't seen or talked to her in sixteen years."

She looked away for a moment, then took a long, slow breath before turning back to me. "I see. I'm sorry. We all... well, let's just say families can be hard work. That's not unrelated to what I have to tell you.

"First, I want you to take the entire fee for Chouteau Village. No, don't object, I'm too sick and tired to argue. I don't want the money, and you deserve every penny. I can't imagine how you managed to deal with that last Imprint. You were in as bad a shape as I was. Yet you didn't hesitate. You have excellent instincts, D, maybe better than mine at this stage in your career."

"I... Thank you, Rosalind. I won't argue with you, although you did more than your fair share. And I don't think I'll be making a career out of this anytime soon."

"Perhaps not. I think that's up to you. But you have the opportunity."

"What do you mean?"

"I'm sick and I'm tired, not just here and now in this damn hospital bed. I'm tired of what this is doing to me, of how I feel every time I erase one of these memories. There's a price, mentally and physically, and I'm tired of paying it. It's been seven years, all by myself. Maybe if you had come along sooner, well, what's the expression? 'If wishes were horses, then beggars would ride.' Still, you're ready, D, to take up the mantle that I'm ready to discard."

"You're going to stop? Just like that?"

"Why not? I don't need to do it. I did it because it needed to be done, and I thought I was helping people. But I also need to help myself and my family."

That floored me. Six months ago I had no idea any of this existed, that there might be some rhyme or reason to all those times I had been disturbed by sensations I couldn't explain. Rosalind had not only opened my eyes, she had also taught me how to deal with it, how I could take this inexplicable skill and use it to do good, like some sort of superpower. I had purpose now, beyond just living what I believed was a normal life. I couldn't imagine following that purpose without her.

She laid a hand on my arm, and I saw a tear welling in her eye. Blurry, because there was a tear in mine.

"I'm not abandoning you," she said, smiling. "I will continue to help you in any way I can, whether it's research or advice. More than that, I consider you my friend, and my friends are very important to me."

"They are to me too," I said, wiping my eye.

"Right!" said Jess, marching back into the room with the vase of flowers and setting them back on the small table in front of the window. "Regardless of where they came from, it's a gorgeous bouquet."

"It is," admitted Rosalind, withdrawing her hand from my arm and wiping her own eyes. "It certainly brightens the room. Thank you, Jess."

"Of course." Jess turned to look at us, hands on hips, and cocked her head. "Now, did either of you see some weird vision of a beaten up black dude surrounded by nuns at Chouteau Village yesterday? Or was that just me?"

ACKNOWLEDGMENTS

It would be fair to say that this book is four decades in the making, harking back to my high school dreams of becoming a novelist. That I have finally published something is a credit to all those who have offered me advice and encouragement over the years. The following list is far from exhaustive, and please know I appreciate each and every one of you.

This story may never have been written at all if it weren't for my daughter, Rhiannon. She didn't wait to graduate high school before publishing her first novel, and she persuaded me to try National Novel Writing Month later that year, 2015 if memory serves. We joined a group of fellow NaNoWriMo writers each Monday evening at a Clayton coffee shop to talk about writing and sometimes even write. The story I worked on then is not this story - that one, while finished, is not (yet) good enough - but it served to clear out the cobwebs and galvanized me to create once again. Rhiannon's still writing too, so I'll have to keep up.

My other daughter, Imogen, is a creator by profession - a visual FX artist for a game studio - and she turned my well-intentioned but clumsy ideas for fonts, logos, and cover designs into concepts that might actually work. She endured a college experience marred by the COVID pandemic and her isolation, at times, mirrored that of D's in the story. Most of this tale was written during lockdown and multiple false recoveries, during which we drove from St. Louis to Savannah, Georgia several times to visit her. Twice, we stayed at The Whitman mansion on Forsyth Park, which proved to be one of my most productive writing environments: I completed the first draft of this story while sitting on a veranda overlooking trees draped with Spanish moss, in a city renowned for its ghost tours.

I am very fortunate to have friends who read later drafts of the story and gave me valuable feedback. Enrique Serrano Valle qualifies as the first person to quote my text back to me - "that's what sigmas are for" - and Geri L Dreiling provided both advice and tools based on her own self-published author journey: check out *Crime Beat Girl* for a great St. Louis-based crime thriller! Rick Wurl was one of the first to read it, and we established a weekly routine over the summer and fall of 2021 where I would print out the latest chapter for his review to be discussed over beers or margaritas at our favorite Mexican restaurant (yes, *that* Mexican restaurant) on Friday evenings. Rick is my source for anything related to the martial arts - any mistakes are entirely mine - and helped choreograph the fight scenes, even conducting re-enactments in my basement. I count myself fortunate to have suffered no damage during these re-enactments: the temptation must have been unbearable.

Self-publishing is not for the faint of heart. There is a lot to do before a book, however well-written, can make it to virtual or physical shelves. I was lucky to find an editor, Gareth Clegg (garethclegg.com), who not only corrected the manuscript and sharpened the story, but did so while taking care to preserve my voice. He was a joy to work with. Michele Khalil of Elite Scribes (elitescribesghostwriting.com) took on the tasks of cover and website design, formatting, and creating my "author brand" - I didn't even know I needed one of those, but she did, and has done a damn fine job too.

Finally, I owe more than I can begin to express to my wife, Sherri. Not only did she read drafts of the book, answer random questions over dinner, and offer her own ideas on everything from terminology to cover design, but she put up with my "obsession" during a pandemic that, in addition to everything else stressful, saw us move from one house to another. The road was far from smooth, but I couldn't imagine a better supporter or anyone with whom I would rather have shared lockdown. I love you, babe.

ABOUT THE AUTHOR

Gareth Ian Davies was born and raised in the south of London, during which time he wrote many terrible things and dreamed of becoming a novelist. Instead, he earned a degree in Physics from the University of Bristol and didn't quite know what to do with it. After moving to the American Midwest he flirted with a career in nuclear engineering before taking the somewhat safer path as a software developer. He spent the next three decades writing code and technical documentation, before finally realizing his dream by publishing his first novel. Gareth lives in St. Louis with his wife, her innumerable fish, two cats, and a cockatiel.

STAY CONNECTED

Want to be one of the first to get all the latest news? Check out Gareth's socials and sign up for his newsletter for upcoming announcements, first looks, and more!

Facebook

Gareth Ian Davies
TikTok

@garethiandaviesauthor
Website

garethiandavies.com

Lightning Source UK Ltd.
Milton Keynes UK
UKHW012148260123
416041UK00018B/257/J